I0543910

# MURDER ON THE LEVELS

A gripping crime thriller full of suspense

# DAVID HODGES

*Detective Kate Hamblin Mystery book 1*

Originally published as *Firetrap*

Revised edition 2019
Joffe Books, London
www.joffebooks.com

First published in Great Britain in 2011
as *Firetrap*

This paperback edition was first published
in Great Britain in 2022

ISBN: 978-1-80405-471-0

*This book is dedicated to my wife, Elizabeth, for all her love, patience and support over so many wonderful years.*

## AUTHOR'S NOTE

Although the action of the story takes place in the Avon & Somerset Constabulary area, the story itself and all the characters in it are entirely fictitious. At the time of writing, there is *no* police station in Highbridge. This has been drawn entirely from the author's imagination to ensure no connection is made between any existing police station or personnel in the force and the content of the novel. Similarly, despite reference to some actual streets and villages, any specific premises mentioned, such as the café and funeral directors in Highbridge and the cottage in Burtle, are all figments of the imagination and any connection between them and existing properties is entirely coincidental.

David Hodges

# BEFORE THE FACT

Moonlight — soft, magical — blazing a pure white trail along the drove, spotlighting the purplish smudge of Glastonbury Tor as it rose like a phallic symbol from shadowed fields, and touching the lattice-work of rhynes with silver. Nothing moved. The world was dead, enfolded in the wings of a primeval night; silent, unknowing.

Twister had reversed his old green van through an open gateway into a field and tucked it behind a hedge; close enough to the farmhouse for him to reach it quickly should anything go wrong, yet far enough away to avoid attracting any unwelcome interest. Not that there was likely to be anyone wandering around the Somerset Levels at this time of the night to *be* interested — unless the dead could walk, of course.

He had watched Joe Mercier being put six feet under that very afternoon and he happened to know that the old farmer's widow had gone to stay with her son in Taunton for a while, which meant that the farm would be unoccupied, visited only once a day by the local herdsman. That was what was so brilliant about the unsavoury profession he had taken over from his late father; you got to know things — like when a house was vacant and could be screwed without fear of discovery. And the added bonus was that no one would ever suspect the local undertaker of being the culprit? It was perfect cover.

Despite his confidence, however, he approached the dilapidated farmhouse cautiously. In two years of serial burglary he had never put a foot wrong and he was not about to start now.

A marsh bird rose with panic-stricken squawks from almost under his feet as he stepped on to the heavy steel plate that had been placed over the rhyne at the entrance to the farm and his heart jumped. But otherwise the night remained perfectly still and, encouraged, he moved on, heading through the open gateway and following the concrete driveway towards the house.

He had actually made the hard-standing separating the house from a cluster of outbuildings and was almost past an open-fronted woodshed when he heard the sharp clinking sound and glimpsed the stab of a flashlight through a gap in the double doors of a large barn opposite.

Ducking into the woodshed, he crouched behind a stack of recently cut logs and froze, eyes narrowed, heart pounding. Who the hell was in the barn, and what were they doing there at this hour? It was hardly likely to be the Merciers or the wandering herdsman at just after one in the morning. So who? Then he saw the vehicle. It was a Land Rover Defender — one of the workhorses regularly used by farmers all over the Levels — and it was parked on a ragged gravel area between the barn and an adjacent cowshed. It was the only vehicle in the farmyard, but it was nothing like old man Mercier's own run-about and it certainly couldn't be confused with the herdsman's distinctive yellow Toyota 4 x 4.

So someone else had decided to pay the farm a visit, had they? Someone who must also have known that it would be unoccupied after the funeral and had chosen to sneak into the place at an hour when most decent folk were tucked up in bed. Twister scowled. It seemed he had a competitor then, but if that was the case, he needed to know who that competitor was.

Leaving the woodshed, he took a chance and darted through the blaze of moonlight to the front of the Land Rover. He put his hand in front of the radiator. Still very warm, so matey hadn't been here long then. Peering at the index plate, he made a mental note of the registration number, just in case.

More clinking from inside the barn and the strong smell of petrol. He crept up to the double doors and peered through the gap. A shadowy figure — a man without doubt, going by his heavy build — was crouching beside a tractor in the light of a powerful flash lamp set on an overturned crate. Around him bits of other machinery intruded into the circle of light — including a large sit-on mower and a digger of some sort — while bales of what looked like hay or straw were dimly visible, stacked in a solid wall behind him. It was difficult to see what the man was up to, but he appeared to be doing something to the tractor's engine.

Could be it was all perfectly legit, of course — a mechanic working late — but somehow that seemed just a little bit too implausible. More likely that this one had come to nick parts off the tractor or lift anything else that was lying around and that posed a problem in itself. Whatever he *was* up to, Twister knew he would have to bide his time until the job was done; breaking into the house was much too risky with matey-boy up to his tricks just a few yards away.

Reluctantly he slipped into a narrow passageway between the barn and a ruined cowshed to wait — and he didn't have to wait long. Just minutes later one of the barn doors opened with a shuddering scraping sound and the mystery man emerged in the full flood of moonlight. Risking a quick glance round the corner, Twister only caught the briefest glimpse of the man's face before jerking back out of sight — but it was enough. He recognized him immediately. How could he forget a past client who had opted for such an elaborate and costly funeral for his mother? Then there was the quick rap of footsteps on the concrete, followed by the crack of door hinges. The Land Rover's engine started up seconds before the driver's door was slammed shut and even as Twister poked his head round the corner of the barn, there was a squeal of tyres as the vehicle pulled away under power.

For a moment Twister watched it lumber away down the driveway, its rear lights only coming on as it turned on to the drove and headed for the main road.

'Well, now, Mr Terry Duval, you were in a bit of a hurry, weren't you, my old son,' he murmured to himself. 'I wonder why.'

Slipping through the still open door of the barn, he produced a masked torch from his pocket and directed the beam round the interior. As he had suspected, the place was jam-packed with machinery of one sort or another and the stench of petrol was overpowering. Holding a handkerchief up against his nose, he focused the beam on the tractor and was surprised to see that it appeared intact. Then he noticed something else: the floor beneath his shoes seemed to be soaking wet. As the beam of his torch jerked sideways in a sudden reflexive movement, he spotted the petrol cans tied together under the tractor and the small oblong box attached to one of them that winked at him knowingly from the shadows with its tiny pulsing eye.

And it was then that he turned and ran.

# CHAPTER 1

Midnight. The inside of the unmarked police Transit van was like a fridge. 'No lights, no noise,' the detective chief inspector had said, which meant no engine, so no heater. Parked on the marshland drove, bordered by rows of skeletal trees on one side and a reed-fringed rhyne on the other, there was little to shield the vehicle from the bitter winter's night, except the overhanging branches. The bodywork of the long wheelbase Ford already bore lacings of hard frost and the frozen surface of the rhyne itself reflected the moonlight like crazed glass.

'Place is dead as a bleedin' dodo,' Detective Constable Alf Cross growled, straightening up from the spy-hole and lowering the night-vision monocular he had been using to study the cottage in the middle of the field. He swivelled round in the chair anchored to the steel floor of the vehicle. 'What a waste of bloody time.'

Detective Sergeant Andy Seldon turned away from the DVR's small screen, only too well aware of the fact that the infra-red camera, cleverly disguised as a rooftop ventilator, had been recording nothing but images of marauding foxes for the past two hours. 'Early days yet, Alf,' he commented. 'Give our man a chance.'

Cross rubbed his hands briskly up and down both arms, more as a gesture of frustration than a genuine attempt to restore the circulation. 'Operation Firetrap,' he snorted. 'What flippin' dickhead gave this job a name like that?'

Seldon treated him to a faint smile. 'I did, as a matter of fact,' he retorted, smoothing his blond, shoulder-length hair back from his face with both hands. 'Seeing as we are targeting an arsonist, I thought it was quite apt — guv'nor thought so too.'

Cross snorted again and picked at the half-day's stubble on his chin. 'If that's what a university degree does for you, Andy, I'm glad I joined the army instead,' he retorted, shivering now despite the heavy coat and woollen hat he was wearing. 'An' talking of the "mob", I'd rather put up with a stinkin' tank in the Gulf than this ice-box any day of the week — I mean, what sort of crap snoop wagon is this anyway? Zero temperatures, yet no ruddy heating.'

'Beggars can't be choosers, Alf,' his colleague admonished. 'HQ workshops are still in the process of fitting this one out and they've had a problem with the ancillary heating system. We were damned lucky to be able to get hold of it at all this weekend.'

He swung back to his screen and zoomed in on the upstairs window of the target premises. As Cross had observed, not a single light showed. 'Getting old, that's your trouble,' the young DS murmured. 'You should pack it in and retire to the seaside.'

Cross grunted, ignoring the jibe. 'I bet an NCS team wouldn't have had to put up with an ancient wreck like this,' he went on. 'They would have had a brand new, state of the art motor.'

Seldon sighed his exasperation. 'Terry Duval is just a local villain, Alf,' he said, 'not a target criminal involved in organized crime. The National Crime Squad wouldn't be interested in him in the first place, so get real, will you?'

There was a chuckle from a corner of the metal box and a young woman, dressed in a hooded fleece and tight blue jeans, leaned across in her own swivel chair to thrust a mug of coffee under Cross's nose. 'Get that down you, Alf,' she said. 'It's got some Irish milk in it.'

The big man accepted the mug with a curt nod. 'Thanks, Kate, you're a star.' He took a gulp, but even the warming effects of the whisky had little effect on his sour mood. 'I bet Duval's laughin' his jockstrap off,' he said, resuming his tirade. 'How many torchin's has he done? Six? Seven? An' we ain't never come close. I bet he even knows we're out here, freezin' our bollocks off, while he snugs it in his pit — I mean, you don't really think a beaten up van, with the words "Water Monitoring Agency" on the side, is goin' to fool a cunnin' bastard like that, do you? He'll have smelled us a mile off.'

'You may be right,' Seldon acknowledged, panning the camera for the umpteenth time, '*if* he has managed to spot us tucked away here in the first place — which I doubt. But what alternative do we have? He's our best bet for this spate of farm fires — the MO is classic Duval — and I reckon a couple of days' surveillance will give us our best chance of catching him at it.'

'So why not just pull him in and save all this hassle?'

Seldon turned again, treating his colleague to a penetrating stare. 'Pull him in for what exactly?'

'Well, he's a queer boy, ain't he? An' he's got plenty of form. What more do we need? Just pull him in an' get it out of him.'

'Right,' Seldon said, nodding slowly. 'So being gay is a crime now, is it?'

'No, but this one's a bleedin' pervert, we all know that. Torchin' places gives him a hard-on — an' he's only just come out the nut-house after doin' six years for the same sort of thing.'

'We can't pull people in just because they're perverts or have form,' Kate interjected with a short laugh. 'What about wrongful arrest — not to mention good old human rights?'

Cross scowled. 'Human rights?' he threw back. 'In my book, scum like him don't have no rights — human or otherwise.'

Seldon gave another sigh. 'Eastbourne,' he said gravely. 'That's the place for you, mate. Nice little bungalow near the sea-front, I think.'

Kate stood up, sensing that the good-natured bantering that usually went on between her two colleagues was about to rack up a notch. 'I need to pee,' she said.

Seldon closed his eyes for a second. 'Fine,' he acknowledged patiently. 'Then maybe you'd better go and do it. But do keep out of sight, won't you?'

For the first time Cross chuckled. 'Do you want me to come and hold your knickers, Kate?' he queried as he carefully unlocked the side door of the vehicle for her. 'You wouldn't want icicles on your bits, now would you?'

Seldon rested his forehead against steepled fingers in a gesture of resignation. 'I can't believe you just said that, Alf,' he breathed. 'Eastbourne it is for you, my man — and as quickly as possible.'

It seemed degrees warmer outside the van than inside, but the ground was rock hard and the short grass, tinged blue in the moonlight, crackled underfoot as Kate picked her way among the ice choked ruts towards a copse bordering the rhyne to one side of the drove a few yards away. It would have been a lot easier to have relieved herself closer to the police vehicle, but she was only too aware of its half-dozen spy-holes and the excellent zoom capability of the infra-red camera, despite the negative effects of the wash of moon-light, and she had no intention of providing Alf Cross with impromptu entertainment.

An owl hooted dismally as she entered the copse and shortly afterwards something scuttled away from her in the gloom. Though slightly unnerved, she stopped only when she could no longer see the police van and therefore could no longer be seen by the pair inside. Crouched in the crisp undergrowth, she felt strangely vulnerable and not a little silly, giggling nervously to herself as she loosened her jeans and did what she had come to do, one hand gripping the lichen encrusted trunk of an alder tree for balance. But her mirth was short-lived, for the next instant the police radio in its harness suddenly spat at her through her plastic earpiece. 'Stay down, Kate,' Seldon's voice warned. 'We seem to have company.'

But she could hear it for herself now — the thudding note of a slow-running engine — and through a gap in the trees in front of her she caught sight of a chunky shadow bumping along the drove skirting the copse, heading in the direction of the surveillance van. The vehicle was not displaying any lights, but in the brief glimpse she was afforded by the moonlight, it looked like a grey Land Rover Defender with a hard-top and a snorkel fitted to the offside in front of the driver's door.

She frowned. What the hell was anyone doing using the drove at this time of the night — especially without lights? A poacher maybe, or some nocturnal twitcher? Hardly likely, and it was certainly the wrong time of year for one of the secretive eel fishermen who liked to harvest the tiny elvers at night with their strangely shaped nets. So who then? Terry Duval on his way home? He did have a Land Rover Defender, after all, didn't he? Could be and that would be a real bummer, for it would mean that if he had intended doing a job, he would already have done it while they sat there on their arses waiting for him.

Not that any of that mattered, of course. Whoever the mystery marauder was, she could not afford to challenge him anyway — especially if it was Duval — for that would risk blowing the whole police operation before it had got started. And the DCI was not known for her forgiving nature.

Hauling up her jeans, she headed back the way she had come, keeping her head low and stumbling through the trees bent almost double; branches and trailing creepers scraping her face and exposed tree roots snatching at her boots.

By the time she reached the edge of the copse, however, the Land Rover was already alongside the Transit van, but instead of continuing on past it, as she would have expected, it came to an abrupt stop, leaving just a small gap between the two vehicles. Mystified, she watched from a crouched position in the undergrowth as an arm appeared through the driver's window and seemed to touch the side of the Transit before being quickly withdrawn.

'What the hell are you up to?' she breathed, for some reason feeling strangely uneasy, yet still unsure as to whether or not she should break cover to challenge the driver. But the answer was not immediately apparent and even as she finally decided on direct action and started back up the track, the Land Rover's wheels slid on the frosty ground and it accelerated away with a sudden and surprising turn of speed, as if the driver had seen her in his rear-view mirror.

Its lights came on as it pulled out on to the main road and she caught a glimpse of one red offside and one white nearside rear light before it turned towards Glastonbury and powered away into the night. Now Kate could see something projecting from the side of the Transit close to where the petrol filler pipe was located. At first she thought the filler pipe flap had been pulled open, which would have suggested the Land Rover driver had been intending to siphon off some fuel, but then she realized that there was actually something stuck on the side of the vehicle, something that seemed to be a lot more substantial than a projecting filler pipe flap.

'What was all that about, Kate?' Seldon queried over the radio. 'Bugger did something to the Transit.'

But Kate was now hot-footing it towards the vehicle to find out. The fact that she didn't quite make it was due entirely to the searing blast that suddenly lifted her off her feet and flung her over the reeds into the rhyne as the Transit van was blown apart by a massive explosion.

# CHAPTER 2

Twister swore, jerking the Land Rover to a halt a hundred yards or so from the mouth of the drove. He had seen the woman in his rear-view mirror at the last minute, just as he'd swung out on to the main road. *Bloody hell*! Where had the bitch come from? He had assumed the surveillance team were all inside the Transit when he'd placed his explosive. Yet there was this slender figure running towards the vehicle just as it went up. She must have seen him drive along the track and stop beside the van, which meant that, if he had unknowingly passed her on the approach, she would not only have got a good look at his Land Rover, but more importantly, caught a glimpse of his face.

OK, so the chances were that she had been caught in the blast — she must have been close enough for that — which, if true, would solve his problem one hundred per cent, but what if she hadn't? What if she was lying on the track nearby, injured, but conscious enough to call up her mates at the nick on her police radio? He had to find out one way or the other and that meant returning to the scene.

He was tempted simply to reverse back, but then decided against it. If she *had* survived, maybe injured, she would be certain to hear his approach and would have time to hide somewhere, making his task a lot more difficult. So he pulled on to the verge instead and switched off. Then, grabbing a flashlight from the front seat, he sprinted back down the road, his feet slipping and sliding on the frosty surface as he ran. 'Now, little lady,' he panted, pausing on the corner of the drove, with one hand raised to shield his eyes from the glare of the funeral pyre he had created, 'let's see where you've got to, shall we?'

Mud — sticky, heavy and deep. Kate had crashed through the thin layer of ice covering the rhyne and was sinking into it fast. The more she struggled, the more she seemed to sink as the evil-smelling water, now lit by the flames of the blazing Transit just feet above her head, sucked and spat around her like an ice-cold geyser. Again and again she tried to pull herself up the steep sides of the rhyne on to the drove, moaning and gasping in her panic, but her clawing fingers found only frosted crumbling mud and clumps of reeds or grass tufts that came away in her hands the moment she took hold of them.

She was going to drown. The seeming inevitability of it all hit her with mind-numbing force. She had narrowly escaped the terrible death that had befallen poor Andy and Alf, only to face a slow painful asphyxiation as her lungs filled with the filthy water of the rhyne. It was as if Fate were playing with her like a cat plays with a mouse and enjoying every minute of it.

The water was up to her waist now and still rising. She had just seconds left to do something, but her boots were so deeply embedded in the mud that there was no way she could extricate them without some form of leverage. And it was then that she turned her head and saw the shadow tracing a ragged line down the bank behind her, slightly to the right of where she was held fast. She had been so obsessed with trying to climb up the bank on the drove side of the rhyne that she had not thought about the opposite bank. Now turning her upper body round in the water, she saw the stunted tree growing out of a clump of reeds, just a couple of feet away. With a new sense of hope, she reached towards it, stretching her arm out until she felt her muscles were about to tear apart. At first her fingers only brushed the frozen bark, but on her second attempt, by leaning to her right as far as she could, she managed to get hold of a lower branch, then extend her reach up the branch towards the trunk. Twisted right round in an agonizing position, she was able to reach the branch with her other hand, more ice covering the surface of the rhyne fracturing with every movement. The tree bent towards her under her weight, but it seemed to be securely anchored to the bank and bit by bit she succeeded in pulling herself towards it until first one boot tore itself free of the mud and then the other. Hanging precariously from the branch for a few moments, she managed to dig the toe of her right boot into a hollow in the bank and pull herself upwards until she found a toe-hold with the left. Then she was clear of the water and, hauling herself up over the edge of the bank, collapsed on the grass in the moonlight, soaking wet and shivering uncontrollably.

That was when she saw him, standing on the drove, silhouetted against the still burning Transit; a sinister apocalyptic figure dressed in a long dark overcoat with a hood pulled up over his head. She could see nothing of his face, just a black featureless oval, as if there was nothing inside the hood at all, and, as she returned his stare, he raised one hand and pointed at her with a slow menacing deliberation that made the hairs rise up on the back of her neck. Then abruptly he wheeled round and began to run, shoulders hunched and head thrust forward like some creature from a horror film, following the edge of the rhyne back towards the mouth of the drove.

In a second she forgot the cold, thrust aside the shock of what had happened to her colleagues, and scrambled to her feet in a rush. He was coming after her. The rhyne was much too wide for him to jump over and the only way into the field in which she now stood was via a five-bar gate she could see in the hedge to her left, adjoining the main road.

Even as realization hit her, she was running; heading across the rough ground towards the very house she and her colleagues had been watching. Tripping over prominent mounds of grass and stumbling into ankle-wrenching hollows, she threw quick terrified glances over her shoulder to see if the nightmare man was on her heels.

She couldn't believe she was fleeing the scene of such a horrendous crime. She was a police officer, for pity's sake, and two of her closest friends had been cremated right in front of her. She should have been chasing the killer, not the other way around. But this wasn't a training school exercise — this was for real — and she knew from the size of the man that she wouldn't stand a chance if he managed to overhaul her. He had already brutally murdered two police officers in what was plainly a premeditated hit, which meant that killing another one would be of little consequence to him.

So she continued running — falling over twice and raking her thigh on a patch of low level brambles that seized her as she stumbled through them. But then she had reached the broken-down fence enclosing Terry Duval's cottage and was following it along towards the far end of the field. The last place she wanted to seek refuge was the arsonist's cottage. The hooded killer was more than likely Duval himself. After all, who else would have not only had a motive for wiping out the police surveillance team, but have known they were operating in the vicinity in the first place? So she kept going until she reached a belt of trees and was able to bury herself in the tangled undergrowth.

She saw him again then. He had stopped in the middle of the field and was staring towards her. His arms were held out from his body like Somerset's sinister Willow Man and he stood there motionless. She shuddered fitfully in her sodden clothes, thrusting her fist into her mouth to stop herself crying out in the hysteria of the moment. If he came for her now, she had nowhere to go. Behind her was another rhyne. She just prayed he didn't know that and couldn't see it through the trees.

The minutes passed. An animal of some sort — a mouse? — scuttled through the undergrowth beside her and she tensed, forcing herself to remain perfectly still. Then something exploded with a loud 'crack' from the direction of the drove and the hooded figure swung round, apparently startled. Kate saw a fiery tongue leap upwards from the burning Transit before abruptly dying. She could smell the acrid smoke even from where she lay and she felt her sobs starting again as she thought of Andy and Alf.

Just then the killer moved again, turning back towards the main road, head thrust forward as before. Unbelievable as it seemed, he had actually given up. Kate breathed a trembling sigh of relief and watched him go through the gateway on to the road, close the gate after him and disappear behind the bordering hedges. Still she remained where she was. Might be a ruse; he could be waiting for her to emerge from hiding. But a few minutes later she heard a vehicle start up and over the low hedge glimpsed the chunky shape of a Land Rover moving off towards Glastonbury. He really had gone.

Climbing to her feet, she felt for her police radio in its harness and depressed the call button. Nothing. She switched to mobile phone and dialled police headquarters. Still nothing. Pulling the radio free, she felt the water dribbling out on to her wrist. Damnation! The rhyne must have totalled the thing. She was stuffed, with no way of alerting her colleagues to her predicament. Were there any telephone kiosks anymore, she wondered, and if so, where was the nearest one? In the village of Mark or Burtle probably, but they had to be several miles away and in opposite directions. That meant a long trek via the main road and the risk of running into the killer again. But she couldn't just stay where she was. She had to get help from somewhere.

In the end, she decided to head back towards Mark. She would have to knock someone up and use their phone; it was the only thing she could do.

She made the main road and paused a moment to study it in both directions before venturing out into the open.

It seemed to be completely empty. She took a chance and turned towards the mouth of the drove, peering along the track through tear-filled eyes. The Transit was wreathed in black smoke now, flames still spurting through it. She knew no one could have survived the terrible blast she had witnessed, but she still had to check to make sure.

She approached the burning vehicle hesitantly and almost on tiptoe, as if she half-expected someone to jump out on her from the smoke which choked the scene. But there was nothing, just the blackened shell, lit from inside by the flames which continued to feed off the seats, fabric and other combustible materials and licked round the frames of the shattered windows with slavering, spitting tongues.

A vile stench hung in the air — a combination of burnt rubber, plastic and scorched metal, together with something much worse, smothering the usual stagnant earthy smell of the marsh and bringing the bile up in her throat in a series of retching spasms.

There was no trace of Andy or Alf, but she hadn't expected there would be. They had never stood a chance. She just hoped they had died instantly in the initial blast. Feeling strangely guilty about leaving her colleagues behind, even though they were dead, she turned on her heel and stumbled back towards the main road, conscious of smoky fingers from the blaze curling after her like spectral entities, driving her from the scene.

Then suddenly she saw the headlights. They were travelling along the main road, coming from the direction of Glastonbury. She froze, wondering whether help was on its way — a late night reveller returning home perhaps, an HGV on an overnight delivery? Or there again, maybe the killer returning to look for her. But she never found out which, for the lights turned off what must have been at least half a mile away and she swore savagely. Couldn't they see the fire? Weren't they in the least bit curious? *Damn, damn, damn!* She felt so helpless and alone.

Her boots slithered on the frosty road and it felt as if her legs and feet were coated in ice as she reluctantly began the long trek back towards civilization. Within yards the doubts started as to whether she would be able to summon enough stamina or will power to enable her to get there, but she knew she owed it to Andy and Alf to at least try.

In fairness, she did manage about half a mile too, and the fact that she got no further than that had nothing at all to do with stamina or will power.

How the Land Rover had got in front of her, she had no idea, but its lights snapped on with a suddenness that rooted her to the spot like a hare transfixed by lamping poachers. The killer had parked in a lay-by just yards away, patiently waiting for her to come within striking distance and even as she stared at those great burning orbs, the big beast erupted from the lay-by with an ear-splitting roar.

It was the noise that shook her out of her reverie, but instead of throwing herself on to the adjacent grass verge, for some reason she dived the other way, crashing on to the hard tarmac and rolling over on to the far side of the road.

The Land Rover very nearly ploughed through the hedge into the rhyne as the killer wrongly anticipated the evasive manoeuvre she was likely to make, tearing great chunks out of the hedge before swerving back on to the road. By then Kate had vaulted a wooden gate and was heading across another field, powered by reserves of panic. But her ordeal was far from over.

The Land Rover burst through the same gate before she had gone more than a few yards. Glancing behind her, she glimpsed it lurching towards her along the track she was following, headlights rising and falling with the uneven contours of the ground.

A rabbit started across the field from almost under her thudding feet and a couple of sheep raced across her path like ghosts. To her right, a skeletal barn reared up stark and ominous in the moonlight. Then quite suddenly it was gone as the moon itself was briefly obscured by scudding clouds. She immediately changed direction, having mentally pinpointed the barn's position. She missed the cattle trough, but apparently the Land Rover didn't and she had the satisfaction of hearing the crash behind her as it ploughed into it a split second afterwards. This gave her some precious time and she reached the barn while the Land Rover was still reversing back from the trough with a harsh crashing of gears before resuming its pursuit.

The huge double doors at the front of the building were not closed properly, but jammed in position and she had only just managed to force herself through the narrow gap before the roar of a powerful diesel engine announced the arrival of her pursuer. She had to find a place to hide and probably had just seconds to make her choice. The barn seemed to be filled with rotting hay and it stank, but she could hardly see a thing, let alone find a hiding-place. She collided with a machine of some sort and swore, then froze as she heard someone trying to force the double doors open. At least being slim had its advantages; the size of her pursuer meant he couldn't squeeze through the gap. But he had strength on his side and it wouldn't take him long to gain an entry through sheer brute force.

Hide. Quickly. But where? She groped around in the gloom, but found only the cold touch of metal on one side and slimy hay bales on the other. Behind her the door shook violently and then she heard a cracking sound. She shrank further into the barn, her throat dry and perspiration pouring down her face despite the coldness of the night air.

Then quite suddenly the moon reappeared from behind the clouds, flooding the place with pale opalescent light through holes in the roof. At once she saw the arm and part of a leg pushing through the gap between the double doors and heard the groan of the door as the killer pushed against it. Throwing wild glances around her, she spotted the ladder at the far end of the building giving access to a loft supported by wooden pillars. The likelihood was that the whole thing was rotten like the rest of the barn, but she had no alternative other than to chance it — unless she fancied burying herself among the bales of hay.

The ladder was also made of wood and the lowest rung snapped the moment she stepped on it. Behind her a splintering crash indicated that one of the barn doors had finally capitulated. In a panic, she went for the next rung, felt it give and transferred her weight to the one above, which also snapped. Halfway up and hanging precariously from the sides of the ladder, she heard the shuddering groan of the barn door being hauled back. With nothing to lose, she went for broke, clambering up the remaining rungs at speed, almost losing her footing as every other one snapped or started to give as she went. But then she was within reach of the loft floor and had pulled herself up over the edge as a powerful flashlight blazed a trail down the middle of the barn like a tongue of fire.

Pressing into the floor, she heard the killer's heavy footsteps advancing down the barn, his flashlight swinging left and right, probing every nook and cranny. She held her breath as he paused at the foot of the ladder, feeling the loft floor tremble as he shook the ladder experimentally. Then the beam of the flashlight grazed the criss-cross of beams supporting the remains of the roof as it traced a path along the edge of the loft floor, pausing for an anxious few seconds just in front of where Kate lay before being withdrawn.

Silence for a moment and then a despairing creak. *Hell's bells!* He was going for the ladder! Kate eased herself further back across the loft, then froze again at the sound of a sharp crack from below, followed by a scrabbling sound and a loud oath. Another of the rungs had snapped. She breathed a sigh of relief. *Thank heavens for rot.*

He didn't try again after that, apparently satisfied that she couldn't have climbed up into the loft by that route, and turned his attention to the rest of the barn instead. Shortly afterwards the barn doors shuddered and, peering over the edge of the loft, she saw his sinister figure framed in the opening for a second before he disappeared, leaving her alone among the shards of moonlight.

But she wasn't fooled by his apparent departure. She felt sure he was still out there in the shadows, waiting patiently for her to show herself, so for what seemed like an age she continued to lay there and it wasn't until she heard the diesel engine actually start up that she realized he was going.

Even then she did not move immediately and the Land Rover's distinctive thudding note had actually faded into a buzz before she plucked up the courage to climb down the remains of the ladder — losing her footing on the broken rungs and falling heavily on to a stack of mushy straw bales piled up on one side at the bottom.

The barn doors stood wide open, moonlight gushing through the opening. Pushing through into the night air, it suddenly dawned on her why the killer had finally decided to depart, leaving his business unfinished. Above the sparsely wooded fields on the other side of the main road, the night sky was lit by a myriad of flashing blue and red lights. As she headed towards the shattered gate at a trot, she heard the shriek of a siren and saw the unmistakable shape of a fire-engine racing past. The troops had arrived at last.

# CHAPTER 3

Cold — Kate had never felt so cold, despite the scorching to her face and hands from the explosion and the insulation provided by the thick woollen blanket in which she was wrapped. Perched on the edge of the police estate car's rear hatch, she could feel the bitter chill creeping up her legs and into her insides from the crisp frosty ground like some anaesthetizing medical probe. Still sodden from her plunge in the rhyne, she needed a change of clothes like yesterday, but there was no way she was going to leave the scene until she had some answers to the horrific crime that had just been perpetrated.

The gutted shell of the police Transit van still smouldered in the light of the halogen lamps trained on it from the nearby fire service tender, despite the force of the fire hoses, and she tried not to think about the blackened dismembered remains that were obviously still tangled up inside the twisted metal of the vehicle, awaiting the farce of a pathologist's examination.

Shivering in uncontrollable spasms, she drew the blanket more tightly about herself, her eyes straying from the Transit van, several yards away behind the blue and white police crime scene tape, to stare across the field on the other side of the drove and the target premises their little team had been watching.

Lights bobbed about in the darkness around Terry Duval's cottage and she visualized what would be happening as her enraged colleagues illegally smashed their way in, looking for him. She was so engrossed that she didn't hear the crunch of footsteps in the stiff frosty grass and she jumped when the voice spoke right beside her.

'Dried out then, young lady?'

The speaker — a thirty-something, hatchet-faced woman with short black hair and a narrow, slightly crooked mouth — leaned against the side of the patrol car, studying her in the light streaming from inside, the flashing roof strobe of the vehicle illuminating the side of her face in rapid pulses of blue, reminding Kate of the witch in the Judy Garland film, *Dorothy and The Wizard of Oz.*

Detective Chief Inspector Rozalind Callow (Roz to her team when she was in a good mood) always made Kate feel uncomfortable. Single, with a sexual preference for her own gender, she had already come on to her slender auburn-haired subordinate twice and Kate's fierce rejection of her advances had created a festering hostility between the two women.

'Not quite, ma'am,' Kate replied, playing safe by addressing her formally. 'Did you find anything at the house?'

Callow shrugged. 'A nice stash of what looks like home-made explosive, plus a collection of timers and detonators, but no sign of the man himself. His motor's gone too, so he's obviously off on his toes.'

'If he *was* the one who actually did this.'

The DCI straightened up and popped something (probably one of the extra strong mints she seemed addicted to) into her mouth. 'Who else would have had a motive?' she said. 'After all, it's pretty obvious from the stuff we found in his cottage that he is our fire-bomber, so he would have had both the reason and the opportunity to waste those who were snooping on his activities.'

Kate shivered as the cold got to her again and the next moment Callow's hand was on her shoulder, gently squeezing it. 'You ought to get out of those wet things, you know,' she advised. 'My place is just down the road at Wedmore. I can easily run you there and I'm sure we can find something to fit you while your clothes dry out.'

Kate shook her head a little too quickly. 'I'm fine,' she replied, cringing into her blanket. 'But thanks anyway.'

The DCI stiffened, her face hardening as she withdrew her hand. 'So tell me again what happened here tonight,' she said, a harsh edge to her voice now. 'We didn't have time to go into it properly when I first arrived, did we?'

Kate took a deep trembling breath. 'Not much else I can tell you. As I said, I got caught short and went for a pee. This Land Rover turned up and stopped alongside the Transit. The driver seemed to reach out towards the Transit, then drove off at speed.' She hesitated, biting her lip. 'Seconds later, "boom" and I ended up in the rhyne.'

'And you still can't describe the man?'

Kate shook her head. 'All I saw at the time was an arm reaching out of the window towards the Transit—'

'When he planted the IED on the side of the Transit?'

'If that's what it was, yes. In the dark, it was impossible to see anything inside the vehicle.'

'But you must have got an idea of what he looked like when he came after you on foot. He would have been in the open and in brilliant moonlight.'

Kate sighed her exasperation. 'Look, all I saw was a tall male figure in a long hooded coat. I didn't see his face. How could I? He was too far away.'

'And still no ideas on the number of the vehicle? We already know Duval uses a Land Rover Defender and it would help if we could confirm it was his motor.'

'As I told you earlier, I can only say that it was a grey-coloured, hard-topped Land Rover Defender with one of those snorkels fitted to the front offside wing. It's rear number plate was unlit and the rear nearside light cover was

obviously broken as it was showing a white light on that side.'
She shrugged. 'That's the lot.'

'But surely you got another look at the motor when it pursued you across the field?'

'Only briefly — and then I was too busy running to see much at all.'

'Doesn't give us a lot to go on, does it?'

'I'm sorry, but that's all I can tell you.'

'And where was it you had this pee?'

Kate pointed down the drove. 'In that copse — you can see it from here.'

'So how did you end up in the rhyne?'

'I was blown off my feet by the blast.'

'But you just said you were in the copse.'

Kate could feel anger surging up inside her. Callow seemed to be trying to trip her up, like a suspect under interrogation. 'I had left the copse by then and was running towards the Land Rover.'

'What made you do that?'

'I thought something was wrong and wanted to check it out.'

'Only then? But I thought you told me you heard the Land Rover approaching? Why not check the motor out before it got to the Transit?'

Kate controlled herself with an effort. 'Because I thought it would compromise the operation — *and*,' she added more forcefully as Callow started to interrupt again, 'Andy Seldon told me over my radio to keep my head down.'

The DCI nodded and abruptly changed tack. 'Strange you didn't think of radioing for assistance though. We were actually alerted by an emergency call from a passing motorist who saw the fire.'

'I couldn't call anyone. My radio was totalled when I went into the rhyne.'

Callow looked unconvinced and, with a sharp hiss of irritation, Kate fumbled for the radio and slapped it into her outstretched hand.

The DCI smiled. 'Maybe you didn't have it switched on?' she gloated, and pressed the transmit button to prove her point. Even from where she was sitting, Kate could hear the answering voice of the police control room. 'Nothing for you,' Callow responded, and handed the radio back to Kate.

'Scared, were you?' she said.

For a moment Kate didn't answer, hardly able to credit that her radio was now actually working and conscious of how this must look to Callow.

'Well, were you?'

Kate glared at her. 'Of course I was bloody scared — the vehicle blew up in front of me, didn't it? And then I was chased by a sodding psycho. Who wouldn't have been scared?'

'If that's what really did happen.'

Kate stumbled to her feet. '*If* it happened?' she grated. 'What the hell are you implying? Anyone would think I was the villain here.'

Callow met her gaze without flinching. 'Simply trying to get my head around things, that's all,' she replied smoothly. 'After all, we don't want the rest of the department to think you ran out on your colleagues, do we?'

Kate gaped at her. 'Ran out on them?' she gasped. 'Ran *out* on them? That's an awful thing to say.'

Callow shrugged and turned away from the police vehicle. 'Just being practical,' she said, without committing herself one way or the other. 'Now, I think it's time you went home to get some rest. Nothing more you can do here.'

'I'm staying,' Kate said stubbornly.

'I'll get you a car,' Callow said even more firmly. 'See you at the nick around ten for a full debrief.'

The streets of Highbridge were understandably deserted when the grey Land Rover Defender turned off the Bridgwater road into a narrow side-street at around 1.30 a.m. Swinging through a gateway in a cul-de-sac shortly afterwards, it pulled up in a private walled car-park at the rear of Wadman & Son

Funeral Directors, and came to an abrupt stop, its headlights blazing back at it from a pair of heavy steel doors. The driver was coughing on a cigarette as he jumped out of the vehicle to open up. Then, snapping on powerful strip-lights, he eased the Land Rover into a long triple-width garage already occupied by a sleek black Daimler hearse and a black Daimler limousine on one side and an old green van on the other.

Cutting the Land Rover's lights and engine simultaneously, he sat there for a few moments, thinking.

The hit had not gone as well as it should have done, that was for sure, and he knew that the woman witness who had escaped him could turn out to be something of a problem later on unless she was found and dealt with PDQ. But he had no idea who she was, where she had come from or what she was doing on the drove at such an hour, so the conclusion of that bit of extra business would have to wait, whether he liked it or not. And anyway, it was time to report in.

Leaving the vehicle, he made his way by flashlight to the end of the garage and through an internal door giving access to the main premises. Beyond lay a small workshop, equipped with a workbench, racks of carpentry tools and a shelf laden with an assortment of tins and bottles. The place could have been any carpenter's workshop, but for the fact that the workbench was occupied by a light oak coffin, which was obviously nearing completion. The room smelled strongly of a combination of varnish and turpentine.

Passing through another door, he entered a long hallway with doors opening off on both sides. The chapel of rest, mortuary and administration offices were, like the workshop, all accommodated on the ground floor and the reception office, its big shop-style windows engraved with the name 'Wadman & Son Funeral Directors', fronted the street at the far end of the hallway. But his funeral business could not have been further from his mind at that moment and he headed for the narrow staircase, giving access to his flat upstairs.

Stepping over a chain, bearing a plastic sign 'Private No Entry', which was suspended between the wall and the banister post, he ascended the staircase with little enthusiasm. Opening the door at the top, he was greeted by the smell of yesterday's fries and crinkled his nose in disgust. Home, sweet home — like hell. He switched on the light and, propping himself on his threadbare settee, lifted the phone and dialled a number. He was answered almost immediately.

'Twister,' he announced, using his agreed nickname. 'Job's done.'

'Any problems?' the voice at the other end queried.

'None,' he lied, after a second's hesitation, unwilling to reveal that he had messed up with the woman who had got away.

'Brilliant. No one saw you then?'

'Only those in the Transit and they're all toast now.'

'You've done well, but we'd better keep our heads down until things quieten down. The police will be out for blood after this.'

He glanced round the shabby room. 'Why would I want to be anywhere else?' he commented with heavy sarcasm, smiling grimly as the phone went dead.

# CHAPTER 4

The police patrol car dropped Kate off outside her Bridgwater flat as it was getting light and her stony-faced 'chauffeur' didn't wait to see her inside, but drove off the moment she slammed the door shut, without a single glance in her direction. The journey home had not been pleasant. She had sensed the hostility in the car the moment she had climbed inside; neither the uniformed constable behind the wheel or his front seat colleague acknowledging her presence or making any attempt at conversation throughout the whole twenty-minute drive. To be fair, that had actually suited her in her semi-traumatized state, but the atmosphere in the vehicle had shocked and unsettled her nevertheless and she was relieved when the police car's tail-lights finally disappeared round the corner in a cloud of diesel.

Despite the coldness of the air and the need to get out of her still sodden clothes, she made no immediate move towards the door of the dismal tower block where she had lived for the past two years. Instead, she stood there for a few moments, shivering fitfully and staring at the curling exhaust plume the police car had left behind as it floated like a wraith in the pool of light cast by a street lamp, her mind in even greater turmoil than before.

What the hell was going on? She had done nothing to warrant the silent treatment she had received — unless the fact that she had survived the Transit blast was seen as reprehensible under the circumstances and her colleagues felt she should have perished in the explosion as well. Could that be what lay behind the DCI's interrogation and the open hostility of the crew of the police car — resentment that she had survived while Andy Seldon and Alf Cross hadn't?

OK, so it could be that she was imagining things — over-reacting due to a combination of trauma and fatigue — and it was possible that the bobbies in the car had not actually been giving her the cold shoulder at all, but just couldn't think of anything to say after all that had happened. Tragedy affected some people like that, making them clam up, reluctant to discuss the circumstances with those involved; she had seen it many times in the job. Yeah, but not this time; this time it was different. That car had radiated hostility and there hadn't been as much as a single 'good morning' or a 'glad to see you're all right' from either of the pair, just a heavy smouldering silence.

As if to reinforce her feelings, the DCI's words hammered away in her brain once more: *'We don't want the rest of the department to think you ran out on your colleagues, do we?'*

Ran out on them? Why on earth would anyone think that? Could it be that Callow had resorted to spite because Kate had rebuffed her sexual advances — spreading poison about her among her colleagues in an attempt to get even? It did not seem possible that an experienced detective chief inspector would do such a thing, but something was certainly wrong and, on top of the acute emotional distress she was already suffering, Kate suddenly felt more alone and vulnerable than she had felt in her life before.

She was so wrapped up in her own misery, in fact, that she failed to notice the shadow lurking in the stairwell — a shadow that remained motionless as she climbed the stone staircase to the first floor and only emerged from hiding when she had slammed the door of her flat shut behind her.

Then, as she wearily slipped out of her wet, badly singed clothes and started to run a bath, the shadow moved out of hiding and slowly, almost hesitantly mounted the staircase towards her floor.

Kate did not hear the bell at first. Her head was already under the shower hose attached to the mixer tap as she tried to wash the evil-smelling gunge from the rhyne out of her hair before climbing into the bath. The sight of herself in the full-length mirror had come as quite a shock — the scorching to her face from the explosion, the ugly bruises now materializing in the form of dirty mauve smudges down one side and along one thigh, the cuts to her hands and both forearms where she had scrambled up the bank out of the water and the ruination of her shoulder-length auburn hair, which had once gleamed like burnished copper when caught in the light and now resembled the matted head of a cleaning mop.

Visitors she certainly did not need and when she finally did hear the bell — which the caller now blatantly chose to lean on — her fury surfaced in a lava-like rush. Pulling on a silk dressing-gown, she wrapped a white towel round her head and marched to the door with murder in mind. Her jaw dropped, however, when she saw who was standing on the doorstep.

The young woman in the long, black hooded coat seemed to shrink before her gaze, sniffing and wiping her dripping nose with the back of one hand. 'Hi, Sis,' she said, looking down at her feet.

'Linda?' she breathed, gaping at the pale emaciated face and blistered lips.

'None other,' her visitor said, affecting a twitchy smile. 'Can I come in?'

Closing her eyes briefly in resignation, Kate stepped back and watched her shuffle inside. 'What the hell are *you* doing here?' she queried, closing the door behind her. 'You should be in rehab.'

The haunted eyes looked away from her and the woman wiped her nose on her sleeve this time, her body noticeably shaking under the long coat. 'I — I'm in trouble, Kate,' she muttered. 'Need some dosh.'

Kate pushed past her into the living room and closed the blinds. 'Oh Linda, look at you,' she whispered as the girl slipped off the hood to reveal a mass of auburn hair that was even dirtier and more tangled than her own. 'You look like a corpse.'

The other treated her to another weak smile and appraised her critically. 'You don't look so hot yourself,' she commented.

Kate muttered an oath. 'Never mind what I look like. I thought you'd be off that crap by now.'

The girl nodded, still snuffling and shaking. 'Bit of bad luck, Sis,' she replied, her voice almost a whisper.

'But you went to rehab?' Kate repeated, frustration now getting the better of her. 'You were doing so well.'

Linda shuddered violently, clutching at her stomach. 'Couldn't hack it,' she mumbled. 'Had to get out.'

Kate leaned against the back of a chair, studying her bitterly. The very last thing she needed was for her junkie twin sister to turn up on her doorstep with more problems for her to sort out. 'So what is it now?' she snapped. 'Coke, "H" or what?'

Linda shuffled forward a few paces. 'Need another fix, Kate,' she said, desperation in her voice. 'Just a few quid — honest. Then I'll — I'll go back.'

Kate snorted. 'What, to rehab? Do me a favour. I'm not that naive.'

Her sister drew her arms about her and rocked on her heels for a moment, her face glistening with perspiration. 'Sis, *please*, just a few quid.'

Kate's mouth hardened. 'Linda, you were sent to rehab as a condition of your suspended sentence. You were lucky you didn't go down again. They'll be looking for you — and I could get into a lot of trouble if you were found here.'

The young woman stared at her fixedly. 'So, you going to turn me in?'

Kate didn't answer her, but swung towards the kitchen. 'First we'll get a meal inside you and then we'll talk. I think I can rustle you up some egg and chips at least.'

Linda shook her head several times. 'Don't want—' she began, but Kate cut her short.

'I don't give a damn what you want. I've got enough problems at the moment without you as well. Now, either you sit and wait while I make you something, or I put in a telephone call to the nick.'

Linda's shakes worsened as she sat down on the edge of the settee. 'Egg and chips then,' she said, forcing a smile and once more wiping her nose with her sleeve.

In the small galley kitchen, Kate could feel the walls closing in on her. She wanted to scream, cry and vomit all at the same time as she gripped the edge of the work surface for support, hyperventilating like some hysterical schoolgirl while her knotted stomach sent waves of acid surging up into her throat.

Broken visions of the blazing police Transit seared across the room in front of her, blotting out the cooker and the chuckling chip pan, and the smell of cooking fat gave way to the sweet nauseating stench of burning flesh as the chips thrust up through the fog like charred fingers. *We don't want the rest of the department to think you ran out on your colleagues, do we?*' Roz Callow mocked again inside her head, as she reeled back against the refrigerator, knocking her egg box off the side with one flailing hand.

Then the bang of a door closing and fantasy and reality merged into one as she stumbled back into the living room. Her handbag gaped at her with malevolent mirth from the table and she saw with a sense of shock that her lipstick and other oddments were scattered across the polished wooden surface. Checking the handbag, she found that her purse was missing. True to form, Linda had seized her chance and gone, snatching her purse containing one of her two sets of keys, her credit cards and over fifty pounds in cash.

Sinking to the floor in a heap, she began to sob hysterically as the eggs in the kitchen bubbled over on to the electric ring and, seconds later, the fire alarm activated.

Twister was in the workshop of his funeral parlour, examining the newly crafted oak coffin, when his mobile rang at just before nine. All the coffins were made on the premises by local pensioner, Tom Grace, who had been with the firm since it had started, but as it was Saturday, the old man was off and Twister had the place to himself — which turned out to be just as well, for the call was not one he would have wanted to answer within the earshot of others.

'You bloody fool,' a familiar voice responded to his terse acknowledgment.

He started. 'What do you mean?'

'You missed one. A woman detective, named Kate Hamblin, was in the copse having a pee when you totalled the Transit. She was unhurt.'

His heart made a sucking noise as he thought about his *faux pas* the previous night. *So the bloody mare was another copper, was she? Just his luck!*

'That's awkward,' he replied, trying to keep the alarm out of his voice.

'Awkward, you stupid prat? It's a lot worse than that. She might have got a look at you.'

'Very unlikely,' he replied, trying to convince himself as much as his caller. 'It was too dark.'

'And what about the motor? She must have clocked that.'

He emitted a short laugh. 'I hope she did.'

'What do you mean?'

'I used an old Land Rover I managed to find—'

'You did what?'

'A Defender, like Duval's, but with replicas of his index plates front and back. A bit of insurance, just in case I was spotted near the scene. If your lady cop did clock the number, it will only put Duval even more in the frame.'

'I didn't tell you to do that.'

'Maybe you didn't, but I only agreed to do the job for you; how I go *about* doing it is *my* business.'

'Not if it means I could be compromised, it isn't. You'd better get rid of that Land Rover pronto.'

He sighed. 'You worry too much. There are dozens of 'drovers like mine all over the Levels.'

'Dump the thing and torch it nevertheless.'

'Bit dodgy with Old Bill swarming all over the place, don't you think?' He paused to light a cigarette. 'And anyway, if I did dump it, I'd have to get another motor and I don't need to tell you, I'm a bit boracic at the moment.'

There was a snort of anger. 'Your financial state will be the least of your worries if it turns out Hamblin can ID you, so you'd better fix her PDQ — just in case.'

'I would if I knew where to find her?'

'She has a flat in Bridgwater. I'll give you the address.'

He breathed a sigh of relief; the information he needed at last. Grabbing a biro and an old newspaper from the workbench holding the coffin, he pinned the phone between his ear and shoulder and quickly took down the details on a piece of white space, adding, 'It would help if I knew what she looked like.'

An irritable hiss. 'Around 5' 6", slim, with auburn hair, blue eyes and lots of freckles. Is that enough for you?'

'Sounds exactly my type — especially the freckles bit.'

'Just fix her, OK. I don't care how you do it — but do it.'

He exhaled slowly. 'Sorted.'

'It had better be — for both our sakes.'

There was a click and, pocketing the mobile, he stood there for several minutes, absent mindedly caressing the brass handles of the coffin and pulling on his cigarette as he thought about his next move.

Kate Hamblin was history — had to be. He couldn't afford to mess up on this contract with his finances the way they were. He had taken over the family firm from his father after an ignominious exit from the SAS had pushed him into working for the mob as an enforcer and earned him a term inside. The old man had run the firm successfully for nearly forty years until he had ended up in one of his own nice oak coffins, and he had obviously thought his only son and heir would carry on the good work when he died. But the confidence he'd expressed in his will had been misplaced.

Twister — as young Larry had been nicknamed by his army comrades for his preferred method of dispatching combat targets by snapping their necks — was no businessman. Drink and gambling had soon depleted the family coffers and even the money he had made out of fencing property burgled from the unoccupied houses of deceased clients had been insufficient to fill the black hole in his finances. Most of his father's long-serving retainers had deserted him following empty promises in lieu of pay. Of the original crew, only Albert Price, his senior assistant who virtually ran what was left of the business for him as his deputy, and master carpenter, Tom Grace remained. With the resignation of Maggie Page, the elderly receptionist who had fronted the business for over thirty years, he had also been forced to rely on single mum, Sue Dennis, to do the job — when she deigned to turn in, that is — and, but for Albert's wife who helped out from time to time, he would have had to do the laying out of the cadavers himself. As a result, his business had been reduced to a basic 'cadaver disposal' service, as Albert Price described it, and he could no longer offer clients the additional frills, like embalming, that his father had been so proud of. Even his pall-bearers were hired in — not that that mattered much, for he'd only had two funeral bookings in the past month anyway.

With the banks and other creditors breathing down his neck, the light oak coffin on the workbench beside him was likely to be the last one old Tom Grace made and he smiled grimly as he ran his fingers over the imitation brass plate on the lid. Poor Mary May was the only cadaver left in his mortuary fridge and she would very shortly be heading for the crematorium anyway. Then what? Bankruptcy, seizure of his

35

cars, his flat and other property and public humiliation? That was unthinkable and now this lucrative contract had come along, offering the solution to all his problems, there was no way he was going to let some bitch of a bluebottle ruin it for him. But first he had to find her.

# CHAPTER 5

The CID office on the ground floor of the new police station in Highbridge was practically dead when Kate pushed through the double doors at just on ten o'clock in the morning after wasting half an hour on the telephone cancelling her stolen credit cards.

'An incident room's been opened on the top floor,' Dick Stacey, the grim-faced office manager, snapped as she walked into the room. 'Briefing in five minutes.'

He hardly raised his eyes from his desk as he spoke and there was no warmth in his tone, no sign of sympathy in his expression.

Tight-lipped, she headed for the stairs and the hubbub of conversation that penetrated even the thick glass of the door on the landing, feeling a bit like a convicted criminal about to walk into court to be sentenced.

The man in the rumpled suit overhauled her halfway up with a shouted, 'Kate!' Detective Constable Hayden Lewis was the oddball of the department, his public school background and old-world courtesy setting him apart from the rest of his more streetwise colleagues, who regarded him with tolerant amusement. Yet he had looked after Kate ever since her arrival and, while he had not so far managed to pluck up the courage to tell her so, his affection for her was common knowledge. The stars in his hazel eyes now clouded over, however, as he studied her from under the mop of unruly flaxen hair that tumbled over his ears and forehead like an uncut hedge.

'You shouldn't be here, you know,' he admonished gently, 'not after what you've been through.'

Her bottom lip trembled and he grabbed her in a sympathetic bear hug, ignoring her tears flooding into the collar of his threadbare shirt.

'I can't believe it,' she choked, 'I just can't believe it.'

He prised himself free, suddenly looking awkward. 'Listen, Kate,' he went on, 'it might be better if you kept out of the briefing — you know, took a back seat for a while.'

She dried her eyes, moving to one side as two uniformed officers approached, obviously heading for the incident room. 'But surely I'm a key witness?' she said, meeting a searching gaze from one of the policemen as he opened the landing door. 'I — I saw the whole thing.'

Lewis looked uncomfortable. 'Kate, there's like — er — rumours going round; you know the sort of thing. Might be best if you spoke to the DCI before going in there.'

'What sort of rumours?' Suddenly there was anger in Kate's blue eyes. 'Rumours about me — is that what you're saying?'

Lewis hesitated. 'People are very upset, Kate. You have to understand that Andy Seldon in particular was a popular bloke.'

The tears were coming again as Kate fought to control her emotions. 'He was popular with me too, Hayden,' she whispered. 'And I nearly died with him on that job.'

He patted her arm. 'I know that, old girl, but there are those on the department who — well — are questioning exactly what happened and why, er—'

'Why I survived? Is that what you're trying to say?'

But Lewis didn't get the chance to respond.

'Ah, Kate,' DCI Callow purred from behind her. 'In early, I see.'

Lewis made a grimace and, nodding towards Callow with a quick 'Morning ma'am,' he headed on up the stairs and disappeared through the landing door.

'I was going to the briefing,' Kate said, her voice now cold and brittle.

The DCI shook her head. 'I don't think that's a good idea, Kate. Not after all you've been through. You told me enough about the hit for the incident room team to be briefed and Detective Superintendent Davey, who has just been appointed Senior Investigating Officer, wants to see you anyway as soon as he's finished at the briefing.' She gave a cobra-like smile. 'Why don't you make yourself a cup of coffee downstairs while you're waiting?'

The office manager was elsewhere when Kate returned to the general office, but the kettle on its tray by the window was already boiling, suggesting he couldn't be far away. She poured herself a black coffee with trembling hands and slumped into the swivel chair at her desk, taking occasional gulps as her mind turned itself inside out.

What was happening to her was like a nightmare. First the horrific murder of Andy Seldon and Alf Cross, then the finger of suspicion pointed at her for absolutely no valid reason at all as far as she could see. And on top of it all, another serious problem arising with her own twin sister, Linda, which had the potential to jeopardize her very career.

In an effort to control her rising panic, she forced Linda from her mind and concentrated instead on the cold-blooded crime that had just been committed — desperately trying to override her emotions and look at things in the clinical deductive way she had been taught.

Why on earth would Terry Duval waste two policemen? It didn't make sense. OK, so as Roz Callow had already pointed out, he did have the motive, drove a Land Rover

Defender *and* had the knowledge and previous where explosives were concerned, which certainly put him in the frame. Furthermore, he had quite a history of violence.

A former quarry blaster, he had suffered a severe beating at the hands of a group of young farmers after forming a sexual relationship with a local sixteen year old boy and had retaliated by using his technical skills to booby-trap each of the cars of his assailants with an incendiary device. One lad had nearly died and two others had suffered multiple injuries, earning him six years in Broadmoor. The spate of farm fires had started within months of his release and his MO was certainly all over them: a timed incendiary device magnetically attached to a tractor or car parked in a barn or other outbuilding in the early hours of the morning, then triggered electronically from somewhere close by — and on two occasions a Land Rover Defender seen driving away from the scene immediately afterwards.

It all fitted nicely together, but what still didn't fit in her mind was why Duval had targeted the police Transit. He must have known that murdering the surveillance team would not halt the operation — only bring down even greater heat on him — so there had to be more to the appalling crime than was immediately obvious, but what, that was the point?

Reaching across to Andy Seldon's desk, which backed on to her own, she picked up the buff folder labelled 'Operation Firetrap', remembering with a faint bitter smile Alf Cross's disparaging comments about the whole exercise.

Terry Duval's photograph stared back at her from the copy of his criminal record file; the square, robot-like face, sparse black hair and half-closed eyes indelibly etched on her memory from detailed pre-surveillance scrutiny.

She knew without having to re-check his file that he was a 42-year-old loner, who had lived with his mother in her cottage on the Levels until her death a year ago — ironically as a result of an accident with a farm tractor shortly after he had been released from Broadmoor. No wonder, given his history, that he had a thing about farms. He was currently unemployed and receiving the usual social security benefits. As far as she knew, he had no surviving relatives and nowhere to go except his cottage, yet he had managed to disappear somewhere and she suspected that finding him was not going to be that easy, especially as he still had his wheels.

Then she started and stared at the file again, the photograph of the Land Rover he was known to be using jumping out at her. She studied it more closely. A green hard-top Defender? She thought back to the incident. Surely the vehicle she had clocked at the crime scene had been grey? Could be mistaken, of course — after all, it had been dark at the time — but something else did not seem quite right either. In her exhausted state, she couldn't at first make out what it was, but then suddenly it dawned on her. The Land Rover she had glimpsed at the murder scene had been fitted with a snorkel, whereas the one in the photograph before her had no snorkel at all. Now that *was* interesting. Either Duval had two Land Rovers or maybe — just maybe — the Land Rover she had spotted on the drove was not his at all, which suggested he might not have been the killer in the first place.

With a frown, she dumped the file back on the desk, just as Stacey shuffled back into the office carrying a carton of computer printer paper.

He threw her a swift searching glance. 'Told you the briefing's upstairs,' he snapped.

'I've been excluded, Dick,' she retorted. 'Any idea why?'

He shrugged and bent over the office printer, turning his back on her — probably to hide his embarrassment. 'Nothing to do with me,' he said. 'I'm only a bloody civvy.' He hesitated and cast her another sidelong glance. 'If I were you though, I'd watch my back,' he added and shuffled from the room again, leaving her staring after him with even greater unease.

Detective Superintendent Steve Davey was one of the new breed of senior police officers and a far cry from the rough, chain-smoking, heavy drinking 'guv'nors' of the past.

Unlike most of the old guard who had cut their teeth on service in the military, he had not so much as sniffed an army barrack block — only private school and university. As a result, instead of a campaign medal, he had gained a first-class honours degree in psychology, enabling him to join the force on the fast-track graduate entry scheme and make superintendent in just ten years.

An attractive, immaculately groomed 36-year-old, with a shock of strikingly unusual white hair, lazy blue eyes and a designer tan to go with his designer smile, he might easily have stepped out of the pages of a romantic Mills & Boon novel; exuding the confidence and charisma that would ultimately guarantee him a ticket to the top echelons of the service. This outward charm, however, concealed a shrewd analytical mind and a ruthless sense of purpose that had earned him the nickname 'Jaws', and Kate was instinctively wary of him when he breezed into the room an hour later, inviting her to join him and Roz Callow in the DCI's office 'for a debrief'.

Her caution proved well-founded too. Following the opening formalities, including just the right amount of arm-patting concern over all that she had been through, he cut to the chase with the aplomb of the true professional. His questions followed much the same line as those of Roz Callow — who sat on the edge of the windowsill behind Kate throughout the whole of the so-called debrief, studying her with undisguised hostility — but they were put in a much more subtle way and probed a lot deeper into the incident and Kate's involvement in it. For all his smiles and empathetic nods, there was a hard glint at the back of Davey's lazy blue eyes and Kate was left feeling drained and for some reason laden with guilt at the end of it all.

When she pointed out that the Land Rover she had seen at the crime scene did not match the vehicle Duval was known to drive and suggested that the killer might therefore not be Duval after all, Davey's benevolent mask slipped even more. It was apparent that he had already made up his mind about the identity of the culprit and didn't want anything to interfere with his preconceptions or prolong what he saw as an open and shut inquiry. As a result, he immediately cut her short, dismissing her suspicions out of hand and leaving Callow to reduce her to shocked silence by blatantly questioning the motives behind her defence of a 'wanted criminal'.

Davey's parting words, as he stood up to go did not help her dismembered spirits either. 'You seem to have been through an awful lot, Kate,' he said, treating her to another of his patronizing smiles, 'so I think it would be a good idea if you took a few days off now to recover.'

She swallowed hard and shook her head. 'I'm fine, thank you, sir,' she said, 'and I want to see this inquiry through.'

He shook his head firmly. 'Sorry, that's out of the question.'

'But — but I'm a key witness.'

'That's exactly why you should *not* be part of the inquiry.'

She clenched her hands in her lap, her body tense. 'Are you suspending me, sir?'

He frowned. 'Don't be silly, Kate. Why would I want to do that?'

She threw a swift accusing glance at Callow, noting with a sense of rising frustration the satisfied smirk on the hard, sallow face. 'Sir, I *have* to stay with this inquiry,' she persisted, doing her best to keep her emotions in check, but unable to prevent the tears welling in her eyes and creating tiny rivulets down her cheeks. 'I need to do my bit.'

There was a tic of irritation at the corner of Davey's mouth now. 'I think I've made the position clear enough, Kate,' he admonished. 'The answer is no. You'll just have to accept that.'

Callow brushed against Kate as she followed her boss out the door. 'Try your hand at knitting,' she murmured close to her ear. 'Very therapeutic, I'm told.'

Kate sat there for several minutes after Davey and Callow had left, staring unseeing into the building's rear yard where both uniformed and plainclothes officers constantly moved to and fro between the back door and the jumble of untidily parked vehicles. The set-up of the incident room would be in full swing by now — with desks hauled into place, banks of computers and photocopying machines plugged in and tested, cork and whiteboards erected for the eventual accommodation of briefing notes and SOCO photographs, and the ubiquitous coffee machines positioned in convenient corners. All the trappings of a major police inquiry, which she should have been part of, but from which she had been coldly and calculatingly excluded. *Bastards*!

Just twenty-six years old, she had thought her career in the force was on a roll until now. Selected under the police graduate entry scheme after leaving university with a first-class honours degree in modern languages, she had established an excellent reputation for herself and had been 'starred' by the hierarchy at HQ Personnel for future high rank. Even before finishing her two years' obligatory police probation, she had been attached to CID and within months appointed a temporary detective constable. She had been made substantive in the post a year later, managing to gain a top grade on the junior detective training course, and it had been intimated that she was likely to achieve detective sergeant rank within a further year if she kept her nose clean.

Not bad for a comprehensive schoolgirl from Ilford, whose dysfunctional family and brutal stepfather had provided the impetus for self-improvement as a means of escape. Now, however, everything seemed to be falling apart and, despite all her hard work, she felt that she was in no better position than poor Linda, who had taken the much easier self-indulgent path to destruction.

She had nearly died back there on the Levels — only a weak bladder had saved her — and yet despite all that, she was being treated like some kind of pariah; almost as if she were being held directly responsible for her colleagues' deaths. It just didn't make sense — or did it? Her eyes widened and she moistened her lips with her tongue. Maybe they were right and she *was* responsible? If she had actually done something instead of just crouching there in the bushes watching the Land Rover approach the Transit, she could have prevented the murders. Maybe Andy and Alf would still be alive now if she had acted sooner.

'*Scared, were you?*' Roz Callow's hateful voice was in her head again and she shuddered. *Was* that it? Is that why she had done nothing — because she was scared? She shook her head violently as if defending herself before an invisible jury. No, that wasn't it at all! She'd had no reason to be scared before the explosion. She couldn't have known what was going to happen — and anyway, Andy had told her to stay down. As for running from the scene afterwards, yes, she fully accepted she had been scared then — who wouldn't have been when faced with a killer twice their size, with no possibility of backup and no means of defending themselves?

She ran her fingers through her hair, trembling fitfully. Why the hell was she seeking to justify her conduct to herself? It was all nonsense, a suggestion the DCI had implanted in her brain when she had interviewed her at the scene. Good grief, she was almost starting to believe it herself. What was wrong with her? She had to get away from this place before she flipped completely.

Dumping her radio on to the desk (she couldn't hang on to that if she was no longer working) she stumbled through the back door of the building, blinking in the fragile strands of sunlight probing the walled yard where she had parked her MX5. She was so wrapped up in her misery that she failed to notice the stocky man in the pork pie hat and rumpled grey overcoat who had just clambered out from behind the wheel of his old Honda Civic. But she soon became aware of him when he shouted after her, 'Oi! And where do you think you're off to, Hamblin?'

She half-turned, meeting the gaze of hard brown eyes. Detective Inspector Ted Roscoe was DCI Callow's number two. A bruiser of a man, who rarely smiled, but tended to glare at people from under his thick, bushy brows, the balding ex-boxer with the fearsome Stalin moustache always reminded Kate of a bad-tempered bulldog and, while he was highly respected by his team for his years of experience and straight-talking no-nonsense approach to everything, he had earned a bad reputation for himself as a womanizer. Furthermore, as one of the old guard, he had shown himself to be totally out of sync with the ethos of the modern police service. His contempt for fast-track university entrants, whom he often referred to as 'educated pricks', was legendary and although Kate had always got on reasonably well with him (probably because she was young and female), she could not forget that he had taken an instant dislike to Andy Seldon, making his life a misery when Seldon refused to back him up following the DI's assault on a local drug-pusher. She wondered how he felt now that Andy had paid the ultimate price — probably relieved that the DS was out of the picture as far as his forthcoming crown court case was concerned.

'You'd better ask the guv'nor,' she threw back over her shoulder and, continuing to her car, hitched up her short skirt to slip behind the wheel As she did so, she couldn't help giving way to a burst of shaky incredulous laughter when she glimpsed his eyes appraising her long legs. Bloody hell, it was unbelievable. Two dead officers, a major manhunt underway and all Roscoe could think about was checking out her thighs. Now sobbing hysterically, she slammed the gear into first, burning rubber as she skated across the yard and out through the entrance — ignoring the 'No Exit' sign and narrowly missing a police traffic motor cyclist turning in.

She could see the traffic man in her rear-view mirror staring after her and half-expected him to gun his powerful machine in pursuit — almost disappointed, in her semi-surreal state, that he didn't — but, as things turned out, it might have saved her further trauma if he had.

# CHAPTER 6

Alf Cross had lived in one of Highbridge's red-brick terraced houses just off the Bridgwater Road ever since finishing his two years' police probation and Kate found herself pulling up outside his place just five minutes later. Unlike Andy Seldon, who had no family as far as anyone knew (apart from a girlfriend living somewhere in Leeds), Alf had left a wife behind and despite the trauma she herself had suffered, Kate felt duty bound to call and see her. She and Pauline had become close friends when Kate had joined CID and she could not even begin to imagine how the poor woman must be feeling now. She was dreading facing her so soon after her tragic loss, but it had to be done and she made an effort to hold her own emotions in check as she stepped up to the front door.

'And what do *you* want?'

The gaunt, blonde-haired woman who answered the door glared at her with open hostility and her belligerent greeting took Kate completely by surprise.

'Pauline?' she queried hesitantly as if the other's uncharacteristic demeanour raised some doubts about that. 'I — I wanted to make sure you were OK and to tell you how sorry I am about Alf.'

'Did you?' The woman stepped aside and motioned her past. 'Then you'd better come inside, hadn't you?'

The curtains were drawn across the bay window in the front room where Kate had spent so many afternoons sharing gossip over a cup of tea and the atmosphere was unusually stale and heavy. She turned as Pauline followed her through, but her natural instinct to embrace her friend in a sympathetic hug was put on hold by the hard expression in the other's blue eyes and the grim set of her jaw. There was no evidence of tears, but shock was clearly etched into her face and a strong sour smell accompanied her into the room, suggesting that she had been drinking.

'Well,' Pauline snapped, almost as a demand, 'exactly what is it you wanted to say?'

Kate felt as if she had been physically slapped in the face and for a moment was stuck for words. 'Just — just to let you know that if there's anything I can do—'

'Do?' Pauline's face twisted into a bitter sneer. 'Haven't you done enough already?'

'Done enough? I don't know what you mean?'

Pauline stared at her with obvious contempt. 'Managed to save your own skin, didn't you, love? Left poor old Alf and Andy to fry.'

Kate felt the room start to close in on her and she grabbed the edge of the door to stop herself pitching sideways. 'That's just not true,' she whispered, and the tears came back again in a flood. 'I couldn't do anything. It all happened too quickly.'

'Yeah, while you were hiding in the bushes.'

'Hiding? I wasn't hiding. I was—'

'Having a pee, I've been told. Lucky old you.'

Kate shook her head brokenly and reached towards her with her free hand. 'Pauline, why are you treating me like this? We've always been friends.'

Pauline ignored her hand and stepped back into the hall with a curt, 'You'd better go.'

For a moment Kate continued to stare at her. 'I don't understand,' she whispered. 'Who have you been talking to?'

Pauline reached for the handle of the front door and threw it open, admitting a shaft of welcome sunlight into the gloomy hallway. 'Get out. And don't ever come back here again.'

There was a barely suppressed violence in her tone that frightened Kate and she edged past her warily, eager to be out in the beckoning sunlight among the reassuring sounds of the street. The front door slammed shut behind her even before she got to the gate.

She dropped her ignition keys as she approached her MX5 and, picking them up, she leaned against the driver's door for a moment, shaking and hyperventilating.

'You all right, love?' The skinny youngster in the hooded fleece had stopped and was peering at her curiously. He couldn't have been more than fifteen or sixteen, but there was a concerned frown on his acne-pitted face.

She treated him to the ghost of a smile. 'Yes, thanks, just had a bit of a shock, that's all.'

He nodded with the sagacity of an old man. 'Coffee, that's what you needs,' he diagnosed. 'Hot 'n sweet. Good for shock that is.'

Then he was on his way again with the cocky springy gait so often adopted by the streetwise hoodies of his gen-eration, cigarette smoke trailing from between the fingers of one hand.

She watched him go with another weak smile, heartened by the concern of a kid who, a few hours ago, she would have written off as nothing more than a complete waste of a skin. His advice was sound too. After her shock encounter with Pauline — on top of everything else that had happened in the past twelve hours — she felt shaky and light-headed and she knew she was in no fit state to get behind the wheel of her car until she had managed to pull herself together. Coffee sounded like the ideal solution.

Leaving the car where she had parked it, she went in search of a café — and she found one within a couple of hundred yards.

The so-called 'tea-room' had faded red and white checked curtains tied back from the grubby window and the doorway, with its half-open scabby blue door, was about as inviting as the entrance to a run-down charity shop. But she was in no mood to be picky and she took a seat in the corner with her back to the counter, heedless of the dirty crockery piled up on the table in front of her.

The place was half-empty, with only three of the dozen or so tables occupied — one in the opposite corner by a rough looking couple who seemed to be arguing over the bill, another by a pair of labourers tucking into a serious fry-up and a third by a quartet of greasers exchanging expletives in a smoky haze of illegally lit cigarettes.

Certainly not the most inspiring company and the waitress in the stained blue apron did little to improve the situation. But at least the coffee and buttered scone arrived very soon after the order had gone in and the girl's surly manner meant Kate did not have to engage her in polite conversation, which suited her fine.

She needed to be left alone — to be given time to think and quell the discordant clamouring of the demons inside her head — and she was trying to do just that when she noticed the sealed yellow envelope on the plate under her scone. Frowning, she tore the flap open and extracted the single sheet of paper from inside. It was a grubby note, written in bold block capitals, as if by someone used to carving their initials on a tree.

I DIDN'T DO IT. MEET ME 2 AM PAVILION PIER BURNHAM SEAFRONT. DON'T TELL YOUR MATES OR I WON'T SHOW . . . TERRY DUVAL

Almost knocking over her cup of coffee, she jerked round in the seat, staring over the counter. The waitress eye-balled her from the doorway of the kitchen and she was behind the counter and in her face within seconds.

'Did you leave this on my plate?' she rapped, waving the envelope at her.

The girl paled and stumbled backwards, gulping. 'Feller said it was a joke,' she blurted. 'Give me a fiver.'

Kate stared past her into the kitchen. A little man in a dirty white tunic and black trousers stared back at her in obvious astonishment.

'What feller?' she demanded, producing her warrant card and holding it up in front of the other's bulging eyes. 'What did he look like?'

'J—just a feller. Wore a long coat an' a woollen hat. Came up to me out back an' said you was a mate of his.'

The girl's eyes strayed to her left and Kate caught sight of the 'Toilets' sign.

'Sod it,' she breathed and lunged for the entrance to a narrow passageway alongside the kitchen.

She checked the single toilet cubicle, but it was empty. Another door opened on to a paved yard with an open gate at the far end and even before she got to it, she knew she would be too late. There was an alleyway beyond, snaking away in both directions between the walls of other premises, and she could see immediately that it was deserted.

'Blast! Missed him,' she said aloud. '*Now* what do I do?'

But she knew the answer to that even as she asked herself the question.

# CHAPTER 7

Moonlight — eerie in its laser-like brilliance — searing the eyes with the intensity of an ice-cold sun. It washed over the glistening mud, beyond the strip of tourist sand from which the frothing saliva of the Bristol Channel had briefly retreated, and blazed a glaring white trail along Burnham-on-Sea's deserted esplanade, where the seaside shelters peered over an anaemic sea wall as if watching for the returning tide.

Kate stopped her MX5 close to the kerb, about a hundred yards from the pier's domed amusement arcade. Switching off, she sat there for a few moments, studying the esplanade and listening to the ticking of the hot engine.

What the hell was she *doing* here? Meeting a suspected double murderer alone on an empty esplanade at two in the morning, with no backup in the wings and, now she no longer had her police radio, with just her own personal mobile phone to fall back on if she needed assistance? It was not only sheer lunacy, but went against every rule in the book. She should have reported the note immediately to Detective Superintendent Davey and left him to sort out a suitable reception committee for Duval, instead of taking on the job single-handed in an effort to redeem herself in the eyes of her colleagues.

OK, so that could have resulted in the threatened 'no show', but at least she would have been playing by the rules, absolving her of any responsibility for the outcome. This way — and she shivered at the salty dankness now creeping into the car — this way, she was not only putting her job on the line if things went pear-shaped, but probably her life as well.

Shaking a cigarette out of the packet she had 'borrowed' from Alf Cross's desk (even though she didn't normally use them), she lit up and choked for a few seconds on the acrid smoke.

Yeah, reporting the note would certainly have been the proper thing to do, but there was one very big drawback to doing the proper thing this time. She was already in the dog-house for allegedly running out on her partners and it didn't take much imagination to envisage the likely reaction of the inquiry team to the revelation that their tainted colleague had now been contacted personally by the suspected killer; she wouldn't just be labelled a coward, but seen as actually complicit in the murder plot itself. What a bloody mess.

Her eyes jerked to the rear-view mirror as headlights flooded the car from behind. Seconds later a souped-up Subaru Imprezza snarled past, the thud of its sound system almost on the pain level as a couple of youths leaned out of the nearside windows, shouting abuse at her silhouette. Then it was gone, the accelerating roar of the powerful engine accompanied by squealing tyres as the car took the corner into a side street towards the town centre at speed.

For a while longer she continued to sit there, drawing on the cigarette and trying to pluck up the courage to leave the car. Then, glancing at her wrist watch, she saw that the luminous dial registered 1.55 am. She had just five minutes to make the rendezvous. Decision time.

Stubbing out the filter-tip in the ashtray, she checked that the torch on the front passenger seat was working and, thrusting it into the pocket of her leather coat, reassured herself that the captor pepper spray she had also brought with her was still in the other. All ready then, so what was it to be — go through with the prearranged meeting, or scuttle back to the security of her flat?

She gave a tight smile and turned up the collar of her coat. 'In for a penny,' she murmured. Throwing open the driver's door, she climbed out into the cold, flinching as the door hinges cracked like pistol shots on the still air.

A stray dog — a grey emaciated-looking thing — limped its way across the road in front of her as she pressed the button on her key fob to activate the central locking mechanism. The animal sniffed once in her direction, then disappeared down the same side street as that taken by the Subaru. Nothing else stirred on the esplanade.

She shivered again and drew her coat more tightly about her. It was almost as if the whole resort was under some sort of lock-down; that she was being watched by scores of eyes from behind the unlit windows of the shops and bay-fronted houses lining the esplanade, eyes that were fixed on her every move, anticipating the drama about to unfold before them.

Her knee-length leather boots rapped out a tattoo on the pavement as she approached the domed pavilion, her hand closing on the captor spray in her pocket in readiness. The site comprised an amusement arcade and several typical seaside shops and takeaways, with the latter end on to the esplanade and the arcade set back several yards across a paved forecourt. She half-expected someone to lunge at her from the shadows of the adjoining sea wall, but there was no one and she released her breath in a rush.

Moving out to the kerb, she scrutinized the esplanade in both directions, but the only sign of life was in the shape of the same stray dog, which suddenly emerged from the side street opposite and stood for a moment staring in her direction. Then, limping across to her car, it blatantly urinated over the nearside front wheel before ambling off again towards a distant set of traffic lights.

Where the bloody hell was Duval? Could it be that the mysterious note was nothing more than a hoax? That someone — her colleagues at the nick perhaps — had played a cruel practical joke on her? Or maybe Duval had got cold feet, simply abandoning the meeting altogether? Either way, it would not only mean humiliation for her, but a complete waste of time and adrenalin, which was now running at full blast.

Muttering her irritation, she was about to return to her car when she heard the piercing whistle. It seemed to come from the other side of the sea wall and it was then repeated twice more. She went closer and scanned the moonlit beach below, one hand shielding her eyes against the glare. At first nothing and then, with a start, she saw the torch flash twice in the blackness under the pavilion pier.

Yet another whistle and a further double flash to which, on impulse, she responded with her own torch. But that was all she was prepared to do. The original invitation had been to meet by the pavilion pier; venturing under it was not an option as far as she was concerned.

Again the torch flashed and again she responded in kind, but made no move towards accepting the invitation. It was at this point that she heard the telephone ring loudly. Initially she thought it was her own mobile, but the next second glimpsed a tiny light flickering on top of the wall a couple of feet to her right. For a moment she just stared into the eye of the abandoned mobile phone as if mesmerized. Then, abruptly snapping out of her reverie, she grabbed it and answered the call.

'Can we get on with this?' The voice at the other end was impatient, belligerent.

She had to swallow several times before the words would come. 'Taking a bit of a risk using your mobile, aren't you?' she exclaimed, trying to hide the slight quaver in her voice.

There was a harsh chuckle. 'Don't worry, love, it ain't mine; I nicked it, so no probs. Now, you coming down or not?'

She shook her head firmly, more to convince herself than anything else. 'No way. Do you think I'm stupid? You come up here.'

A loud snort. 'An' I ain't stupid neither. Come up there an' show meself to your tame pigs? Do me a favour, lady.'

'I'm alone.'

''Course you are, but you still got only three minutes an' then I'm out of here. Got it?'

Before she could say anything else, the phone went dead.

*Bugger it*! There was no way she could allow a murder suspect to simply fade into the night, but at the same time, what guarantee did she have that he just wanted to talk rather than up his body count? After all, she was the only witness to the crime and that made her target number one — even if she had very little evidence to offer. And as she turned things over in her mind, it suddenly struck her that she really didn't have a proper plan of action anyway. What had she intended doing when she met Duval face to face? Make a lone arrest by squirting pepper spray up his nostrils? Hardly realistic under the circumstances, was it?

Yeah, well, you should have thought about that before deciding to go it alone, shouldn't you, DC Hamblin? Walking out on the thing is no longer an option. You're stuck with it, whether you like it or not. Anyway, you're a copper, aren't you? This is what coppers do, so get on with it, love, even if you are terrified at the prospect.

The grey dog had come back and was in the process of checking out the rear nearside wheel of her car as she turned to retrace her steps, but it made off again at a limping run the moment it saw her, denying her the opportunity of giving it a swift kick in passing.

A few yards from the pavilion a railed plinth marked one of several access points to the beach through a gap in the sea wall. On the other side stone steps dropped down to a walkway topping stepped sea defences, which ran the whole length of the wall, like the seating of an ancient Roman arena.

Anxious to avoid going on to the beach in her expensive leather boots until she ran out of concrete and conscious of the fact that her earlier dip in the rhyne had already ruined her only other pair, she turned sharp right at the bottom of the steps to follow the walkway along the wall, until further progress was prevented by a wooden fence, forcing her down to the beach.

She made a face as her boots sank into the crumbly sand and stopped for a moment to listen. At first she thought she could hear the sound of the returning tide, but then put this down to a low, newly arisen wind. She moved on, picking her way carefully round pieces of driftwood.

Strands of moonlight probed the blackness beneath the pier, touching on silvery pools of water among the forest of supporting piles and creating sinister shadows that seemed to retreat before those tentative laser fingers.

'Where are you?' she demanded, her voice husky and uncertain.

There was no reply. She gritted her teeth in a futile effort to control the heavy pumping sensation in her chest and throat. 'I warn you, I'm armed,' she lied, fumbling for the captor spray in her pocket.

Something moved in the gloom in front of her — a shape denser than the blackness — and she heard the slosh of water. She swung her torch in the direction of the sound, but the beam picked out nothing more than the rows of piles.

She moved closer. 'I'm not going to play games with you, mister.' she grated.

The face of the moon was blotted out by the pier's superstructure as she advanced a few more steps, the beam of her torch sweeping left to right and back again.

'OK, that's it — you can get stuffed, you stupid arsehole.'

She turned back towards the moonlit beach, angry at being trifled with, yet somehow relieved that Duval had decided not to show. It was then that the muscular arm reached out from behind to pin her arms by her sides and a large calloused hand clamped itself over her mouth and nose, cutting off her air supply.

# CHAPTER 8

Linda Hamblin stood in the shadows of the little wooden porch, listening to the rhythmic snores emanating from the open fanlight a couple of feet away. She affected a fleeting smirk. It seemed that the old farts were well under and that couldn't be better as far as she was concerned; while they snored on, she would slip inside and help herself.

This was not the first time she had paid a visit to the retirement bungalows in 'Cemetery Close', as she had cruelly nicknamed the small development on the outskirts of Bridgwater, and she knew they were always worth screwing. The majority of the elderly residents were either disabled or doolally — or both — and, like many older people, tended to distrust banks, especially after the latest economic meltdown. That meant there was usually plenty of cash stashed away in cupboards and drawers — and she needed that cash badly.

She had already used up the fifty she had lifted from Kate's handbag and the ecstasy of her last fix was fast wearing off. Worse still, the tell-tale sweating and shaking, marking the start of the downer which always followed the brief drug-induced 'high', had already begun. Soon the nausea and agonizing cramps that accompanied what addicts liked to refer to as cold turkey would set in. Time was running out and although she knew where she could get more of the stuff, even at two in the morning, it was likely to cost her a lot more; it always did. She could only hope that the wrinklies she had selected this time were loaded — and careless.

She felt no guilt about stealing from elderly people — taking money that they could ill-afford to lose — any more than she felt guilty about stealing from Kate, her own twin sister. She felt no sense of satisfaction either. Ruled by her addiction, it was simply a matter of necessity — of survival even. They had what she needed and because they were old, they were an easy touch; it was that simple — expediency.

Not that heroin was entirely to blame for the way she was. She had always been weak and self-centred, opting for the easy way out rather than facing up to the challenges of life. Expelled from school at fifteen for pushing cannabis, she had fallen for a crack dealer and then become pregnant by him. She had suffered a miscarriage following her addiction to heroin and after her boyfriend had ditched her, had embarked on a life of crime and prostitution to feed her habit, ending up in a variety of institutions, including nine months in prison for a bungled burglary. During enforced rehab, she had been virtually weaned off the drug. But it hadn't lasted long and, following her release, she was soon back to her old ways.

Now twenty-six years old and suffering from the insidious onslaught of hepatitis B and chlamydia, she had been given one last chance to kick the habit and receive proper medical treatment with a lenient suspended sentence for shoplifting. But, true to form, Linda had been unable to face up to the harsh regime of detoxification, which was a condition of her sentence, and had simply walked away from rehab after just a month. She knew her future was bleak, but her slavery to heroin put her craving above all else and it certainly dominated her mind now.

Creeping past the bedroom window of the little bungalow, she headed down the sideway that separated it from its detached single garage. The back gate opened without protest and she found herself on a moonlit patio accessed from the lounge-diner by aluminium-framed doors. The manicured postage-stamp garden, with the ubiquitous bird bath and timber shed, was enclosed by a high fence, which, though obviously designed to put paid to prying eyes, meant that none of the neighbours could see her either. She smirked again in spite of her deteriorating condition. Couldn't be better.

The catch on the kitchen window was broken and, like the gate, opened without a sound. She could hardly believe her luck and there was even a convenient stack of bricks beneath the window to help her to climb in over the sill.

The stainless-steel draining-board creaked under her weight and her trainers squeaked once on the vinyl floor. Otherwise, she managed the entry with the stealth of a shadow. Yeah, a shadow; she liked that.

The kitchen door was ajar and from the hall she could hear the sound of a clock ticking. Producing the masked torch she always carried with her, she went through each drawer in turn, starting at the bottom and working up like the true professional, enabling her to work faster without being obstructed by drawers already opened.

She found the tenners first — a whole wad of crisp ones in the back of a housekeeping diary — then a tin of one pound coins, which she carefully emptied, one by one.

The cramps started as she straightened up and she swayed for a moment, gripping her stomach with a silent cry as her senses swam. But the scent of money was too strong to resist, greed overruling caution. Finding nothing in any of the cupboards, she crept along the carpeted hall and slipped into the lounge-diner.

Delicate porcelain figures adorned the middle shelf of a teak unit housing a Bang & Olufsen stereo system, and a couple of oil paintings in flashy gilt frames occupied one wall. Her heart quickened. The porcelain and paintings looked expensive and she knew that the Bang & Olufsen *certainly* was. This had to be a well-heeled couple, which probably meant a lot more money tucked away — not that she was given the chance to find out, for she was rudely interrupted even before she managed to dip her hand into the drawer she had bent down to open.

She hadn't heard the soft footfalls in the thick hall carpet and only realized she had been rumbled when the lounge's twin chandeliers blazed, temporarily blinding her and sending her lurching to her feet. The rotund little man standing in the doorway looked vulnerable and faintly ridiculous in his knee-length dressing-gown and slippers, his bandy white legs supported by a steel walking stick in each gnarled hand.

'Gotcha, you thievin' bitch,' he grated, his watery blue eyes fixed on his unwelcome intruder with obvious glee.

Seeing what she was up against, Linda's fear quickly faded. 'Out of my way, old man,' she said, moving towards the door. 'I don't want to hurt you.'

'Oh you won't hurt me,' the other retorted, standing his ground. 'My guardian angel will see to that.'

Linda felt the cramps intensifying and she felt sick, but she couldn't help releasing a short inane laugh. 'And which guardian angel would that be?' she sneered. 'The Archangel Gabriel?'

'No,' the old man replied, with a grim smile and pushed the door further back to allow something big and black to push past him into the room. 'Just Daphne, my Rottweiler!'

Kate could feel her senses slipping away as she desperately tore her hands free and attempted unsuccessfully to prise the assailant's hand away from her face. She tried to remember the self-defence techniques she had learned all that time ago at police training school, but her mind was freezing up and all she could manage was a half-hearted backward kick at his shins. Then his foul breath enveloped her as he bent down close to her ear. 'Pack it in, you silly cow,' he hissed. 'You'll only get me mad.'

There were cartwheels of light in front of her eyes now and she seemed to be spinning into a black void. His hard voice came again, but more distant. 'I'm goin' to take my hand away. Make a sound an' I'll wring your neck.'

The next instant fresh salty air was gushing with painful force into her lungs and she bent over almost double, gasping and retching.

'Heard noises,' Duval growled. 'Thought someone else was here.'

She straightened slowly, reaching out to steady herself against one of the piles, and turned to face him. 'You bastard,' she gasped, peering myopically at the ominous black shape behind the torch that was trained on her face. 'I told you I was alone.'

'Yeah,' he sneered, 'but pardon me if I don't believe everythin' a copper tells me — comes from personal experience.'

Her hand slid into her pocket, feeling for the captor spray, but it wasn't there and she stopped short, suddenly remembering that she had dropped the thing with her torch when Duval had grabbed her from behind. 'So why ask me to meet you if you don't trust me?' she countered.

She heard him grunt. 'What choice do I have?' he retorted. 'You're the only one who saw what really happened to them two coppers.'

'Apart from you, you mean.'

She saw the torch jerk and his tone was harsh and gritty when he replied. 'I had nothin' to do with that job. It was a bleedin' set-up.'

'Who by?'

'An' how the hell would I know? Maybe someone with a grudge.'

'Might be quite a few of those around,' she acknowledged with more than a hint of sarcasm, but he seemed not to have heard her.

'Yesterday afternoon,' he went on, 'someone left a note under the windscreen wiper of me Land Rover while it were parked round the back of my place.' He hesitated. 'The note weren't signed, but whoever wrote it said they had evidence I'd torched a farm near Glastonbury couple of weeks back—'

'And had you?'

He ignored her. 'They threatened to hand the lot over to Old Bill 'less I met 'em at midnight last night to sort out a price. Then, a few hours later, I gets a phone call from some geezer askin' if I'd got the note an' tellin' me to make sure I turned up for the meet.'

'And where was this meet?'

'The car-park below Brean Down.'

'And you went?'

''Course I bloody went, but when I got there no one showed. I hung around for nearly an hour an' was on me way back when I heard the newsflash on local radio about them coppers in the Transit. I knew you lot had been there snoopin' on my place—'

'You *knew* we were there?'

He gave a contemptuous snort. 'Do me a favour, love, I can smell Ol' Bill a mile off. Anyway, I put two and two together and sussed I'd been set up — got out the way, so the job could be pinned on me — an' I did the only thing I could an' pissed off.'

'And this note you mentioned, what happened to that?'

He released his breath in an exasperated hiss. 'Stuck it in the pocket of me fleece I left hangin' on the kitchen door, didn't I? Didn't think I'd need it again.'

Kate gave a disparaging grunt, for a moment forgetting her vulnerability. 'A convenient story, I'll give you that — almost believable.'

He swore. 'It's the bloody truth, you disbelieving cow. An' unless your lot have already found it, that note will still be where I left it.'

His anger was palpable even in the gloom and Kate shrank away from him, stopping only when she found one of the pier's piles at her back. 'But — but why are you telling *me* all this?' she blurted, as he towered over her. 'I'm not even on the inquiry team.'

He snorted again. 'Not very bright for the filth, are you?'

She frowned, unsure as to what he was getting at, but it was only for a moment and as realization abruptly dawned, she stared at him in disbelief. 'Holy Moses, you want me to recover it for you, don't you?' she breathed. 'You actually want me to go in there and bring it out for you?'

'No, I want you to run away with me to South America,' he threw back. 'What the hell do you think I want you to do? I can hardly go back for the bloody thing meself, can I?' He pressed something into her hand. 'The key to the back door, OK? You just got time to do the bus' before it gets light.'

Kate's mind was racing. She was in a cleft-stick. There was no way she could overpower this giant of a man and take him in single-handed. If, on the other hand, she refused to co-operate, he would simply disappear, leaving her with nothing to show for her lone initiative but eventual dismissal from the force and possible criminal charges for obstructing an official police inquiry.

'And what makes you think I would help you?' she went on quickly, playing for time as she tried to work out what to do next. 'Two of my best friends died in that bomb blast.'

He gave a short humourless laugh. 'Maybe, but from what I hear, you're in enough cack yourself. Your mates think you run out on them two coppers, don't they? Which means you need all the Brownie points you can get. So dig out that note for me an' I'll turn meself in. That way I gets a chance of proving me innocence an' DC Hamblin gets a nice bit of personal glory. You savvy?'

'And how am I supposed to let you know I've got the note?' she went on, trying to keep him talking.

He grunted. 'Don't you worry about that, love, I'll get hold of *you* — just give me your mobile number.'

She hesitated and he swore. 'I ain't got all day, you know,' he warned.

Making a sudden decision, she rummaged in her pocket and reluctantly handed over one of her business cards, commenting, 'Be a lot more sensible if you let the investigation team have the note and turned yourself in right now.'

Another cynical laugh. 'Oh yeah? An' have one of your lot burn it so they can get a quick conviction? Do me a favour. At least you've got too much to lose to stitch me up.'

'But who's to say you didn't write the note yourself as a sort of insurance policy before you did the job?'

But suddenly he was no longer listening and she felt him tense in the gloom. 'I thought you said you come here alone,' he grated.

'But I did.'

'Is that right?' Grabbing her by the hair, he jerked her head to one side so that she was staring back at the beach she had crossed just a short time before. At once she saw the policeman. He was only yards away from the pier, his tunic buttons glinting in the moonlight as he approached. 'What's *he* doin' here then?'

Without waiting for her answer, he threw her roughly to one side and took to his heels, the elastic blackness springing back into place after him as the rapid sloshing of water accompanied his flight towards the other side of the pier.

Then, as she struggled up on to her knees in the wet sand, a powerful flashlight blazed in her face, forcing her to throw up an arm to shield her eyes from the sudden whiteout. 'OK, miss,' an authoritative voice rapped. 'Out here where I can see you.'

Flaming woodentop, she mused uncharitably, but complied with a resigned shrug of her shoulders. Where he had come from she hadn't the faintest idea — no doubt the local plod who checked out the pier for the customary winos and junkies as a matter of course. But he had certainly cocked up any chance she might have had of persuading Duval to hand himself in and given her one hell of a job of trying to explain to her superiors what she was doing under a seafront pier at after two in the morning.

The policeman's free hand was already cupped around the radio projecting above the lapel of his tunic and she closed her eyes in despair as he called for female backup.

'Quick shag, was it, eh?' he said, when he'd finished his request, the possibility that she could actually have been a victim of rape something he had apparently not even considered. 'Your punter done a runner then?'

Kate shook her head in the manner of someone humouring a small child and produced her warrant card. 'Not quite, Constable,' she said with emphasis on her mispronunciation of his office. 'DC Kate Hamblin.'

He gaped. 'You're a police officer?' he exclaimed.

'No,' she replied drily, pocketing her card. 'I'm a bloody mermaid.'

# CHAPTER 9

The man in the hooded coat had been standing for so long under the canopy of the esplanade shelter that he could hardly feel his legs and feet. But it had been worth it. From his vantage point Twister had been provided with a good view of the beach and, more importantly, the pavilion pier, and his night-sight binoculars had enabled him to keep even closer tabs on Kate Hamblin as she cut across the sand towards the forest of supporting piles.

Staking out her Bridgwater pad throughout the afternoon and evening had certainly paid off and he was pleased that the patience of his old army days was still with him. He had thought about breaking into the little tart's flat and doing her in there and then, but was glad that he had held back an extra thirty minutes. To be honest, he had been surprised to see her leave home at well after one in the morning, but it suited his purpose admirably and because of the GPS tracking device previously fitted under her car, he had been able to follow her at a discreet distance, leaving his Land Rover out of sight in a side street when he saw she had parked on the esplanade.

He had no idea who she was meeting; it had to be a meet of some sort surely — unless she was into moonlight skinny-dipping — but he was content to wait until she finished what it was she was here to do, just so long as she started back to her car before his legs and feet froze completely.

The arrival of the cop car was completely unexpected and he shrank back into the shadows of the shelter, silently cursing his luck as it stopped behind Kate Hamblin's MX5. The young policeman was obviously surprised to see the solitary sports car parked on the esplanade and he walked round it several times, shining his torch through the windows and peering at the licence plate. Then, still not satisfied, he strolled over to the sea wall and peered down on to the beach. Twister saw him stiffen at the same moment as he himself saw the torch flash under the pier. *Bugger it!* That was bound to arouse the copper's curiosity and could totally foul up his plans for the night.

He watched as the policeman headed for the gap in the sea wall and the steps down to the beach like a hound on the scent, seeing him emerge on the sand moments later and stumble diagonally towards the pier. Using his binoculars, he saw Kate Hamblin materialize from under the pier on the invitation of the policeman's flashlight and stand talking to her colleague. From her body language, it was apparent that she was not at all happy at being disturbed and, lowering his binoculars for a second, Twister frowned. 'Now what have you been up to down there, miss?' he murmured quietly to himself.

His answer was not long in coming and it was delivered from a totally unexpected source. Sudden movement on the very edge of his field of vision drew his attention away sharply from the action below the pier to another of the railed plinths marking a beach access point 2-300 yards beyond the pavilion. A dark figure had emerged through the gap in the sea wall and was stumbling in near panic down the steps to the esplanade.

'And who the devil are you?' he exclaimed, and quickly trained his binoculars on the figure as it ran across the road to disappear into a side street opposite. 'Well, I'm damned,' he breathed, 'Terry Duval. Now that *is* interesting.'

But interesting or not, he didn't get much of a chance to ponder the possible implications attached to Duval's sudden appearance. Instinctively swinging back to the beach, he saw Kate brush the young copper aside and start back across the sand towards the esplanade. It was time to go.

His Land Rover was parked in a side street on the other side of the road and he made it comfortably, slipping behind the wheel and sinking down in the driving seat as much as he could to avoid attracting attention. From its position near the mouth of the junction, he was afforded a clear view of his target climbing into her car. The copper arrived shortly afterwards, but drove off shaking his head even before she had started her engine. As she pulled away, Twister smiled. Everything seemed to be falling into place for him. Maybe he would even get to bed ahead of first light now, but before that he had a nice little 'accident' to arrange.

Two local coppers came for Linda, a regular and a special, and they seemed surprised to find that their burglar was not some hardened thug, but an emaciated young woman who looked about as problematic as a truanting schoolgirl. Maybe that was why they made their big mistake.

By rights they should have handcuffed her, but they obviously thought this slip of a girl, shaking and retching in the throes of cold turkey, would be no problem at all for them and they were almost casual in their approach.

'Right, love,' the bearded overweight regular said, shifting gum from one side of his mouth to the other. 'You're nicked, OK?'

There was no caution, no attempt to search her — which for male officers would have been out of order anyway, seeing as their prisoner was female — just the single gruff comment in the best traditions of a television crime drama and a brief nod to the special, who took hold of Linda's arm to wheel her out to the waiting police car. The Rottweiler, denied its pound of flesh and rumbling its disappointment from behind a mesh panel fixed across the open kitchen door, watched her leave with as much interest as the old man, who came to the door to see her escorted down the garden path. His face was set into a grim smile of satisfaction as the special opened the door of the police car and gently pushed Linda's head down to prevent her hurting herself when she climbed inside, but his satisfaction was short-lived.

Neither of the policemen had considered that their twitching emaciated prisoner might actually be capable of resistance. The regular officer had already gone round to the driver's door, assuming that his colleague was quite able to deal with her on his own, and the last thing the special expected was for the prisoner to suddenly turn on him while he was doing his best to ensure that she didn't injure herself. But Linda was a lot more streetwise than was apparent. As a result, the part-time policeman was caught completely off guard and the next instant doubled up in agony against the side of the car as she reached behind her to grab his testicles through his nicely creased trousers.

Then she was gone, vanishing into the night even before the regular officer had time to spit out his gum. But, as she staggered drunkenly across town, heading for the backstreet semi where her newly acquired cash could buy her the one thing capable of satisfying the craving that was now tearing her apart, she had no means of knowing that escaping from police custody would turn out to be an even bigger mistake than that made by the two police officers in underestimating her capabilities.

Kate waited until the police car's rear lights had faded into nothing along the esplanade before moving off. The acrimonious encounter with one of her own had shaken her almost as much as the meeting with Duval and she regretted brushing the young copper aside as she had done. He was bound to report her presence on the beach and it would not take long before that got back to Detective Superintendent Davey and DCI Callow. With nothing to show for her night's reckless escapade, she would be hung out to dry.

There was only one way out of the mess: find Duval's note. Ironically, that meant getting even deeper into the hole she was digging for herself, but at least then she would have something positive to produce and if it also resulted in Duval turning himself in, then maybe — just maybe — DC Kate Hamblin would be seen in a much more favourable light. Maybe.

She would have to be very careful though. Duval's cottage would almost certainly still be under surveillance on the chance that he might go back there and if she were to be spotted by one of her colleagues before she could get what she wanted, it would be all over for her.

A dead badger lay partially flattened in the middle of the road — a recent non-statistical casualty — and a fox sniffing at the remains turned its head quickly towards the approaching car, its eyes glittering for a moment in the headlights before it streaked away into adjacent undergrowth.

Kate hardly noticed either animal and her wheels just missed the corpse — passing on either side of it — more by luck than judgement. She was even less aware of the headlights following her at a discreet distance, as she left the sleeping seaside resort behind and headed along the black ribbon that was the grandly named Queen's Drive towards the roundabout at Edith Mead where the A38 linked up with the twin slip roads to the M5 motorway.

In the Land Rover that was tailing her, Twister swore. Where the hell was the silly bitch going now? He had expected her to cut through Burnham's backstreets to Highbridge and then take the A38 to Bridgwater. He had already decided where he was going to drive her off the road — another non-stop fatal accident that would hardly raise an official eyebrow — but that was completely out of the window now. All he could do was to follow her and look for another suitable opportunity.

Yet at the same time something was nagging at him. Why had she met up with Duval under the pier? What had he told her? What *could* he tell her? Maybe it would be best to put off the accident for the time being — see where she went first? Yeah, a stay of execution until he could suss out what madam was up to; that was the best plan. After all, what was there to lose? There would be no chance of getting to bed before dawn now anyway.

Twister watched as Kate turned left at the Edith Mead roundabout, but stayed well back as she headed along the A38 towards Bristol. It was as well that he did, for just a quarter of a mile further on she turned sharp right, cutting through a gap in a concrete safety island and disappearing into a lane on the other side of the road. He gave a brutal smile as he followed her. 'Harp Road, eh?' he muttered to himself, glimpsing the sign at the mouth of the junction. 'How very apt.' Angels were fond of playing harps, weren't they? Well, he fully intended to ensure that this particular angel joined the ranks of the heavenly harpists a lot sooner than she had ever anticipated.

The burned out police Transit was no longer at the murder scene when Kate drove slowly past. She guessed SOCO had finished their examination of the immediate area and had had the vehicle and its gruesome contents moved to a more secure location — both for forensic examination and to deter the press and other ghouls from camping out in the vicinity. Nothing now remained to mark the spot save the blue and white 'Police Crime Scene' tapes hanging limply from their poles between the hedgerow bordering one side of the drove and the adjacent rhyne, which glittered coldly in the moonlight as it angled right to follow the line of the road.

She was not taken in by the apparent emptiness of the scene, however, and moments later spotted the plain CID car tucked into a gateway opposite the entrance to Duval's cottage. There seemed to be no one in the vehicle, which meant that either her colleague was relieving himself behind the hedge or — more likely — was hidden away close to the cottage itself, waiting for Duval's return.

She mouthed a soft 'Not very clever, boys', as she followed the rhyne along the front of the property and accelerated towards Glastonbury. If Duval *had* chosen to drop by, he would have spotted the plain car in an instant; he was not a fool after all. It was the sort of ham-fisted and predictable setup she would have expected from a television cop story rather than a professional CID team and she guessed the whole thing was more of a formality exercise — a case of going through the motions to forestall later criticism — than anything else.

Nevertheless, the presence of one of her colleagues somewhere in the vicinity did make her job that much more hazardous, particularly as she had no idea whether he was closeted in the cottage itself or lurking about in the shadows outside. It was always a possibility that there was more than one of them too — even though, with manpower the way it was, this seemed pretty unlikely — but she tried not to think about such things as, in a few hundred yards, she turned off the main drag into a narrower lane that thrust its way across the marsh between the familiar skeletal hedges, extinguishing her lights and relying on just the moon to light her way.

She found another gateway a few yards further on and pulled in on to a grassy bridge that had been built over another arm of the rhyne, which enclosed the field in which Duval's cottage stood. Patches of frozen water glittered in the moonlight amid the green invasive duckweed choking the ditch and she climbed out of her car very carefully, shivering as she remembered her nightmare experience in the icy water on the other side of Duval's cottage the night before.

The cottage itself was clearly visible in the middle of a huge field, set well back from the main road and crouching into the stubble grass, as if trying to hide itself from scrutiny. Nothing moved and no lights showed in the vicinity, but she knew one of her colleagues would be hiding there, with his police radio connected to his ear by its thin plastic tube and earpiece. It was just on three, so he would probably be close to dozing off by now; bored, tired, eyelids heavy and half-closed. She knew the score from her own experience of observation duties like this. Between two and four in the morning, life was always at its lowest ebb and it was a constant battle to keep awake. If you *did* fall asleep, even for just a few minutes, you regretted it when you woke up again — cold, dispirited, every muscle aching for relief and with your mouth tasting, as poor old Alf Cross had once succinctly put it, like a camel's armpit. After four, sleep was no longer the priority; you became irritable, restless and impatient for the dawn when your early turn relief was due to arrive, which gave you a renewed sense of alertness.

To be on the safe side, it was imperative that she got in and out of the cottage before that phase cut in and she hadn't much time in which to do it.

Despite the need for haste, she forced herself to follow the hedgerow all the way round the edge of the field to where it joined the fenced boundary of the cottage, then down the fence to the side of the cottage, which was set back some forty feet from the road. A diagonal route would have been more direct, but it would also have been more risky too — especially if the obs man was not one prone to falling asleep like the rest and had brought night sight binoculars with him. But her caution cost her precious minutes and it was nearly twenty past three when she finally reached the bottom end of the cottage fence and peered through one of the gaps.

*Take it steady. Stop. Listen. Don't be in too much of a rush.*

The warning voice in her brain urged even more caution, but the only sound to intrude upon the still air was the sudden sharp cry of some nocturnal winged marauder that flew low over her head with a thump of heavy wings and disappeared into the night as if it had never existed.

Taking a deep breath, she ducked through the opening and moved swiftly across a neglected lawn to the side of the cottage — only to freeze again and press herself into the brickwork when she heard a loud cough close by. Seconds later there was the fizz of a match and she smelled cigarette smoke.

*Damn it!* He had to be just yards away, maybe hidden by the corrugated iron water butt she could see to her right. How on earth had he missed seeing her cross the lawn?

Placing her feet with extreme care into the tufted grass, she leaned against the brickwork with one hand for support and crept along the wall towards the rear of the cottage in the manner of an astronaut negotiating the barren airless surface of the moon, anticipating the moment when her foot collided noisily with some half buried object *en route*. But to her relief that didn't happen and she made it without mishap.

The back door of the house was tucked into a rickety porch and with cold trembling fingers she tried the key Duval had given her in the lock. The door opened without difficulty and she found herself peering into a tiny curtained room which at one time would have been called a scullery. As she stepped inside, her nostrils were assailed by a rank odour and she was not long in discovering the source. She saw the eyes first — a whole row of them, glaring at her in the torchlight — and she recoiled with a sharp intake of breath. The rabbits had not yet been skinned and were hanging by their ears from the hooks of an antiquated Welsh dresser. *Nice.*

With a grimace she tore her gaze away from them and turned her attention to an internal door a few feet in front of her. The door creaked as she opened it, admitting her to the kitchen. *At last.*

She saw the coat hanging on the back of another door directly opposite her and crept towards it as if she thought it was a live thing that might take off in fright at any moment.

Another loud cough from just outside the kitchen window. She switched off her torch and thrust a hand into one pocket. Nothing. A flashlight grazed the window as a bulky silhouette moved past. She froze. The flashlight disappeared, leaving her with just obstructed moonlight. She tried the other pocket and felt the crackle of paper.

Exhaling her relief, she tugged the piece of paper free and flicked it open with the fingers of one hand. Then, switching on the torch in her other hand, she quickly masked the beam with her fingers and scanned the note. The words jumped out at her: '... *know about arson ... meet me Brean Down car-park* ...' It was enough. She had what she had come for. All she had to do now was get clear of the cottage without being spotted.

In fact, she did quite well initially and had actually managed to relock the back door and partially retrace her steps round the side of the cottage before things fell apart. How the obs man had sussed her presence she never did find out, but his flashlight blazed in her face before she had gone more than a few feet.

'Kate?' Hayden Lewis exclaimed, his surprise only fractionally greater than hers. 'What the hell are *you* doing here?'

# CHAPTER 10

Within sight of Duval's cottage Twister pulled into the side of the road, then carefully reversed into a gap in the hedge, cutting the engine and lights. If his assumptions were correct and the police were staking out the place on the chance of Duval returning, going any closer in the sort of vehicle he was driving would be suicidal. At least where he had parked up he was hidden from the view of any passing police patrol and there was no need for him to get any closer at this stage anyway, for he knew exactly where his quarry had gone. The road in front of him was straight for at least a couple of miles and he had seen Kate's MX5 swing off into another signposted lane several hundred yards beyond the cottage. Furthermore, the clever little GPS monitor in his Land Rover, which was tracking the device fitted to her car, indicated that she had stopped for some reason.

First the clandestine meeting with Duval under the pier and now what looked like being a nocturnal visit to his cottage. Things were getting more interesting by the hour.

Quitting the driving seat, he went to the front of the vehicle and clambered up on to the bonnet, focusing his night-sight binoculars on the field in which the cottage stood — his gaze passing over the drove where he had callously totalled the police Transit without giving it a second's thought.

From his slightly more elevated position he was able to spot Kate just entering the field, but then lost her seconds later as she moved swiftly into the cover of the roadside hedge. It was obvious that she was heading towards Duval's place, her covert approach indicating that she was fully aware of the likely police presence. But he had no chance of picking her up again, for his view was blocked by the cottage itself and the fence that enclosed it. 'Going in by the back door then, are we, my little treasure?' he murmured to himself. 'Well, I'll just have to wait until you come out again, won't I?'

Returning to the driving seat, he lit a cigarette and sat watching the smoke curl upwards in the moonlit cab while he waited patiently for the GPS tracker monitor attached to the dashboard to activate.

Hayden Lewis seemed more indignant than angry and Kate slumped back against the wall of the cottage, feeling a bit like a recalcitrant public-school boarder caught sneaking out of the dormitory for an illicit liaison.

'You're supposed to be off the inquiry,' he expostulated. 'You shouldn't be anywhere near here.'

She nodded lamely. 'I know, Hayden. I — I just had to check the place out.'

'Check it out? Whatever for? That's why *I'm* here.'

She gently pushed his flashlight downwards, so that the powerful beam no longer blinded her. 'I just don't think Terry Duval was responsible for the Transit blast,' she said without thinking.

'What?' She saw him stiffen. 'Why on earth would you say that?'

She hesitated. She wanted so much to tell *someone* about the note — to wash her hands of the thing she had got involved in and hand the responsibility over to another colleague before she crossed the line that would put her in the frame for assisting an offender. Hayden would certainly have been her choice if she had had to choose anyone, but she was terrified of how he might react. She knew he was sweet on her, but *how* sweet? Would he jeopardize his own career to help her or simply throw up his hands in horror and run to the guv'nor? And was it fair to lumber him with the responsibility of having to make that decision anyway?

He was staring at her now, saying nothing, just staring; waiting for an answer to his question.

'I — I just think it's all too pat,' she blurted suddenly, throwing away her one chance of absolution. 'Why would Duval crap on his own doorstep *knowing* he would be the number one suspect? And what would be the point in murdering the surveillance team anyway? It doesn't add up.'

'Perhaps he just lost it and decided to get even.'

She shook her head quickly. 'I don't buy that, Hayden. And anyway, even the Land Rover I saw was totally different to the one he owns. It was grey and had a snorkel fitted. His doesn't have a snorkel and it's green.'

'So he owns another Land Rover we don't know about.'

'In which case, why have we never seen it? And where does he keep it?'

Suddenly she stopped short, conscious of the fact that her argument was beginning to sound like the sort of passionate defence of Duval that Callow had homed in on earlier.

He grunted and she could tell he was not happy about her answers. Hayden was an intelligent man and she had inadvertently only added to his suspicions.

'Kate,' he said finally, 'you're not doing something you shouldn't be doing, are you? I mean, you're in so much trouble already and—'

She reached forward and quickly squeezed his arm, cutting him off. ''Course not,' she replied, forcing a husky laugh. 'I just don't think it all adds up, that's all, and — and I wanted to see if I could get some answers by coming here.'

There was another long pause and she could sense the battle going on inside his head. She was out of order being on the property and it would have been pretty obvious to anyone that she was up to something. By rights he should report the circumstances straightaway. The problem was, could he bring himself to do it and not only welsh on a colleague, but destroy the career of someone he had fallen for in such a big way?

She squeezed his arm tighter. 'Are you going to turn me in, Hayden?' she said, the tremble in her voice genuine as she remembered her own twin sister saying the same thing just a short time before.

He took a deep breath. 'Flippin' heck, Kate,' he said tightly. 'Did you have to put me in this position? Just bugger off, will you, and don't let anyone else see you or I'm in the poo big time.'

On impulse, she stood on tiptoe and kissed him on the cheek. 'Thanks, Hayden,' she whispered, feeling an absolute heel. 'I owe you one.'

He was still looking after her as she slipped through the hedge and made her way back across the field, gnawing her lip in frustration. Why the hell hadn't she told him the truth? He was the one person she could have trusted and she had not only thrown the chance away, but had played on his feelings for her own purposes. She couldn't have felt more despicable.

Throwing open the door of her car, she slumped into the seat and sat there for a moment, her eyes tightly closed and her head pressed back against the headrest as she tried to blank off her emotions and think positively — but failing miserably.

So she had the note, but without Duval what good was it to her? She had allowed herself to be inveigled into following his agenda, letting a vicious arsonist and suspected murderer dictate the terms of his own surrender. What had she been thinking of? She had made the worst possible decisions all the way through and now she had no alternative but to stick with the course she had chosen.

Starting the engine, she pulled forward into the lane before carefully reversing into the open gateway where she had parked. Then, returning to the main road, she headed back the way she had come, past the parked CID car and Duval's cottage.

Unfortunately she failed to notice the Land Rover Defender parked in the field as she drove past and she had gone a few hundred yards before she glimpsed its distinctive cumbersome bulk in her rear-view mirror. The vehicle was not displaying any lights and was gaining on her fast, but — perhaps through tiredness — the significance of its sudden appearance behind her didn't really register. Land Rovers were a common sight on the Levels at all times of the day and night, so it was natural she should assume that this one belonged to a farmer out on an early morning stock check who had forgotten to switch on his lights, and she slowed to let him pass. But the driver made no attempt to overtake and by the time it dawned on her that something was terribly wrong, it was too late.

The next instant over a ton of heavy steel smashed into the rear of the MX5, hauling her back in her seat, before propelling her forward into the cruel burning embrace of her seat belt and sending her car careering across the road on to the opposite grass verge.

For some reason her airbag did not inflate with the impact and she successfully managed to wrestle the car back on to the road on the approach to a sharp left-hand bend, but she was unable to gain her correct side before the Land Rover pulled alongside and slammed into her passenger door. As her airbag now exploded with painful force and her car mounted the verge for the second time, she glimpsed the Land Rover's driver through her passenger side window and her last conscious recollection was of his bearded face, brilliantly illuminated by the moonlight, grinning at her with malicious satisfaction before her car left the verge on the apex of the bend and plunged straight into the rhyne.

The man in the Land Rover pulled into the side of the road just yards from where he had forced Kate's car off the road and turned round in his seat to stare back at the spot, his heavy brows crinkled in a frown. Twister could just see part of the roof and a corner of the boot of her MX5 and realized that the small vehicle had somehow become wedged between the steep banks of the rhyne at an angle. With a bit of luck, the front end, including the woman copper's head, would be under water or so badly damaged that she had been crushed to death by the impact, but he knew he had to make sure.

His feet slithered on the frosty road surface when he stepped out of the car and he drew his coat more tightly about him as he crossed the road diagonally to the churned up grass verge, a pocket torch in one hand. Part of a rear light unit lay on the road side, which he picked up and tossed into the rhyne — no sense advertising the crash — before approaching the edge of the bank and peering over.

The front of the car had smashed through the thin layer of ice and was buried up to its windscreen in the water, the driver's side well below the surface and the windscreen crazed over with the force of the impact, but he could see little of the interior, which was in dense shadow.

Checking that the road in both directions was empty, he got down on to his hands and knees, wincing at the cold rising from the crisp grass, and leaned against the edge of the roof for support. Then, thrusting his face to within a few inches of the strip of front passenger window that projected above the bank, he directed the beam of his torch into the car with his other hand.

At once he was able to make out Kate's motionless figure, partially buried by the inflated airbag. Her body seemed to have been forced sideways in the confined space between the airbag and the seat, her head twisted round and turned towards him at what looked like an impossible angle and one limp arm hanging down beside the seat, partially submerged in the water swirling into the car through the shattered driver's window. She did not stir even when he hammered the roof with the butt of his torch and her eyes were wide open and vacant. He had seen death many times in his army service — had been responsible for it on a number of occasions too — and although the sunken position of the car made it impossible for him to get closer to his victim to actually check her pulse, he could tell from the look of her that she was dead, and he smiled grimly as he stood up. 'Job done,' he murmured.

OK, so he had not been able to find out why she had met Duval under the pier or why she had made her clandestine visit to his cottage, but that was academic now anyway. The only people she would be able talk to about it were the angels.

Seeing headlights approaching from the direction of Glastonbury, he patted the roof of the car in mock farewell and headed back to his Land Rover at a run. By the time the HGV thundered past the scene, he was gone and the lorry driver was too busy studying the screen of his own GPS to notice the car in the rhyne on the other side of the road.

Danny Mogg was still hung over from a night out with the lads and, as the lonely marshland road opened up to his headlights in the gathering dawn, he shivered. He was looking forward to the next eight hours like a hole in the head. He had never liked observation duty and he certainly hadn't joined CID to babysit a villain's house on the Levels. OK, so he was only a *temporary* detective constable, but that didn't mean he should be dumped on like this. Obs was a uniform job, surely, so why couldn't one of the plods have been given it instead?

He grinned as he approached a sharp right-hand bend, slowing as his tyres began to slide on the frosty road surface. Still, at least he had missed the bloody graveyard shift, which was one good thing anyway. Poor old Hayden had clicked for that and it couldn't have happened to a more deserving bloke. The Don, as he was called, was always claiming how hard life had been at public school and how cold the dormitories were. Maybe this would teach him a lesson, for he would more than likely have frozen his bollocks off by now

— *if* public schoolboys had them in the first place, of course. And Mogg laughed out loud at the thought.

He wasn't laughing as he rounded the bend, however. In fact, all the humour went out of him when he caught a glimpse of the shiny roof of the MX5 in the rhyne, and he swung on to the verge with a slither of locked wheels, nearly ending up in the ditch himself.

The powerful flashlight he carried in his car pinpointed the hunched figure in the crushed driving seat as soon as he bent down to scrape some of the frost off the strip of visible passenger window and he scrambled to his feet with a sharp intake of breath, depressing the button of his police radio with a shaking hand. Police control responded immediately. 'TDC Mogg,' he said unnecessarily and without realizing he was shouting. 'I've got a possible FATACC.[1]' Quickly giving his location, he added: 'I think the driver is DC Kate Hamblin.'

[1] FATACC — fatal accident

# CHAPTER 11

The needle had not been particularly clean — in fact, there were traces of something even on the body of the hypodermic syringe she had been given — but Linda didn't care. The euphoria she'd got from the blast of heroin as it coursed through her veins was enough and she'd barely had time to loosen the strap on her thigh before Mr H took over completely and she sank into oblivion in the corner of the church porch.

She came round in fragile afternoon sunlight to find an elderly woman with an armful of flowers bending over her. Her jeans were still round her ankles, exposing the collapsed veins in one leg, and the old biddy had an open mouth you could have practically driven a hearse through. Lurching drunkenly to her feet, Linda yanked up her trousers and pushed past the woman into the cemetery.

'My dear!' the querulous voice called after her, but she kept going, hugging her open coat around her against the cold and trying to focus properly on the gateway at the end of the path. Where the hell was she? She thought she knew Bridgwater, but this part was foreign territory to her.

A police car drove past the church at speed as she gained the street and she shrank into the doorway of an adjacent house, waiting for the car's stop-lights to flash, indicating he had clocked her and was coming back. But he kept going and she breathed a sigh of relief, cursing herself for over-reacting. Old Bill had a lot more to think about than some junkie absconder, hadn't he? Yeah, maybe he had, but police patrols would still be on the lookout for her and sooner or later some eagle-eyed plod would get lucky. She needed to find a place where she could lie low for a bit. The money she had lifted from the bungalow had bought her a couple of extra fixes, so she was all right for a few hours. After that though, it was anybody's guess.

So cold, she felt so bloody cold — and hungry too — and the shakes that were starting all over again were not just due to the temperature either. *Shit! Not already?* Her last fix had only been a few hours ago. It couldn't be time so soon, surely?

She grabbed a bottle of milk from a doorstep (no doubt a morning delivery left there after someone had already gone to work. Shame to waste it, she mused cynically, and gulped it down as she kept walking, hardly aware of the fact that the milk was already off. Eventually she made it to a wide main road clogged with traffic. Ah, the A39. Now she knew where she was. A couple of the drivers leered at her through their windows and she glared back at them, knowing full well what they were thinking. Dirty bastards. Yeah, but it might come to that later if she couldn't get another fix after she'd run out again. A quick screw used to be a good source of bread, but she had no illusions about herself. She might look OK with her clothes on, but naked, it was a different story. Needle tracks and collapsed veins had taken their toll on her physical appearance and her only pick-ups now had to be knee-tremblers well after dark, or with her own diseased kind.

Another police car drove past and this time the stop-lights came on a little too quickly. The uniformed passenger's head was turned in her direction. They'd clocked her!

She cast them a quick sidelong glance (stupid, it only made her look even more guilty) and saw they were now trying to turn round, blue lights flashing at the clogged traffic. As she darted into another side-road and ran, she heard the scream of the siren. But they were too late. She was through a broken gate and had ducked down behind a four foot high wall even as they raced past.

But she felt no sense of triumph. Crouched among piles of rubble on the dismal piece of waste-ground that had given her temporary refuge, she found herself frantically trying to breathe as she fought against the panic that threatened to engulf her. OK, so she had managed to elude the plods this time, but the odds on her being able to do the same thing again were a bookie's nightmare. Her only hope was to drop out of sight until all the fuss died down. Trouble was, she wasn't exactly flush with options as to where to go.

It was burned into Kate Hamblin's subconscious. Pain, bitter cold, swirling choking water, accompanied by a confusion of pulsing blue and red lights. Doors banging, loud unintelligible voices, followed by movement all around her. The scream of machinery, metal tearing, someone tugging and lifting; more pain and . . . emptiness.

Then quite suddenly unexpected warmth, blazing lights, a choking antiseptic smell, and again the sound of unintelligible voices, this time soft and reassuring. She opened her eyes, but saw only pale blobs floating around her like ethereal balloons, blobs that seemed to lurch towards her, before fading into a pastel blue nothingness. Finally, nausea, a spinning sensation and a return to oblivion.

More voices — this time stronger — and someone calling her name. She found herself struggling upwards through a heavy blackness; surfacing, responding, seeking. And as the darkness began to fade, just one disembodied white face materializing from nowhere and drifting towards her — a face strangely distorted, unrecognizable, like that viewed through a badly focused camera lens. Then suddenly her vision adjusting, as if someone had manipulated a hidden switch, and everything snapping into place with a jolt.

The bearded Asian man in the turban and long white coat smiled down at her and she forced a smile back. She was lying on a trolley of some sort, dressed in a cotton gown. She could hear the hubbub of conversation all around her and the sound of footsteps coming and going on hard uncarpeted floors.

'Feeling better?' he said. 'You were very lucky. Some minor concussion we think and a little bit of whiplash, plus superficial bruising to your ribs, but that's all. You've been out for quite a while.'

'Where am I?' she queried weakly, trying to put things together in her disordered mind.

'A & E,' he replied. 'You had a nasty accident, remember?'

She turned her head, noticing the curtains drawn around her for the first time. *Hospital?* Now something began to stir in her befuddled brain, began to push up through the mental fog. Moonlight, the gleam of icy water, a sinister black shadow rising up over her — no, not a shadow, a Land Rover, and a man grinning through the driver's window; bearded, heavy-set, wearing a thick coat and baseball cap.

Then abruptly, a nightmare montage of flashbacks coming together with bludgeoning force. The police Transit blast, the meeting with Duval under the pier, the run-in with Hayden at the suspect's house and the collision with the Land Rover which had forced her off the road. All now recalled with sickening clarity.

'We'd like to do a CT scan and blood tests just to make sure,' the doctor continued. 'Then we'll be keeping you in overnight for observation. If all goes well, you should be out of here sometime tomorrow.'

*Keeping me in until tomorrow?*

Kate's eyes widened as she thought of Duval and his note. What if he had been trying to contact her and thought she had reneged on their agreement? He could disappear for good. Then what? 'Tomorrow?' she gasped. 'But I need . . .' Her voice trailed off as she tried to sit up, but fell back on to her pillow with a gasp of pain.

He frowned reprovingly. 'Not a good idea to do that,' he said. 'Best to lie still and rest. You've got some quite nasty bruises. I'll get you some painkillers and we'll speak again later.'

The CT scan took longer than she had expected and, dosed up with strong painkillers, she fell into a deep sleep again as she was wheeled away from the unit; lost in a recurring nightmare of blazing headlights, moonlight on dark water and the screeching of tortured metal. When she awoke she found herself in a small sunlit room, lying in a proper bed — with Roz Callow sitting in a chair beside her, wearing an expression of cynical amusement.

'Well, well, well,' Callow drawled. 'The voyager returns. You had us all worried.'

Kate closed her eyes tightly for a second as if she wanted to shut out the vision of the DCI's cold hard face.

'I must admit though,' Callow continued, 'I am rather curious as to what you were doing roaming around the Levels in the early hours of the morning.'

'Went for a drive,' Kate replied sullenly, her voice distant and slightly slurred.

Callow raised an eyebrow. 'Strange that your drive should take you to within spitting distance of Terry Duval's place though, isn't it?'

Kate blinked several times, trying to clear the fug clouding her brain, then winced at the pain in her chest and neck. 'Wanted to look at murder scene again,' she mumbled. 'Needed to lay a ghost.'

'Right,' the DCI said, nodding slowly. 'And precisely what ghost are we talking about?'

Kate managed to ease herself up higher on to the pillow, teeth gritted against her pain. 'Wanted to see if I could remember anything else,' she said, her voice now strengthening in spite of her condition.

'And did you?'

'Only what I've already told you.'

Callow sat back in her chair, her dark eyes boring into her. 'You do seem to like rhynes though, don't you?' she said. 'This is the second time you've put yourself in one. Fall asleep at the wheel, did you?'

Kate felt a spurt of irritation, which had the effect of clearing the last vestiges of fug trying to reinfect her brain. 'I didn't put myself in the rhyne,' she retorted, 'and I wasn't asleep. I was hit from behind by another vehicle and driven off the road.'

Callow feigned puzzlement. 'But Traffic tell me your car had gone into the rhyne facing in the wrong direction and that, judging by your tyre tracks, you must have crossed from the other side of the road to end up in that position.'

'I did.'

Callow shook her head. 'Bit of a strange accident though, you have to agree? If you were struck by another vehicle, I would have thought you'd have ended up in the rhyne on your own side of the road.'

Kate grimaced as the flashbacks steadied into a more solid picture. 'It wasn't an accident,' she disputed. 'It was deliberate — an attempt to silence me as a possible witness — and the motor was the same Land Rover I saw at the murder scene.'

'Was it indeed? And did you get the number this time?'

'No, everything happened too quickly.'

'Then how can you possibly say it was the same Land Rover?'

'I recognized it; I'd know it anywhere.'

'What, in the dark — with the vehicle behind you?'

Kate forced herself to remain controlled. 'After shunting me into the bend,' she said patiently, 'it came alongside and slammed into my nearside wing, forcing me across the road into the rhyne.'

Callow smirked. 'Oh, how very convenient,' she sneered. 'And what about the driver?'

Kate met her gaze without flinching. 'Heavy build, with a full beard and wearing a coat and baseball cap,' she replied. 'So, nothing like Terry Duval.'

The DCI raised an eyebrow. 'Remarkable description, considering it was dark at the time and you were heading into the rhyne.'

'I know what I saw.'

Callow leaned towards her. 'You have a vivid imagination, young lady, I'll give you that,' she said, her tone suddenly menacing. 'But you and I know that that's all it is, don't we? Why can't you just accept that Terry Duval is the man we want and stop trying to protect him?'

'I'm not trying to protect anyone,' Kate flared, then immediately flinched with a sharp exclamation as her anger triggered more pain in her head and chest. 'I just want the people who murdered Andy and Alf nailed and I don't happen to think Terry Duval is the culprit.'

Heedless of her obvious discomfort, Callow pressed on with her ruthless interrogation. 'Oh don't you? Well, whatever you choose to think, Miss Hamblin, the investigation has nothing to do with you anyway, so my advice is to keep your nose out of it.' She sat back and popped one of her customary mints into her mouth. 'But on to another matter. A little bird tells me you were checked by a patrol on the beach at Burnham just before the accident. Mind telling me what you were doing there at between two and three in the morning?'

For a moment Kate was thrown and she seemed to dissolve before Callow's hard stare. 'I — I went for a walk to clear my head,' she said finally.

The DCI grunted. 'Is that right? And what were you doing under the pier? Collecting sea shells?'

Kate swallowed several times. 'I got caught short and—'

'What *again*?' Callow gave a harsh laugh. 'While you're in here, you should tell the doctor about your bladder problem. He might be able to give you something for it.'

She snapped to her feet and stood over Kate like some predatory bird. 'You're up to something, my girl,' she grated, 'and in the end you're going to tell me exactly what it is, I promise you.'

But that was as far as she got, for her interrogation was suddenly and dramatically cut short by an imperious voice from the door behind her. 'What the devil is going on here?'

The sister was lean, middle-aged and bristling with indignation as she strode into the room.

Callow threw her a contemptuous glance and waved her warrant card airily in her direction. 'Police,' she said, 'DCI Callow.'

'I don't give a damn who you are,' the sister blazed. 'This patient is under my care and you have no business being in here.'

Callow's eyes flashed dangerously. 'I don't think you realize who I am,' she retorted.

But the sister was incapable of being intimidated. 'I don't need to realize anything,' she cut in again. 'In this hospital I am in charge and you will leave here immediately or I will call security and have you ejected. Is that clear?'

Callow's expression dripped more venom than a rattlesnake's fangs as she wheeled and marched from the room, but Kate took no satisfaction from her humiliation. She knew that, as of now, her DCI would be really out for blood and if she failed to deliver Terry Duval at the end of it all, she could say goodbye to everything she had ever worked for. She was still thinking about that when she drifted off into another troubled sleep.

The local newspaper screamed its headline from the battered billboard:

## MURDER COP IN CRASH

Twister left his Land Rover on double yellow lines with the engine running and hurried into the newsagents twenty yards away. He re-emerged with a grim face and climbed back into his vehicle, scanning the story and noting, with a tightening of his facial muscles, the photograph beneath the headline showing Kate Hamblin's MX5 being winched out of the rhyne by a breakdown truck bearing the sign: 'Jury's of Bridgwater'.

*Unbelievable. The bitch got out alive.*

He dropped the newspaper on to the front passenger seat and sat there for a few minutes, staring out of the windscreen, but seeing nothing as he tapped the steering wheel rhythmically with the fingers of one hand. When his mobile rang, he gave a twisted grin. Right on cue.

'Where the hell have you been?' a familiar voice snarled. 'Been trying to get you all morning.'

'Have to kip sometime,' he retorted, unrepentant. 'Been up all night.'

'My heart bleeds for you,' the caller sneered. 'Especially as you seem to have cocked up yet again. Papers are full of Hamblin's miraculous escape.'

Twister's eyes flicked to the rear-view mirror and a traffic warden making her way slowly along the pavement towards him. 'Yeah, I know. Non-stop accident, they're saying. At least they haven't put it down to anything else.'

The voice at the other end dropped to a hiss. 'They're looking for a bloody Land Rover, you prat. I told you to get rid of that thing.'

'Don't worry. Hamblin obviously didn't get my number, otherwise they'd have said.'

'But what if some bright spark makes a connection with the other job?'

'What can they do? As I told you before, there are loads of Land Rovers round here and I've already replaced the dented bumper, so they've got nothing to go on. Anyway, if they do begin to suspect anything, it's Duval who'll get the blame.'

'*When* they finally manage to catch him. He seems to have disappeared.'

Twister's jaw tightened as he remembered seeing the arsonist running away from Burnham pier. He should have said about that and about Kate Hamblin's shenanigans at the murder scene, but he had enough on his plate at present without introducing complications. So he kept quiet.

'What's your marvellous plan now then?' his caller went on.

Twister smiled without humour. 'I thought I might do a hospital visit — once I've got some grapes, of course.'

There was a disparaging snort. 'Just make sure the patient is not in a fit state to eat them, OK? Try to do something right for once.'

He didn't bother to reply, but cut the call and turned quickly as the traffic warden appeared at his window. 'You're illegally parked,' the short, fat woman snapped, reaching for her ticket wallet.

He forced a smile. 'Sorry, love, just getting some chocolates for my good lady. Had an accident and she's in hospital.'

The traffic warden hesitated, then returned her wallet to her handbag, her disappointment showing. 'Go on then, but watch where you park in future.'

He nodded and started the engine. 'You're an angel.'

His compliment was met with a scowl. 'You just make sure you take good care of that lady of yours.'

'Oh yes,' he replied over his shoulder as he drove off. 'I'm going to take really good care of *her*.'

# CHAPTER 12

Kate awoke to find she had another visitor — though this one was a lot more than welcome.

Hayden Lewis had parked himself in the chair beside her bed, hair awry as usual and the frayed collar of his shirt crumpled by the V neck of a baggy sweater.

'Hi, Kate,' he greeted and smiled a little uncertainly. ''Fraid your car's a bit of a write-off, old girl, but you're OK, which is the main thing.'

'The car's the least of my worries,' she said, thinking of Callow. 'I had a visit from our lovable DCI earlier.'

Lewis whistled. 'What, the "Wicked Witch of the North" doing welfare? That must be a first.'

'It was no welfare visit. She was in interrogation mode.'

'Don't I know it,' he said ruefully. 'Had me in a couple of hours ago. I got quite a grilling.'

'*You* were grilled? Whatever for?'

He shrugged. 'She knows we're — er — friends and suggested I might know why you were in the area of the crime scene when you had your TA.'

'You didn't tell her anything, did you?'

He looked horrified. 'What do you take me for? As I told you before, if it gets out that I caught you sneaking around Duval's place and didn't report it, I'm in very deep poo.'

'*I'm* hardly likely to say anything, now am I?'

He gave a weak grin. 'Well, that's a relief anyway. So, how are you feeling?'

'Rough.'

'Hardly surprising really. It was a bad accident and you were lucky my relief came by and found you in time.'

'It was no accident, Hayden,' she said. 'I was run off the road by the same arsehole who blasted the Transit.'

His jaw dropped. 'What? Oh come on, Kate, how can you possibly say that?'

She tried to wriggle up into a sitting position, riled by his incredulity, but gave up when the pain in her head and ribcage started again.

'Hayden, it was the *same Land Rover*,' she grated. 'You must believe me. Someone is trying to shut me up for good.'

He snorted. '*Someone*, Kate?' he echoed. 'Surely you're not still hung up on this idea that Terry Duval is innocent?'

She forced herself up on to one elbow, gripping his wrist tightly with her other hand. 'Hayden, I saw the driver this time. He had a beard. He was nothing like Duval.'

Lewis ran his fingers through his hair in a gesture of frustration. 'But — but even if you are right in what you say,' he countered, 'why would anyone want to kill you? You didn't get the number of the Land Rover when the Transit was targeted and you said you couldn't describe the driver, so you're hardly likely to be seen as much of a threat to anyone.'

'Maybe the killer doesn't know that, or just isn't taking any chances.'

'Fine, but whether he is or he isn't, if you didn't get the number of the Land Rover in the first place, how can you know it was the same vehicle that ran you off the road this time?'

'You're beginning to sound like Callow, Hayden,' Kate snapped. 'But I'll tell you what I told her — I would know that wagon anywhere.'

Lewis hesitated, choosing his words carefully. 'Listen, Kate,' he patronized, 'you've been through a lot lately, but don't you think you're seeing things that aren't there? You were involved in a non-stop RTA, nothing more than that, and the driver probably didn't stop because he was over the limit.'

But Kate was no longer listening; something far more important had thrust itself into her mind like the point of an icy needle. Duval. What about Duval? And what about the note she had slipped into her coat pocket with her mobile? What if it had fallen out or been found by someone else?

'My clothes, Hayden,' she said urgently, trying to pull back the sheets, 'where are they?'

He placed a restraining hand on her wrist. 'Steady, old girl. You're in no fit state to get up yet.'

She pulled her hand free, ignoring his concern. 'Hayden, I said, where are my bloody clothes?'

He flinched, taken aback by her aggression, and nodded towards a slim wooden locker next to her bedside cabinet. 'In — in there I expect. Hospitals usually—'

She clutched at the sides of the bed as her head swam. 'Will you please check?'

He looked shocked. 'Check your clothes? I — I can't do that, Kate. It's not right.'

She closed her eyes tightly for a second, her own frustration showing. At any other time she would have found his old-fashioned sensibilities endearing, but right now they irritated the hell out of her. 'I'm not asking you to wear my bloody bra, Hayden,' she said heavily, wincing as a sharp stabbing pain now lanced through her head and neck again. 'Just take a look, will you?'

With an unhappy frown, he stood up and crossed to the locker, opening the door as if he believed it might suddenly explode in his hand.

'What's inside?' she demanded.

He flushed with obvious embarrassment. 'Just a pair of trousers, a sweater and — and other . . . sort of undie things.'

*Nothing else?* She felt a stab of apprehension. 'So what happened to my leather coat?'

He shut the door in the manner of someone closing the covers of a dirty book. Suddenly he was back in his comfort zone. 'Ah that. You should have said. Sorry, but I seem to remember it got badly ripped when the fire service had to cut you free. It must have been left in the car.'

She stared at him aghast. *Left in the car?* 'And where's my motor now?'

'Jury's Yard at Bridgwater. They'll hang on to it until you sort out disposal with your insurance company.'

'Hayden, I've got to get out of here — fast.'

He looked annoyed. 'Don't be silly, Kate. Hospital will want to you keep you in under observation at least until tomorrow.'

'Bugger the hospital,' she retorted and, rolling over on to one elbow, swung her legs over the edge of the bed and forced herself up into a sitting position, fists clenched and face contorted in a fierce grimace as she waited a few seconds in the hope that the nausea and eroding pain would subside.

He gaped at her in disbelief. 'Kate, it's a coat! For goodness' sake, it's only a coat.'

But she took no notice and, levering herself up off the bed, swayed past him to her locker, where she paused with one hand on the metal door and her head leaning weakly against her forearm. 'Hayden, you're very sweet,' she said with an effort, 'but I am going to get dressed, so would you mind leaving.'

He shook his head defiantly. 'No,' he said. 'I can't let you do this.'

She closed her eyes again for a few seconds, feeling too ill to argue the point. 'Suit yourself then,' she breathed and, pulling her nightdress up over her head, tossed it on to the floor and reached into the locker for her underclothes.

Lewis simply stood there, transfixed, unable to take his eyes off her slim naked figure.

'Kate,' he protested finally when he managed to find his voice. 'This — this is just not on. I mean . . .'

'Told you to leave, didn't I?' she muttered, pulling her sweater over her head with great difficulty and stumbling back against the locker before managing to regain her balance. 'Now, you can take me to Jury's.'

Lewis shook his head again. 'Jury's? Not a chance.'

She studied him for a moment, her leather boots in her hands. 'Then I'll get a taxi.'

He stepped in front of her. 'You'll have to get past me first,' he said.

Her jaw hardened. 'You can't stop me, Hayden, and if you try, I'll scream the place down.'

The flush drained from his face and there was panic in his eyes. 'Don't you dare,' he exclaimed. 'No one even knows I slipped in here.'

'Then don't interfere.'

Lewis capitulated with a groan. 'OK, OK,' he said hastily. 'I'll take you there, damn it — as if I'm not in enough trouble over you already.'

For the first time there was a hint of mischief in her blue eyes. Straining on tiptoe, she grabbed his arm to steady herself and gave him a quick peck on the cheek. 'Thanks, Hayden, I owe you.'

He nodded, the sulks still written into his expression. 'Let's just get out of here, if we're going,' he growled. 'That bitch of a DCI might decide to come back.'

She glanced down at her bare feet and slapped her boots into his chest. 'Then you'd better help me on with my socks and boots, hadn't you?' she replied.

# CHAPTER 13

Lewis had an old red Mk 2 Jaguar, much like the one used by the fictional police detective, Inspector Morse, and he had parked it in the hospital car-park, close to the exit. With characteristic old-fashioned courtesy, he opened the front passenger door and stood to one side, holding on to Kate's arm, as she carefully climbed into the seat.

The man in the Land Rover saw them leaving as he turned into the car-park and he swung in quickly alongside the first double row of parked cars, out of sight, until the Jaguar had gone through the exit barrier towards the main road. Twister realized his mistake when he got to the barrier himself, staring with barely suppressed fury at the red and white arm, which came down blocking his way. He had been to the hospital before and should have remembered you had to pay for the car-park and validate the ticket in the hospital foyer before you could exit.

*Lost them, sod it.*

Reversing into a nearby car-parking space, he sprinted across the service road through the automatic doors and into the building itself, inserting his ticket into the machine just inside the entrance. It seemed to take ages to respond, then the illuminated display told him there was nothing to pay;

the first twenty minutes were apparently free. Snarling his frustration, he snatched the ticket back when it grudgingly reappeared and brushed roughly against an elderly man with a stick as he swung for the doors.

Even as he sprinted back to his car, however, he knew he was wasting his time — the Jag was long gone — and, finally driving out through the hospital exit, he cursed his luck and the fact that this time there was no tracking device fitted to the target vehicle to enable him to keep tabs on his quarry. Then his stomach practically slammed up into his ribcage, suddenly reminding him of something else.

*Bloody hell, the tracking device on the MX5.*

If it hadn't fallen off into the rhyne with the force of the collision, it had to be still attached to the underside of the vehicle — almost certainly busted as it was not registering on his monitor — and just waiting for some plod traffic accident investigator to spot it. And that was the last thing he could afford to happen.

Reaching the roundabout and the junction with the A370, he deliberately cut up another car on the roundabout itself, furious with himself for his stupidity and determined to take it out on anyone in the vicinity. How could he have forgotten about the blasted tracker? He was supposed to be a professional. This business was doing his head in. One thing was clear, however: he had to get to the car before anyone had a chance of examining it too closely. According to the picture in the paper it had been collected by a breakdown truck from Jury's of Bridgwater and he just hoped that was where it had been taken. A prayer might have helped had he been vaguely Christian, but in addition to being a non-believer, he knew that, with his record, he could hardly expect to find a listening ear above, even if there *was* someone in residence to pray to.

In fact, as he took the third exit off the busy roundabout, a disjointed assortment of pictures flashed through his brain; gruesome images he knew he would never forget — would never want to forget. He had been an assassin most of his adult life and though he liked to blame the SAS for that, his penchant for murder had actually started long before he'd reached adulthood and joined the army.

A quiet retiring boy with few friends, there had never been anything in his behaviour to suggest he was other than a normal teenager who simply preferred his own company. He was always polite, never got into trouble with the more rebellious crowd at school and consistently achieved good examination results. Though an only child, he also enjoyed an apparently happy stable family life, with all the love and support that went with it, even after the death of his mother when he was ten. On the surface then, he had everything going for him.

But beneath the inoffensive wholesome persona that Larry projected lurked the seriously deranged mind of the psychopath; a cold, calculating mentality driven by absolute self-interest, a complete lack of empathy towards anyone or anything and an inbuilt ambivalence towards basic moral norms — including the sanctity of human life. Unlike Terry Duval's motivation for arson, for Larry killing was not an overtly sexual or vengeful thing. True, it imbued him with a sense of power and fulfilment, and he took great pride in doing the job properly, but he did not get a hard-on from the act — any more than he felt the slightest remorse for carrying it out. He killed because it fitted in with what he wanted to do at the time and if a psychiatrist were to have asked him why he had taken the life of another human being, he would probably have shrugged and answered simply: 'Why not?'

During his early childhood, he had actually managed to resist the strengthening voice in his head urging him to kill someone, contenting himself instead with shooting birds, cats and small rodents with his airgun or incinerating them with a blowtorch after they had been trapped. But by the time he reached his last year in school, this no longer satisfied him and the voice had become so painfully insistent that he knew it could no longer be ignored.

As a result, he befriended a lower year fat boy, named Jerome Cassidy, and, luring him to the municipal park near the school on the pretext of showing him some dirty pictures, he plunged a chisel he had stolen from the woodwork class into the boy's throat. Then he sat quietly on a tree stump and, with dispassionate clinical interest, watched him die in a bubbling choking haemorrhage, feeling no connection between himself and his victim, other than through the experiment he had set up.

He killed twice more after that in separate parts of the county, first a young woman out jogging in a lonely country lane and then a middle-aged hospital nurse on her way to work. Both victims were selected at random and strangled. Both were pretty too, but neither the nurse or the scantily clad jogger stirred his juices and he made no attempt to interfere with either of them sexually. It was the act of killing that interested him, plus the satisfaction he gained from watching the light go out in the eyes of his victims as they choked their last; rape was nowhere on his agenda.

More murders would undoubtedly have followed too, had he not spotted a railway hoarding bearing an advertisement for the army with its apparent limitless opportunities for legalized murder. His application was in within four days.

Soldiering — and more particularly the SAS — taught him how to kill silently and efficiently: to slice through someone's windpipe from behind with a length of wire, to crush a target's Adam's apple with the edge of the hand, or — his chosen method — to snap a spinal cord with a sharp powerful twist of the neck.

But while he proved to be a ruthless and dependable assassin, supremely fit and very quickly combat hardened, it soon became apparent to his lords and masters that he was a loose cannon; someone for whom the kill was more important than the purpose of the operation and whose reckless disregard for rules and adherence to orders put others in jeopardy. Inevitably, he messed up in a big way during a key training exercise, which resulted in the death of another soldier, and, following a court martial, he was dishonourably discharged from the service.

For several years after that he simply drifted, claiming social security benefits, while working — first for a Manchester villain as an enforcer and then as a so-called security officer for a dodgy night club in Liverpool. Despite all the efforts of the then regional crime squad to nail him, he was never tied in to any of the crimes he had committed, but ironically, like Al Capone, he was finally indicted for fraud — in his case for evading income tax and dishonestly claiming benefits while employed by the night club — and he received eighteen months inside as a result.

But prison had no effect on him and following his release, he returned home, ostensibly to support his father who was developing Parkinson's disease. Instead, within three months he had smothered the old man in bed to enable him to take over the family business. The death had gone down as natural causes, of course, despite police reservations, and he had initially congratulated himself on a pretty smart move. But that was before he had run the business into the ground and put himself in the position he was in now — no money, a precarious future and a termination contract that had gone badly wrong — something he had to rectify PDQ if he was to maintain his own self-respect as the ultimate killing machine.

His father's face and the faces of the rest of his many victims now floated before him like gossamer on a breeze, or foam on a slow-moving sea current. Not that he was distressed by them — psychopaths like him were not troubled by conscience. Instead, he saw those past hits as 'friends' who accompanied him on his journeys, a spectral entourage he was confident Kate Hamblin would soon be joining, just as soon as he had worked out the detail on the deadly new plan that was forming in his twisted brain.

Jury's was not actually in Bridgwater itself; it was some way outside the town, within a short distance of the curiously named Dumball Wharf. The former petrol station had become a graveyard for crashed motor vehicles and its two to three acres of flattened scrub held several hundred broken shells waiting to be consigned to the huge crusher Ray Jury had installed at the far end of the property.

Dusk was creeping in across the misty fields that enclosed the place as Lewis carefully eased his Jaguar through the half-closed iron gates and pulled up before the caravan that served as an office.

Ray Jury was a fat little man, almost as wide as he was tall. He was dressed in a woollen hat, an old donkey jacket, corduroys and what looked like oversize wellington boots. His florid face wore a perpetual frown and his unlit cigarette stub seemed to be stuck permanently to his bottom lip, even when he was speaking in his thick Somerset accent.

He took in Lewis's old Jaguar with a look of hunger and seemed disappointed when Hayden's opening shot revealed that they had not come to dump his car, but to look at Kate's MX5.

The sports car was parked with half-a-dozen others on a concrete apron, away from the car graveyard. 'We close at five,' Jury warned, after leading them to the vehicle. Then, seeing there was no new business to be had, he waddled away, shaking his head.

'Bit of a mess, eh?' Lewis commented unnecessarily, looking critically at the crushed bonnet and front wings. 'You were lucky to get out of this in one piece.'

But Kate was not interested in his assessment and immediately turned her attention to the gaping hole where the passenger door had once been. The fire service had done a thorough job as usual. Not only had the door been removed, but part of the nearside rear panel as well and most of the hard-top roof had also been cut away. She found her leather coat almost at once, badly ripped, as Hayden had said, and dumped in the passenger foot-well, and her heart was pumping madly as she checked the pockets. She recovered her mobile immediately, apparently intact and still switched on, but when she slipped her hand into the same pocket, she found nothing save a small tear in the lining. She was on the point of withdrawing her hand and checking the other pocket when her probing fingers touched crumpled paper.

Her heart pounding even harder, she carefully extracted the piece of paper, then, making sure Hayden was still fully occupied, peeled it open and glanced at the contents. At once she breathed a sigh of relief. *Thank heavens*. It was what she had come for. Panic over.

'What have you got there then?'

Lewis was standing directly behind her and she quickly slipped the note into her pocket with the mobile. 'Oh, nothing. Just my mobile and a bill I left in my coat,' she lied.

As she straightened up, she saw him frown. 'Don't you want your coat then? You came all this way for it.'

She shook her head. 'No point. Pity, but it's ruined. And there's nothing else here that I want.'

He threw her a quizzical look, plainly not satisfied with her answer, but he did not pursue it, instead holding out his gloved hand with theatrical aplomb. 'I wouldn't say that, Kate,' he contradicted politely. 'I found this attached to one of the frame members.'

Peering into his palm, she found herself staring at a badly split black oblong box, maybe 5x2x1" in size, with part of a silvery disc that looked very much like a battery visible through the split. 'Whatever is that?'

He grunted. 'Well, I'm no technical whizz kid, but I *have* seen something similar to it before and I would say it's a bug.'

'A what?'

'Most likely a magnetic GPS tracking device,' he added, staring about him uneasily.

'You can't be serious?'

'Oh I'm serious enough.' He studied her fixedly. 'It seems that someone has been keeping very close tabs on your movements, old girl, and I think you owe me an explanation, don't you?'

Twister pulled up in front of the padlocked gates and stared sourly at the sign, 'Jury's Auto Recoveries', which seemed to be mocking him in the headlights trained on the seven-foot-high chain-link fence. He was too late; the bastards had gone home. Still, that wasn't too much of a problem — padlocked gates had never been a barrier to him in the past and they were not going to be now — but he needed to check for any possible opposition first, even though the arrival of the Land Rover, with its headlights blazing, should have been enough to advertise his presence already.

Leaving the engine running, he climbed from the vehicle and walked right up to the gates, shaking them as noisily as he could several times. Nothing. No sudden blaze of a flashlight, challenging shout from a security officer or growls from a roaming guard dog and the caravan just inside the compound was fast fading into the deepening gloom of early evening, suggesting that the place was as deserted as it looked. Maybe Jury just wasn't used to receiving nocturnal visitors, so didn't worry about security.

Returning to the Land Rover, he opened the back door and rummaged among the selection of tools he kept in the old army ammunition box hidden beneath a couple of tarpaulins. The bolt cutters were old, but still serviceable and it took him just a few minutes to find a weak spot in the padlock chain and snap it in two.

The gates shuddered as he pushed them open and seconds later he drove through and parked out of sight behind the caravan, switching off the engine and lights and opening the driver's door to listen again. Still nothing, save the distant drone of an aircraft. For a few moments he watched the flash of the plane's red navigation light as it dropped towards Bristol Airport on its final approach, then climbed out of the vehicle with his torch and began his search.

He found the MX5 almost immediately, parked as it was on a concrete hard-standing away from the alleyways of wrecks that stretched right to the back of the site, and it took him even less time to discover that the tracking device was no longer attached to the sports car or lying underneath it. *Shit!* Either the thing was in the rhyne or had dropped off somewhere en *route* — was maybe even lying on the floor of the breakdown truck itself. He scowled and lit a cigarette, considering his next move, but he only managed a single pull on the filter-tip before the voice rapped at him from behind. 'OK, mister, you stay right there!'

He turned slowly into the flickering beam of a torch — maybe someone should have told his challenger to change his batteries — and glimpsed a short, fat figure behind the light.

'I been watching you,' Ray Jury said triumphantly. 'You come back here screwing once too often. I've already rung the police.'

'Have you indeed?'

'Yeah, an' you better stay put. I got a shotgun here.'

The torch was lowered briefly to reveal the barrel of the weapon and Twister took another pull on his cigarette and smiled. 'So are you going to shoot me?' he queried and flicked the still glowing ember into the gloom.

For a second the torch wavered as Jury was briefly distracted by the red spot trailing away into the darkness and that was enough.

Twister was on him before he realized it, knocking the length of pipe, which had served as his 'shotgun', out of his hands and bowling him over on to the concrete hard-standing.

'Now, my friend,' his antagonist breathed, sitting astride him with one steely hand gripping his throat, 'you're going to tell me all you know about that MX5. And as you say the police are on their way, you've got exactly two minutes to talk before I kill you.'

# CHAPTER 14

'Right, Kate, what's really going on?' Hayden Lewis demanded, dropping into the single armchair and studying her expectantly as she slumped among the cushions on the settee opposite. 'I have to get back to the nick soon or there'll be questions.'

Kate didn't answer him, instead allowing her gaze to travel round the low-ceilinged living room in which they were now closeted.

With its oak beams, open log fire and thick pile carpet, the one-bed thatched cottage in the tiny village of Burtle was exactly the sort of place she had always imagined someone like Hayden would choose for his pad. Horse brasses and other ornaments winked from the hearth and chimney breast and on the bowed shelves of the bookcase occupying the whole of one wall, leather-bound books charged into each other in the glorious confusion of a routed army. Outside on the Levels it was now sleeting and the leaded-light windows rattled under the onslaught of a filthy night that funnelled its icy detritus down the wide chimney, spitting into the maw of the open fire with the continuous 'phut, phut' of a silenced pistol.

Kate cradled her half empty brandy glass in both hands, still feeling the warming effects of the fiery spirit spreading through her body. She knew she shouldn't be drinking after what she had been through — especially at this early hour — and Hayden himself had been unhappy about giving her the brandy in the first place, but, as she had pointed out, it was her body, so her decision. What the hell was she doing in his cottage anyway? She should have gone home straightaway instead. Trouble was, passing out in his car and refusing to return to the hospital for fear of running into Roz Callow had left her with little alternative but to humour him and accept his offer of hospitality. But for how long, that was the point? Not that she was given much time to ponder the point.

'Well, are you going to answer my question, or not?' Lewis snapped, breaking in on her reverie. 'What is going on?'

Kate's gaze returned to his face and after a moment's hesitation, she rummaged in her pocket and produced the note she had retrieved for Terry Duval, holding it out limply in front of her.

He leaned forward to take it, looking puzzled even after he had read it twice. 'I — I don't understand,' he said.

Kate took another gulp from her glass and wriggled painfully into a more upright position. 'You will,' she retorted and quietly — at first tremulously but gaining in strength as she progressed — she told him everything.

There was an awkward silence for several long seconds after she had finished and Lewis's face was white in spite of the heat of the room as he sat rigidly in his seat gaping at her.

A log on the fire exploded and sprayed burning embers on to the wide stone hearth. Neither of them took any notice.

Lewis finally closed his mouth and ran a hand through his hair. 'Kate, what on earth have you done?' he whispered. 'You could be crucified for this.'

'Don't you think I know that?' she choked, then clenched her teeth tightly together in frustration, as she leaned forward. 'But what was I *supposed* to do? Bloody Nora, Hayden, the knives were out for me — I had to do something.' She bit her lip. 'I'm just sorry I had to involve you.'

He made a face, drained his glass and refilled it from the bottle on the coffee table. 'So am I, old girl,' he said, wheezing slightly as the spirit went down a lot faster than he had intended. 'But what's done is done. It's what we do now that matters.'

'So what do you suggest?'

He took a deep breath and shook his head. 'I really don't know. The best thing would be to unload the whole lot on Davey and seek forgiveness.'

She emitted a short laugh, instantly regretting it as pain gripped her chest again. 'Oh you mean, hang *myself* out to dry. No thanks, Hayden. That isn't even close to a solution.'

He frowned and, reaching in his pocket, produced the broken tracking device. 'I must admit,' he said, 'I am more than a bit curious about this little baby. After all, Davey or Callow may privately believe you — er — let your team mates down—'

'Thanks, Hayden.'

He flushed again. 'Well, you know what I mean — but that wouldn't justify putting you under electronic surveillance.'

She shook her head. 'This has nothing to do with them, Hayden. The person who put that tracking thingumajig on my car is obviously the same one who tried to run me off the road; that's how he was able to keep tabs on me in the first place.'

He looked even more worried now. 'Then that certainly raises the stakes, old girl. This chap must be someone with a pretty good knowledge of electronic surveillance kit and, more importantly, he must want to snuff you out pretty badly.'

She nodded now and stared at him. 'Which proves my point, doesn't it? The killer isn't Duval at all. He was telling the truth when he said he was set up.'

He still looked more than a little dubious. 'Well, it goes some way towards it, I agree, but Duval could still be our man; might even have written this note himself as future insurance.'

'I've already considered that possibility, but it doesn't hold water. Why didn't he just write the note after absconding and hand it to me when we met? Sending me back to his place to retrieve it was just too elaborate to be a fix.' Sensing his continuing scepticism, she raised her eyes to the ceiling. 'Look, Hayden, we went through all this at the hospital. I actually saw the driver of the Land Rover when he cannoned into me, remember? And, as I said before, he was nothing like Duval to look at and he had a full beard.'

'But why would this chap want to kill poor old Andy Seldon and Alf Cross in the first place?'

'If I knew that, I'd be halfway to solving the bloody crime. Anyway, I'm not so sure it is just him.'

'What the devil do you mean by that?'

She stared at him, hesitating for a moment. 'What if he's just the hired killer? What if someone else behind the scenes is actually pulling the strings?'

'Like who, for instance?'

She shrugged. 'Could be an organized crime thing — someone either Andy or Alf upset. But, more importantly, how come the killer *knew* the surveillance van would be there at that time on that particular night?'

'I'm not with you.'

'Oh come on, Hayden, think! Someone within the organization must have blabbed about the job. We're dealing with a serious leak here — a hit set up on the basis of intelligence given out either deliberately or unintentionally by someone in the know.'

Lewis snorted. 'You mean a member of the team? Do me a favour, Kate. Let's keep this thing in perspective, shall we? Not venture into the realms of fantasy.'

'Why should it be fantasy? Gangland killings go on all the time and institutional corruption is often a contributory factor.'

'Not in rural Somerset it isn't. As far as I'm aware, neither Andy or Alf have ever worked on anything other than local crime stuff — and certainly not any NCS or

SOCA[2] investigations. And as for the idea that someone at Highbridge nick could be in league with our killer that is too ridiculous for words.'

She made an irritable face. 'Ridiculous or not, I think there's a lot more to this affair than a local grudge killing. In fact, it has all the hallmarks of a professional hit.'

He sighed his exasperation. 'You'd be well advised to come up with something a bit more rational than that, Kate,' he warned, 'especially if you're to keep Roz Callow at bay. Once she gets her claws into you, you're done for.'

'Not if I can bring home the bacon, I'm not.'

'What, Duval, you mean?' He gave a cynical laugh. 'You don't seriously believe he will hand himself in once he has the note, do you?'

'I don't see why not. It's no good to him otherwise.'

'It's not much good to him on its own anyway. I'm just surprised he thought it would be.'

'Does that matter? As long he *thinks* it could get him off the hook, he has a reason for turning himself in.'

'I admire your faith.' Lewis picked up the tracking device again. 'And this? What do we do with this? Ideally, we should hand it in for forensic analysis—'

'No way. That would really get Callow's nose going and the whole thing could unravel around me.'

Lewis nodded. 'Maybe you're right, but we do need to have it checked out. There might be a print or two on it — apart from mine, that is. Could help us to identify your would-be assassin.' He sighed and slipped the device back into his pocket. 'Leave it with me. There's someone in SOCO who owes me a favour . . .'

Suddenly the worry was back in her eyes. 'Do you think that's wise? You could drop yourself in it.'

He laughed. 'I'm already "in it", as you put it, Kate. Might as well go the whole hog. But, more importantly, what

---

[2] SOCA — Serious Organized Crime Agency

are we going to do about your present situation? I don't like the idea of you being in that flat on your own with this character on the loose.'

She drained her brandy glass and carefully levered herself up off the settee, trying hard not to let him see her wincing at the pain ripping through her chest and desperate to extricate herself from a potentially awkward situation. 'I'll be fine,' she said. 'I need to go home to get a hot bath and some rest.'

He hesitated. 'You could always stay here the night,' he said hopefully, then immediately coloured up at his own suggestion. 'I would sleep on the settee, of course.'

She smiled faintly. His offer sounded like a line from a romantic Hollywood movie. The only thing was, Cary Grant had no part in this one, just poor old homespun Hayden. Reaching forward, she picked up the keys of his Jag from the coffee table and dangled them in front of him. 'Home, Jeeves,' she said soberly. 'And don't spare the horses.'

Twister stood for a long time in the shadows of the bus shelter, even though the sudden sleet storm had now abated. Only the tip of his cigarette revealed his presence and he hardly moved a muscle. The bus had already gone, but he was not there to catch buses — just to watch the tower block opposite. The first-floor windows facing him across the road had held his gaze for the past fifteen minutes and not a glimmer of light or a sign of movement had showed in all that time. Kate Hamblin had obviously still not returned home and that suited him to a tee. He would have the time to make himself comfortable in her flat — ready to welcome her back. Dropping the cigarette in front of him, he extinguished it with the toe of one shoe and, turning up the collar of his coat, headed across the road with quick business-like steps.

Twister knew he was in trouble. He hated to admit it, but he had seriously underestimated Kate Hamblin. Before snapping Ray Jury's neck, he had learned from the terrified little proprietor of the breaker's yard all about her visit to the pound with the man in the Jag — including the fact that the pair had apparently found something under the MX5 and taken it with them when they'd left. *The tracking device; it had to be* — which meant that his target must now be well aware that she was under surveillance and would be watching her back. Worse still, it was almost certain she had the bloody tracking device to flash around too, not to mention having got a pretty good look at the Land Rover — maybe even himself — when he had driven her into the rhyne. Things were stacking up against him and he was beginning to feel vulnerable.

The one saving grace was that Hamblin seemed to be doing her own thing rather than working as part of the police investigation. It was common knowledge — in all the papers — that she was in deeps with the murder team and the fact that she had not sorted out some backup for her meeting with Duval under the pier suggested she had not been able to. It was unlikely then that she would be running to her mates with the information she had, but just the same, bit by bit she was putting things together all on her own and she was getting much too close for comfort. This time he had to make sure he croaked her and retrieved the tracking device. No more mistakes or contrived bloody accidents; a straightforward hit was the only option. And seeing as she'd quit the hospital, the best place to look for her was at her flat. The only complication was the arsehole with the Jag. He needed to find out who he was and fix him too — just in case. Maybe he'd get little Miss Kate to tell him what he wanted to know before he shut out her lights. Pulling on a pair of gloves, he licked his lips in anticipation. Yeah, he liked that idea, liked it a lot.

There was no alarm on the flat and the lock on the door was easily sprung — good old council properties — but he was careful to close the door properly behind him. Once inside, he removed the light bulbs from the chandelier in the living room, closed the blinds on the single window and poured himself a stiff whisky from the kitchen cupboard.

Then, swinging an armchair round to face the door, he settled back to wait.

The street was deserted when Kate was dropped off outside
the tower block and the nearby street lamp, its glow reflected
in a pavement that once more gleamed with a thin covering
of ice after the recent sleet storm, seemed to be watching her
with a cold cyclopean eye.

Lewis had offered to see her in, but she had politely but
firmly declined the humiliation of being escorted to her own
flat and he had driven off in a huff.

She sighed as she approached the main door of the
building. Poor old Hayden. He was a real brick, but she
knew what would have happened if she had agreed to his
offer. He would have been through her door ('just make sure
everything is OK in here') and one thing would have led to
another. She liked Hayden a lot, but she had only just ended
one long-term relationship with local solicitor, Alan Morey,
after finding him sharing his bed with two call-girls, and she
wasn't ready for another romantic entanglement just yet —
especially in her present fragile emotional state.

She shivered as she climbed the stone stairs to the first
floor, screwing her nose up at the dank atmosphere of the
place and wondering why the stairways of council tower
blocks always smelled like urinals. Maybe she would be able
to find some little country cottage, like Hayden's, to rent
when this awful business was over. That was, of course, if
she still had a job by then — or, more importantly, a life!

She hadn't admitted it to Hayden, but the revelation that
someone had actually taken the trouble to bug her car had
unnerved her almost as much as the sinister circumstances
of her so-called accident. The realization that she was being
stalked gave her a funny jittery feeling, adding to her sense
of insecurity — not just because of the obvious risk to her
person, but because of the intrusive nature of the thing; the
knowledge that her every move was being closely monitored
by someone who had invaded her life and her privacy. There

was also a sense of indignation, despite the fear factor, that some low-life had had the audacity to put a police officer under surveillance, rather than the other way around.

She wondered just how much the killer knew about her and what she had been doing. Had he seen her pick up the note in the Highbridge café for instance? Had he seen her meet Duval under the pier? And did he know that she had found his tracking device? At the same time, the strange irony attached to the situation was not lost on her, for by targeting her in the first place, he had only lent weight to Duval's claim that he was innocent of the murders of the police surveillance team. But that in turn raised another question — if not Duval, then who and, just as important, why?

The timer controlling the lights activated as she fumbled in her pocket for her key, plunging the stairs and landing in darkness, and she had to press the plastic stud in the wall to switch the lot back on again. But by then she had found her key and, inserting it in the lock, pushed the door open. The interior of the flat was in darkness and she tried the light switch several times before irritably accepting the fact that the ceiling chandelier was not working. With a soft curse, she kicked the door shut behind her and felt her way across the room — and into a nightmare.

Twister had heard the hollow sound of footsteps on the concrete floor outside the flat seconds before someone turned the key in the door. He smiled as the hand fumbled for the light switch and heard a muffled curse when, after several clicks, it dawned on the young woman, whose long auburn hair was briefly backlit in the doorway by the landing light, that the cheap chandelier in the living room was not working.

He sat very still in his corner as she shut the door behind her, then clumsily felt her way across the room to the kitchen as if she couldn't walk properly. Maybe the car crash had done her some harm then. Good! He heard her try the kitchen light and curse even louder when she found that that was out too, rapidly flicking the switch on and off in obvious temper. Her voice was uneven, catching sobs every few seconds, and, though he couldn't see, it was evident that she had made for the sink, because he heard a tap being turned on and a loud splashing sound, suggesting she was dashing water over her face.

Very carefully he climbed out of the chair and edged along the wall past the window to one side of the kitchen door and waited, controlling his breathing and remaining motionless.

She appeared suddenly in the doorway, apparently holding on to the frame. He could hear her breathing, smell the sweat on her, and was surprised that he couldn't catch a single whiff of perfume. But there again, she had probably discharged herself in the same clothes she had been wearing at the time of the crash and hadn't had time to freshen up. Pity, for she wouldn't get another chance now.

She took a couple of steps into the room and stopped. It was almost as if she could smell him too and he inwardly jumped when she spoke. 'Who's there?'

Clever girl. She had keen senses — but not keen enough. One powerful arm had encircled her chest in a crushing embrace before she knew what was happening and even as she opened her mouth to scream, he had found the vital pressure point in her neck and she was out cold.

In the darkness he smiled to himself as he dragged her across the room to the armchair he had vacated and dumped her into it. A length of nylon cord ripped from the blinds on the adjacent window and cut in two with his pocket knife provided him with the means to lash her thin wrists to the chair arms and a piece torn from her blouse and stuffed with tissues from one of her pockets made an excellent gag. Now all he had to do was wait until she regained consciousness and then the interrogation could begin. He felt a most unprofessional, but almost sexual, thrill at the thought of it and he quietly hummed to himself as he switched on the standard lamp behind the chair. 'Now, Miss Katie,' he murmured, 'I wonder what you've got to tell me, eh?'

Terry Duval had been crouched in the tiny maintenance cupboard for the best part of an hour and a half, waiting for Kate Hamblin to return home. From his cramped position, he had been afforded a clear view of the flat across the landing through a tiny gap between the edge of the door and the frame and his patience seemed to have been rewarded when the slender auburn-haired girl let herself into the flat just as he was about to give up on his uncomfortable vigil. He had been ringing Kate on the mobile number she had given him at various times throughout the day, but without success and had decided on the more direct approach in a mood of desperation. He needed to know whether she had managed to retrieve the note before he could decide on anything. Without it he was on to a hiding to nothing, but time was fast running out for him. Twice he had only avoided being spotted by a police patrol by the skin of his teeth and he knew that the odds on his luck continuing were pretty bleak. Kate Hamblin was his one chance, but could he count on her? He wasn't so sure about that, but he sure as hell was going to ask her.

He waited a further ten minutes before deciding to leave his hiding-place and only then after listening carefully for the slightest sound that would indicate someone was using the now blacked-out stairs. But all he could hear was the blare of a television coming from the floor above. Satisfied, he very gently pushed the door open and began to squeeze through — only to freeze again when a shaft of light suddenly sprang out across the landing as the door of the flat he was watching was pulled open. The next instant a tall, powerfully built man, dressed in a hooded coat, emerged and stood there for a second, apparently checking out the landing. Easing the cupboard door closed, Duval remained in a half-crouched position, balancing on one leg, but afraid to move in case he gave himself away.

But he was in luck this time and the next moment he heard footsteps ringing on the stone stairs, followed by the sound of the main entrance door in the lobby downstairs closing with a resounding bang. Taking a calculated risk, he peered out again, but the landing was deserted. The mysterious visitor had apparently switched on the landing lights as he left, but the automatic timer cut them off even as Duval straightened up and shut the cupboard door behind him. He made no effort to hit the switch again, however; sometimes the dark could be a useful ally and right now he sensed that things were best left the way they were.

The door of Kate Hamblin's flat was ajar and he frowned. Who the hell had she been entertaining? Her departing visitor had not looked like the sort she would be interested in romantically and Duval had been involved with the police long enough to know that it hadn't been Old Bill either. So who then? His instinct told him something was very wrong and he should get out while he could, but curiosity got the better of him and he couldn't resist pushing the door back to peer inside.

At first he was partially dazzled by the standard lamp in the corner, but his eyes quickly adjusted to the light and, suddenly realizing that the woman sitting in the armchair beneath it must have seen him, he lurched across the room towards her, kicking the door shut behind him. 'Don't make a sound,' he snarled, 'or I'll kill you.'

But even as he got to her, it became apparent to him that someone else had beaten him to it. He saw the cords binding her wrists to the chair arms first and when he bent down beside her to gingerly pull the long hair away from her battered face, he saw the gag in her mouth and found himself staring into wide-open sightless eyes.

His gruesome discovery sent him staggering back from the corpse with a choking cry, colliding with a wall and another piece of furniture on the way. Then, wrenching open the front door with shaking fingers, he blundered out on to the landing, slamming the door behind him as if seeking to contain some unimaginable horror that was in pursuit.

He snapped the landing light on again as he stumbled towards the stairs, his eyes wild and unseeing, the perspiration pouring down his face in the panic of the moment. The elderly man going through his post-box in the lobby stared after him in astonishment as he crashed through the main door and out into the street, but he hardly noticed him.

Kate Hamblin was dead, that was all Duval could think of — *dead* — which meant that he had lost the one chance he had of proving his innocence. As he climbed behind the wheel of his Land Rover and churned away into the night, however, something else hit him with almost physical force: he had just stumbled upon a murder scene and, like a fool, he had left his prints all over it.

Dick Stacey, the office manager, was sorting through some files on his desk when Hayden Lewis pushed through the door of the otherwise empty CID office.

Lewis raised an eyebrow. 'Still here, Dick?' he queried. 'I thought you'd be home in front of the telly long before now.'

The admin man shrugged. 'Asked to stay on,' he replied. 'Bit of a flap going down at the moment. DI's been trying to get hold of you.'

Lewis poured himself a coffee from the machine, keeping his back towards Stacey to hide the alarm that must have registered in his expression. 'Yeah, got a problem with my mobile,' he lied, adding a little too casually, 'What sort of a flap?'

Stacey grunted and Lewis heard him push his chair back as he got to his feet. 'Only another murder,' the other replied drily.

'Murder?' Lewis turned quickly, the coffee cup partially shielding his face as he took a sip.

Stacey studied him with a kind of grim amusement, then shrugged again as he crossed the room towards a half-open filing cabinet in the far corner, a wad of files under his arm. 'Yeah, a Bridgwater car-recovery merchant by the name of Ray Jury.'

'Jury?' Lewis choked the name through his coffee, then pulled out a handkerchief to wipe his chin.

Stacey bent over the cabinet, apparently inserting the files inside in some sort of set order. 'Local plods got an "intruder on premises" call,' he said, 'but when they got there, they found Jury lying in the yard with a broken neck.'

The admin man slammed the drawer of the cabinet shut. 'Detective Super and DCI are down there now. Nasty business.'

But Lewis was no longer listening — all he could think about was Kate — and when Stacey turned back towards his desk, he was surprised to find the detective had gone, his footsteps thumping off down the corridor outside, leaving his cup of coffee leaking through the screwed up paper in one of the office's cane wastepaper bins.

'Dirty bastard,' Stacey growled, grabbing some kitchen roll from the coffee tray to clear up the mess and briefly cocking an eye towards the door as a vehicle left the car-park outside with a screech of tyres.

# CHAPTER 15

Hayden Lewis was scared — not for himself, but for Kate. He had to admit that at first he had been pretty sceptical about her claim that she was being targeted by some shadowy assassin, but discovering the bug on her car had changed all that and the fact that the murder of Ray Jury must have been committed within an hour or so of their visit to the car-breaker's yard was just too much of a coincidence. Kate was in deadly peril, he was convinced of it, and he feared that the clock was already ticking. Why the hell hadn't he over-ruled her protests and insisted on escorting her to her flat in the first place? He would never forgive himself if anything had happened to her.

'Weak, weak, weak,' he blazed at himself, hammering the steering wheel with the palm of one hand. 'Always so damned spineless.'

He continued to beat himself up most of the way to Bridgwater and it was because of his angry recriminations that he failed to spot the Land Rover in time. It passed him on the opposite side of the dual carriageway just after he had left Dumball Wharf behind and even as it disappeared into the elastic darkness, his wide-eyed stare confirmed that the vehicle was identical to the one Kate had earlier described to him: a grey coloured, hard-top Defender, with a snorkel fitted, showing one red and one white light to the rear.

Travelling at speed on the opposite side of a substantial central reservation, he had no chance of picking out the driver or even part of the index number, but he knew instinctively that it was the right vehicle and his skin crawled at the thought of where it must have just come from. *Gordon Bennett — Kate!*

Deep down he knew he was already too late, but that didn't stop his right foot from trying to push the accelerator pedal all the way through the floor to the road surface and the milk tanker negotiating the big roundabout on the outskirts of Bridgwater had to slam on its brakes to avoid him as he emerged from the dual carriageway in a blur. But Lewis was unrepentant. Careless driving or speeding tickets he could deal with, but the corpse of Kate Hamblin he could not.

Seconds later he pulled up with a slither of tyres in front of the grim tower block where Kate had her flat and leaped from the car like a madman, skidding on the icy pavement as he headed for the main door and almost bowling over a young couple in the process of leaving the building.

Beat music thudded out from somewhere above his head and the smell of curry greeted him as he bounded up the stairs. Everything seemed so refreshingly normal and he began to wonder whether he was about to make a prize ass of himself. But that thought was immediately discarded the moment he reached the door of Kate's flat. It was half open.

'Kate?' he called, his voice cracked and unnatural as he carefully pushed the door right back. 'It's Hayden. Are you OK?'

There was no reply and he saw that the flat was in darkness save for a pool of light cast by a standard lamp in the far corner, which illuminated a solitary armchair. His hand fumbled for the main light switch just inside the door, but flicking the switch produced no response. *Damn it!*

Then, as his eyes adjusted to his surroundings, he saw for the first time what looked like someone sitting in the armchair under the standard lamp and his heart missed a beat when he caught the gleam of auburn hair.

'Kate!' he shouted, only to realize when he stumbled across the room that she was not sitting in the chair at all, but lolling forward, her head resting on her chest and her shoulder-length hair hanging down over her face.

Kneeling beside her, he saw that her wrists were tied to the chair arms with some kind of nylon cord that cut right into the flesh and she did not appear to be breathing. Gripped by panic, he rummaged in his pocket for his clasp knife and quickly severed her bonds before trying to push her back in the chair. But the moment he took his hands away from her, she fell forward on to his shoulder, limp and unresponsive. Her hair in his face smelled strangely earthy and her body emanated a coldness that terrified him. He grasped her wrist and felt for a pulse, but could detect nothing.

'Come on, Kate,' he pleaded and, supporting her with the palm of one hand against her shoulder, used the other to feel for a pulse in her neck. But there was not the faintest tremor and even as the horrible truth hit him with sledge-hammer force, a familiar voice in the gloom behind the chair confirmed his worst fears.

'You're too late. She's dead.'

DCI Roz Callow had had a long tiring day and now, with the murder of Ray Jury, it looked like getting a lot longer. Her situation was not helped by the press either. Descending on the crime scene like a pack of jackals within minutes of her arrival, they had been clamouring for information ever since — kept at bay solely by the perimeter fence and a pair of wire gates, which had required wedging shut with a police Transit van after the crew of the initial response car had found them standing wide open.

Ray Jury still lay where he had been found, within a few yards of his caravan, shielded from the media's flash cameras by a couple of police accident signs and a few bollards pending the arrival of the pathologist and forensic team.

The doctor the uniformed officers had called out to certify death had already given the cause as a broken neck and since there was nothing Jury could have fallen from, it didn't need the expertise of Sherlock Holmes to deduce that his death must have been due to foul play — and that in itself worried Callow.

As an experienced detective, she knew that it was not that easy to break a person's neck without using a weapon of some sort and the doctor had already pointed out that there were no signs of any external injuries consistent with a blow. This suggested that the former proprietor of the breaker's yard had been killed by someone with the skill to do the job with his bare hands. An ex-army man perhaps? Special Services maybe? But why? Jury was known to the police for ringing cars and he was suspected of doing a nice little trade in forged documents too, but he was nevertheless small fry — not someone who would have attracted a contract from one of the big-time villains.

All very perplexing, but with her boss tucked up at head-quarters on a briefing with the assistant chief constable in charge of territorial policing and the current double murder investigation floundering due to the failure of her team to flush out the main suspect, she reckoned she had quite enough on her plate without falling for another complicated murder inquiry. Her sour mood was plainly reflected in her expression when the SOCO team arrived and set up their powerful spotlights, but her transformation turned out to be just a few steps away and it was unwittingly brought about by Detective Inspector Roscoe, who approached her from the caravan.

'Thought you should hear this, ma'am,' he said, nodding towards a greasy-looking man in an anorak who was trailing behind him.

Callow studied the man with undisguised contempt. 'So who is he?' she snapped, as if he wasn't there.

'Lenny Stallard, one of Ray Jury's men,' Roscoe replied, then nodded to the man again. 'Tell the boss what you told me.'

Stallard shrugged. 'Ain't much to tell. Left the yard when Ray closed the place at five. Ray stayed be'ind an' I locked him in. Never saw him again.'

Callow frowned. 'Why did he stay behind?'

Stallard grinned, seemingly unaffected by Jury's death. 'Fievein'. We'd 'ad a lot of stuff nicked lately an' Ray said 'e was goin' to nail 'em.'

'And the rest,' Roscoe encouraged. 'Tell her the rest.'

'Oh yeah, we 'ad a visitor just afore Ray closed up — some bird an' a bloke. They come to look at the MX5 job over there.' He waved an arm towards the concrete hard-standing.

Callow turned quickly to look in the direction he was indicating. 'That's Kate Hamblin's car, isn't it?' she snapped at Roscoe.

'Yeah,' Stallard cut in before Roscoe could reply, 'I fink that's what the bird's name was. Anyways, I saw the bloke bend down and pull somefink off from underneaf. Then the pair of 'em looked at it afore drivin' away. Told Ray they'd 'alf-inched somefink, but 'e said it was the bird's motor, so she could take whatever she liked.'

Callow's eyes were gleaming now. 'What did the man with her look like?'

'Dunno. Didn't pay too much attention like. Tall, lot of 'air.' He chuckled. 'Looked a bit like that London mayor geezer — Boris Johnson. But I clocked the car — nice red Mk2 Jag it was. Not many of them about today — 'cept the one that used to be driven by that copper, Inspector Morse, on the telly.'

Callow wore a triumphant smile as she turned away from him and popped an extra strong peppermint into her mouth. 'Now that *is* interesting,' she murmured, 'very interesting indeed.'

Kate Hamblin looked like a ghost on the fringes of the light from the standard lamp, her eyes hollow black depressions in a cold white mask that quivered spasmodically. She was right on the edge of reason and Lewis lunged round the armchair to catch her as she suddenly collapsed into his arms.

He carried her across the room and through a door into what turned out to be a bedroom and flicked on the light — one that worked this time — before laying her gently on the bed. She lay there, eyes wide open, lips trembling, trying to speak, but somehow unable to form the words.

'Thank God you're safe,' Lewis gasped, sitting on the bed beside her. 'For a moment I thought—'

'Took out the other light bulbs,' Kate blurted suddenly. 'Waited for me to come home.'

'Who is she?' Lewis asked gently, shuddering as he remembered the battered face, bloodied nose, and the tell-tale scars on the dead girl's thin white wrists. 'She looks so much like you.'

Kate's eyes focused on his face with a peculiar intensity, then abruptly drifted away, staring at the ceiling. 'My twin, Linda,' she whispered. 'Must have come here looking for help and in the dark he thought she was me. Looks like he roughed her up before—'

Lewis patted her hand and stood up. 'I have to get some help,' he said. 'You stay here, OK?'

He went outside on to the landing to make his mobile call to headquarters control room, requesting backup and an ambulance. His voice was shaking as he provided the necessary information and he had only just slipped his mobile back into his pocket and returned to the flat, when he heard a sound and saw Kate standing in the bedroom doorway.

'No, old girl,' he said, stepping quickly towards her and guiding her back into the bedroom, 'you have to lie down. You've had a terrible shock.'

To his surprise, she shook her head. 'No tears, Hayden,' she whispered and bit her lip in pain, one hand darting to her still badly bruised chest as she began to sway unsteadily in front of him. 'No tears. Waste of time.' She stared at him, again with that same intense expression. 'No love between us,' she said. 'Unusual for a twin, isn't it? Tried to help her to quit, but she was too far gone.' She hesitated. 'At peace now.'

He was conscious of the fact that he was gaping at her. This wasn't the sort of reaction he would have expected from someone who had just found her sister brutally murdered, but it was apparent that the shock was still there and she was dangerously close to collapsing again. Getting a grip on his own emotions, he more or less forced her down into a sitting position on the edge of the bed. Somewhere outside he could hear the distant scream of sirens.

'Do you think it would have been quick for Linda?' she asked.

He nodded automatically, feeling tears of his own coming. 'Yes, old girl. It would have been quick,' he said, without knowing whether it would have been quick or not.

'We've got to find him, Hayden,' she said, sudden unexpected venom in her tone. 'The murdering bastard mustn't get away with this.'

He patted her hand again, his face grim. 'We'll find him, never fear, old girl,' he said. 'But first we've got to prepare ourselves for some awkward questions from the team, you do realize that, don't you?'

She gave a faint humourless smile. 'And the Wicked Witch of the North,' she added.

''Fraid so,' he replied, 'especially the Wicked Witch.'

Then the time for conversation was over. Heavy footsteps racing up the stairs as a powerful flashing blue light stained the walls of the bedroom from below. Help had finally arrived and he should have felt relieved. So why then did the prospect fill him with such foreboding?

# CHAPTER 16

Twister just couldn't believe it; he had cocked up again. What was it about this job? It was almost as if it were jinxed.

Pulling into the wayside pub on the edge of the Levels, he ordered a pint and a whisky chaser before slumping into a corner by the open fire. The bar was virtually empty and, after one curious glance in his direction, the girl who had served him rejoined the long-haired youth at the other end of the counter to continue chatting him up.

Twister took a long pull on his pint, then in a sudden spasm of anger picked up his glass of whisky and drained it in a gulp.

Part of the problem was that he had only ever seen Kate Hamblin at a distance. The kid who had waltzed into her flat had looked just like her in the poor light — had actually appeared to be the living spit of her when he'd dumped her in the chair under the standard lamp. As it had turned out, she was her bloody twin, so it had been easy to make that initial mistake. But he'd soon realized he'd got the wrong person when he'd seen the needle tracks and the ruptured veins, and he had cursed himself for an idiot. He should have sussed it earlier; the earthy unwashed smell of someone used to sleeping rough was like no other — and her hair — ugh! Filthy.

He took another gulp of his beer and rolled it around his mouth for a moment. He had probably done her a favour by snuffing out her lights, but she would never know anyway; he'd snapped her neck just like Ray Jury, after they'd had a 'little chat' about things. Had to. Couldn't afford to risk being picked out by her on some future ID parade.

So where did he go from here? He was tempted to keep on driving. The job now had as bad a smell to it as the junkie he'd just stiffed. Another mistake and he could end up in stir. Trouble was, there was too much money at stake to simply bail out and he was in too deep. Topping a few A-rabs in the desert was one thing when you were under the colours, but the cold-blooded murder of a couple of British coppers was in a totally different league. Old Bill would never let this one go, so he would need every penny of the pay-off he was expecting to fix up a new identity for himself and then to get out of the country.

At least he'd covered his tracks well enough. He was pretty certain no one had seen him break into the flat or leave it afterwards and he had been careful to avoid making Old Bill a gift of his prints or DNA — even washing up his whisky glass, despite the fact that he had been wearing gloves. That meant he was in the clear for another crack at Miss Lucky Knickers. This time though it couldn't be just another hit; the dynamics had changed. He needed that little chat with her first to find out what had happened to his tracking device and who the guy in the Jag was. And now that she was still alive, it was suddenly very important to find out why she had met Terry Duval under Burnham pier and what he had told her. No loose ends, he was definite about that. But getting the thing done with the sort of bad luck he had been having lately wouldn't be easy.

Draining his pint, he nodded towards the girl behind the bar and headed back out to the car-park and his Land Rover. Finding Kate Hamblin again would be his first real challenge. Her flat would now be a crime scene and it was very unlikely that she would be able — or want — to return there in the immediate future. But she'd have to go somewhere and his best bet was the guy who had collected her from the hospital and run her out to Jury's place — after all, there couldn't be that many local Samaritans around with a red Mk 2 Jaguar.

Kate was in a hole and even in her shocked ethereal state, she knew it. By rejecting the advice of the paramedics attending the murder scene that she should return to hospital with them in the ambulance for a check-up, she had played right into DCI Callow's hands. As a result, she had been left with no option but to submit to what promised to be a dismembering interrogation back at the station.

Callow had questioned Lewis first, but had got nowhere; his carefully  worded replies convincing her that he knew nothing of what Kate was up to and, as she put it crudely to DI Roscoe afterwards, was simply 'sticking with the little tart in the hope of getting into her knickers'.

Callow had saved Kate until last, leaving her to sweat in another office while she finished a second cup of coffee and reviewed the facts the detective sergeant at the flat had given her. When she finally collected her and sat her in the chair on the other side of the interview- room desk, there was a gleam of malicious anticipation in the dark eyes as she popped a mint into her mouth with the relish of a cobra devouring a mouse.

'So young lady, here we are again — you and I, eh?'

Kate said nothing, but stared unseeing at the far wall.

'You found the dead woman, I understand?'

Kate nodded and returned her intense gaze with a strange indifference, the debilitating shock she had suffered reasserting itself and numbing her senses — as well as her susceptibility to intimidation.

Callow seemed irritated by her disconnected manner. 'And what time was that?' she snapped.

There was a long pause before Kate surfaced from her comfortable dreamlike state, her brows knitted together in a frown, as if she had trouble extracting the information from her short-term memory. 'About — about an hour and a half ago,' she said distantly. 'Came home and she was in the chair — dead.'

'What did you do?'

'Do?'

Callow hissed her frustration. 'Did you cut the bloody cords around her wrists, damn it?'

The DCI's sharp aggressive response seemed to have the effect of shaking Kate out of her semi-reverie and her focus suddenly snapped back into place.

'No,' she blurted, as if she had been given a mental shove. 'Hayden did. He called by and found the door open. Thought Linda was me.'

'He tells me she was your twin. Is that correct?'

Kate nodded again.

'A junkie, eh? I saw the tramlines.'

There was a flicker of resentment in Kate's eyes. 'She was a heroin addict, yes.'

'So what was your *junkie* sister doing in your flat?'

Kate flinched, her mouth tightening as anger now began to sharpen her senses. 'Probably looking for me for help.'

'She had a key then?'

Kate took a deep breath. 'She turned up the other night out of the blue; probably took it when she raided my handbag for cash while I was out of the room.'

'According to my information, she was supposed to be on compulsory rehab.'

Kate shrugged. 'Possibly.'

'Yet you didn't report her visit, even though she was an absconder in breach of the conditions of her suspended sentence.'

Kate stared at her wearily. 'You *have* been busy, haven't you?'

Callow's eyes became mere slits. 'Don't get clever with me, miss; you're already in deep shit.'

Kate stared at her with contempt. 'So shoot me, why don't you?'

Callow stiffened in her seat, fazed slightly by Kate's uncharacteristic behaviour, and when she continued, her approach was more measured. 'The ambulance crew reckon she died from a broken neck. The pathologist will obviously confirm or otherwise later, but for now, any idea why someone would want to do that?'

Kate shuddered, conscious of her hands trembling as she remembered walking in on Linda's corpse, but for some reason found herself fresh out of tears. 'How could I?' she breathed.

'You don't seem particularly upset by the tragedy.'

'That's not fair.'

Callow's face hardened. 'No, it isn't, is it?' she grated. 'But then neither is murder and I am curious as to why someone would gag and tie up a young woman, subject her to a beating, then snap her spine like twig. As it seems to have happened in your flat, maybe you could help me there?'

Kate sensed danger and swallowed quickly. 'I told you, Hayden thought Linda was me. Her killer probably thought the same thing.'

'And why would this person — whoever he is — want to kill you?'

'For the same reason he ran me off the road—'

'Oh come on,' Callow cut in. 'You're not still claiming that your accident was the work of some shadowy bogey man trying to prevent you rubbishing the case against Duval?'

Kate shrugged. 'Mock as much as you like, but I know it was and I still don't believe Duval is our killer either.'

Callow's thin lips twisted into a sneer. 'Don't you?' she retorted. 'And I suppose this bogey man was the same one who followed you all the way to Jury's yard and stiffed Ray Jury?'

In an instant Kate was thrown off balance and she stared at Callow as if mesmerized. 'Ray Jury?' she gasped. 'Ray Jury's dead?'

The DCI nodded, pleased that she had finally managed to rattle her. 'As mutton, my dear. Looks like his neck was broken too.'

'But — but he was alive when we left his place.'

Callow lurched forward across the desk. 'Is that right? Well, I think it mighty coincidental that you and your boyfriend should have dropped in at the yard minutes before he called for police assistance.'

Now Kate could feel the fear building up inside her like an ice-cold cramp. 'Surely you don't think Hayden and I—?'

Callow sat back in her chair and studied her over steepled fingers. 'Why not? Maybe you panicked when Jury saw what you'd found underneath your car and you decided to shut him up.'

For a second Kate's guard slipped and she nearly fell into Callow's trap by telling her about the tracking device. Just in time she bit her tongue. 'I — I don't know what you're talking about.'

'Don't you? We have a witness who saw you remove something from under the car and take it with you when you left. What was that all about?'

Despite her traumatized state, Kate's defence mechanism, sharpened by Callow's bullying tactics, came to her aid, alerting her to the flaw in the DCI's *Dr Watson*-style analysis. Skilfully turning the tables without answering her question, she said, 'We were seen to leave then, were we? So at that stage Ray Jury must obviously have still been alive, which puts a nice big spike in your theory, doesn't it?'

'You could have doubled back.'

Now Kate was incredulous. 'Do me a favour, Chief Inspector. You've been watching too many TV cop films.'

Callow's face twisted into a spiteful mask, but before she could respond, the interview was interrupted by the discordant blast of the mobile she had placed on the desk in front of her.

Without taking her eyes off Kate, she spat an acknowledgment into the phone and listened intently, her face softening as she did so, until a triumphant smile replaced the venom in her expression and she ended the call in a positively upbeat mood.

'That was DI Roscoe at your little flat,' she now purred. 'Apparently SOCO have so far found some interesting fibres and lots of nice marks, so it will be necessary for you and your boyfriend to come in here tomorrow to provide the usual elimination prints.'

'As serving police officers, our fingerprints will already be on file,' Kate cut in.

Callow's smile became even more pronounced. 'Maybe so,' she agreed, 'but since your flat has now become a crime scene, *I* require you to provide elim prints anyway — *if* that's not too much trouble, for you?'

Kate nodded and studied her warily, knowing from Callow's change in attitude that something else was coming that she wouldn't like.

The DCI paused for a moment to slip another mint into her mouth, obviously enjoying the tension she had created. 'The prints and fibres are all good stuff, of course,' she went on, 'but not of immediate value to the investigation as conclusive results will take time. But' — and she leaned forward again across the desk — 'what is of immediate value is the fact that we have a witness.'

'A witness?' Kate could not help a sharp intake of breath.

The gleam in the DCI's eyes became more intense. 'An elderly resident who not only saw a man run away from the scene at about the right time, but was able to give us a detailed description of him — and guess what? That description fits Terry Duval to a tee.' She crunched her mint once like a dry bone. 'So much for your phantom bogeyman, eh?'

The fire was nearly out when Lewis ushered Kate into the living room of his cottage and she sank on to the settee while he stoked up the dying flames again.

They had hardly spoken on the way back from Highbridge, each busy with their own thoughts, and Lewis's opening remark of 'So how was it?' as he had helped her into his car had been greeted with a hostile 'Just don't go there'. He knew all about Duval being tied to the crime scene by a witness — news travels fast in the police service and the skeleton crew in the general office had been full of it — but he had known better than to broach the subject to Kate. She was obsessed with the idea that Duval was innocent and in her present fragile condition and with Lewis himself on the verge of exhaustion, this was not the time for a heated debate.

There were other considerations too. The killer had obviously been after Kate when he had confronted Linda and he would know he had made a bad mistake. That meant he was bound to be looking for Kate again and a thatched cottage stuck out on the Levels at Burtle was not the ideal refuge for a vulnerable target. Lewis frowned as he turned to look at his charge. She had slumped sideways on the settee, with her eyes closed, and appeared to be out for the count. 'Gordon Bennett!' he muttered. 'An assassin on one side and the Wicked Witch of the North on the other. Which leaves us both right up the creek without a paddle.'

Grabbing a duvet from his bed, he trailed it down the stairs into the room and draped it over Kate's prostrate form, carefully sliding a cushion under her head. Then, checking that the doors and windows were locked, he dropped into a chair by the fire and awaited developments, a heavy poker in one hand.

The pub was a well-known haunt of local police officers finishing the late shift and Twister propped himself on a rickety stool at the bar with a pint in front of him. The place was packed, despite the fact that it was well after the usual drinking hours. A couple of the force's finest, civilian coats over their uniforms, were already well oiled, their voices loud and slurred. He wondered if they intended driving home afterwards.

'Got a light, mate?' he asked a spotty-faced youngster next to him, noting that his pint glass was nearly empty.

The policeman frowned. 'Can't smoke in pubs no more,' he declared in a thick voice.

Twister swore. 'Just my luck,' he growled. 'Better have a chaser instead then.' He raised his hand to beckon the bartender and glanced quickly at his new acquaintance. 'Want to join me?'

The other swayed slightly, turning away from his colleagues. 'Yeah, don't mind if I do — beer, thanks.'

Twister watched with grim satisfaction as the policeman downed half of his pint in a gulp. 'You can certainly hold the old sherbet,' he commented.

The youngster puffed out his chest. 'Don't affect me no more,' he boasted. 'Been on it too long.'

Twister nodded. 'Local Bill, are you?'

The kid's eyes narrowed. 'Why do you ask?'

Twister shrugged, staring into his glass. 'No reason really. Only, one of my mates is in your lot.'

'Oh?'

'Yeah, Highbridge CID.'

The other gave a good-natured grin. 'What the "defective" squad? Load of poofs, they are.'

Twister forced a laugh. 'Yeah, I'll drink to that. He must be to drive the motor he's got — bloody Inspector Morse Jag, I ask you.'

'What, a red one?'

Twister glanced at him. 'Yeah, good-looking car though. You know him?'

The policeman chuckled. 'What, Hayden Lewis? Now he really *is* a poof. Ex-pubic schoolboy.' And he laughed again at his unsavoury pun, turning back to his colleagues. 'Hey, guys, this chap knows ol' Hayden Lewis.'

Twister's mouth tightened. He didn't want the whole crowd in on the conversation. But he need not have worried; they were too interested in a joke one of them was telling to be diverted and they ignored their workmate's shout.

'Got a nice pad though, hasn't he?'

Another snort. 'If you like the Levels — I mean, who'd want to live in a place with a grass roof?' He chuckled again. 'Especially one with a name like The Retreat — sounds like an old folks' home.'

'Maybe he likes village life.'

The policeman finished his pint and grabbed hold of the counter for support. 'Life? Ain't no life at Burtle — just bloody marsh.'

*Time to go.* Twister finished his whisky and stretched. 'Call it a night, I think,' he said.

His drinking partner grinned again. 'What, you on to a promise?'

Twister clapped him on the shoulder. 'More likely a threat at my age, old son. Have a nice life.'

Then he was gone, weaving between the drinkers to the door. Outside he lit a cigarette before heading off down the street to the empty car-park where he had parked his Land Rover in the shadows — and it was his turn to grin as he climbed behind the wheel. So, the man with the Jag was called Hayden Lewis, was he, and he lived in a thatched cottage in Burtle called The Retreat? Well, he shouldn't be too difficult to find, should he? And finding him would almost certainly mean finding little Miss Katie.

He glanced at his watch. He was tempted to head for Burtle right there and then, but checked himself in time. No sense in rushing things, however important recovery of the tracker was. What was done was done and if Kate and her boyfriend still had the device, they wouldn't be doing much with it in the middle of the night, would they? And anyway, if they were both home, he could hardly just go up to the cottage in the early hours of the morning and knock them up; that would be plain dumb. No, he would have to handle this last tidying up operation with a bit more aplomb than he had managed so far — check the place out for the tracker first and deal with the two coppers afterwards. Daylight was the best time. Lewis was likely to be at work then and there was an even chance that little Miss Katie would be there on her own. His mouth almost watered at the thought. Ideal. And if she *wasn't* actually staying there as he'd assumed, then he could sit and wait for either of the pair to show up, couldn't he? After all, what had he to lose more than he could have lost already?

He started the engine and eased out into the road, armed with a new sense of purpose. At last he felt good again and after a nice kip, he knew he would feel a whole lot better — well enough, in fact, to embrace a brand new fulfilling day.

CHAPTER 17

The police station at Highbridge was virtually deserted when Kate and Lewis put in an appearance at just after eleven in the morning and, slipping in the back door to avoid the press camped out the front, they learned from Dick Stacey that the inquiry team was engaged in house-to-house inquiries in the vicinity of Kate's flat and not expected back until the afternoon, which suited them just fine.

Kate had passed the rest of the night on Lewis's settee without waking once and the few hours' sleep she had managed, followed by the shower and the coffee and buttered-toast breakfast Hayden had then set before her, had certainly helped to restore some of her former resilience. But she remained in a lot of pain from her accident, despite the strong pain-killers she had been taking, and the dark smudges under her eyes, coupled with the haunted expression on her pale, drawn face, reflected the torment that was going on inside her head over the brutal death of her sister and the fact that she could still not find it within herself to feel any real sense of loss.

It was true that Linda's death had come as a terrible shock to her, but no more than the death of any murder victim in such circumstances, and while her feelings of pity and regret for a life so tragically wasted were genuine, there was none of the agonizing gut-wrenching sorrow that one twin is traditionally expected to suffer following the demise of the other. Looking back, she remembered that she and her sister had never been very close anyway and when Linda had gone off the rails and turned to drugs, effectively destroying the lives of her mother and father as well as her own, the coldness between them had turned to mutual hostility — a sentiment that had been made a lot worse by Kate's own decision to join the police. Maybe the day would come when Linda's death would finally hit her, enabling her to shed tears for her sister in the same way as she had shed them for Andy Seldon and Alf Cross, but right now her mind was partially anaesthetized by the shock and the pain of the last few days and she had no more tears left; only a burning hatred for the person responsible for so much carnage and a determination to bring him down, whatever the cost.

The SOCO man who took Kate's elimination finger-prints had very little to say — no doubt because he had already been briefed about her alleged cowardice by the rest of the team and was too embarrassed to try and make polite conversation. Lewis fared only fractionally better and it was clear that his association with Kate had now tainted him in the eyes of his colleagues, which only added to her feelings of guilt, and she squeezed his arm as they left the SOCO office. 'Sorry, Hayden,' she said. 'I've spoiled things for you too.'

He forced a grin. 'Cup of coffee, old girl!' he said firmly, sensing her mood. 'And maybe even a currant bun, eh?'

Kate smiled faintly. 'You should be at work now. You'll be getting into trouble.'

Another grin. 'You worry too much, Kate,' he said. 'The guv'nor and the Wicked Witch are still down at the crime scene and, according to good old Dick Stacey in there, the DI is now back to covering things at Jury's Yard. What better time for a currant bun, eh?'

The café Kate had visited before was almost empty and Lewis chose a corner table, apparently unaware of the sullen glance the waitress cast in Kate's direction as she took their order.

'Point is,' Hayden began in a conspiratorial whisper after an awkward silence, 'we need to sort you out, don't we? You can't go back to your flat, so it looks like you'll have to stay with me at Burtle until things settle down.'

Kate shook her head. 'You're very kind, Hayden,' she began, 'but I can't—'

'That's settled then,' he beamed, cutting her off and taking the laden tray from the waitress as she approached. 'And the next thing we have to do is to get you another car. Can't have you walking, can we?'

'My insurance company will sort that out,' she replied. 'Terms of my policy provide for a temporary replacement.'

'No need,' he said, cutting open his bun and buttering it lavishly. 'I've got another motor — a little Mini — at my place and it should do you until the insurance company pays out.'

'No, Hayden,' she said firmly. 'I won't allow it.'

'I'll drop you off there,' he said, butter oozing through his fingers as he bit into his bun, 'then hotfoot it back to the nick before the posse returns. Now don't forget your coffee; it'll get cold.'

But Kate was no longer listening. Her gaze was directed over his shoulder to the door. Pauline Cross had just entered the café and to Kate's alarm, was walking straight over to her.

'Hello, Kate,' she said, nodding to Lewis as he half struggled to his feet with characteristic courtesy.

Kate swallowed her mouthful of coffee in a solid lump. 'Hello, Pauline,' she responded, blurting an automatic, 'How are you feeling?'

Pauline shrugged. 'May I join you?'

Kate's jaw dropped. 'Join us?'

Pauline nodded, giving a tight-lipped smile. 'Just been in to collect Alf's personal effects and saw you through the window.'

Kate squirmed. 'I'm so terribly sorry,' she whispered.

Pauline made a face. 'So am I, Kate,' she said. 'But I think I owe you an apology.'

Hayden coughed, sensing the tension between the two women and trying to hide his embarrassment. 'Look, Kate,' he put in quickly, 'you sit and have a chat with Pauline. I — I'm supposed to be at work, so I should really go back to the incident room. Pop by when you're ready and I'll take you' — he hesitated, swallowing the words 'back to Burtle', and quickly substituting — 'home.'

Before Kate could think of a suitable excuse, he had clumsily pushed his chair back into the next table and was edging for the door, smiling and nodding his discomfort as he went.

'Nice man,' Pauline commented, taking his vacated chair and raising a finger in the direction of the waitress.

Ordering a cup of coffee, she sat back in her chair, eyeing Kate quizzically. 'Heard about your accident and the terrible business at your flat,' she went on. 'You look dreadful.'

Kate nodded. 'I don't feel so good,' she admitted, then added, 'Look, Pauline, what they're saying about me, it just isn't true.'

'I realize that.'

'You do? Then why—?'

Pauline laid a hand on her wrist. 'Kate, I was distraught, can you understand that? I said things that were — well, totally unfair, and I'm sorry. I know you wouldn't have deserted poor Alf and Andy.'

Kate felt as if a heavy weight had been lifted off her shoulders. 'So we're still friends?'

Pauline smiled, turning to take her cup of coffee off the waitress. 'What else?'

Kate took a deep breath. 'That means so much to me, Pauline, it really does.'

Pauline took a sip from her coffee, possibly to hide her own embarrassment. 'You must come round and see me again, Kate,' she said, and made a face at her own coffee. 'Then I can make you a proper cuppa.'

'I'd like that.'

Pauline set her cup down. 'Kate,' she said earnestly, 'I'd really like to know what happened on the night of — of . . . you know.'

Kate felt her stomach churning as the images returned, but for a moment she said nothing, simply stared into space.

Pauline reached across to put her hand on her wrist again. 'I know this must be terribly difficult for you, Kate,' she persisted, 'but it would help me to understand things a little. Can you see that?'

So Kate told her, slowly and distinctly, stirring her coffee idly as she did so and watching the specks of undissolved granules chasing each other round the half-empty cup like tiny renegade atoms.

When she had finished, Pauline sat for a moment in silence, tears brimming in her eyes. Then she swallowed hard, wiped her eyes with the back of her hand and gave a brief smile. 'I gather the police are looking for someone called Duval?' she said.

Kate nodded. 'But I believe they're on the wrong track,' she replied.

Pauline stared at her. 'You're saying it was someone else?'

'I — I think it's possible Terry Duval was deliberately framed.'

'Good heavens. What makes you think that?'

Kate lowered her gaze. 'It's just a hunch.'

'But DCI Callow tells me you didn't get the number of the Land Rover that was used or see what the driver looked like.'

*Ah, so the Wicked Witch had been talking to her. Surprise, surprise.*

'That's true. It was too dark and he was wearing a hooded coat.'

'But surely you must have seen *something*?'

Kate bit her lip at the implied criticism, then said almost as a defence, 'Well, I *did* get a glimpse of him when he ran me off the road last night and it wasn't Terry Duval, I know that much.'

Now Pauline was all ears and she stared at her intently. 'Brilliant. What did he look like?'

Kate shrugged. 'Heavy build, bearded — I reckon about forty — and wearing a heavy coat and a baseball cap.'

Pauline's face fell. 'Not much to go on there, is there? Oh, sorry, I didn't mean to criticize.'

Kate gave a faint smile. 'Much the same view the DCI had anyway,' she replied, 'so don't let that worry you.'

She was tempted to unload the rest of her story on Pauline, desperate to convince her that she had not walked away from Alf's murder, but was doing her level best to nail his killer on her own. But in the end she decided against it. Pauline's change of attitude towards her was a relief, but sharing too much with Alf's widow at this stage could be dangerous, especially if, as Kate suspected, she had Callow's ear.

'And you think Alf's killer is after you as well then?' Pauline went on, apparently unaware of Kate's hesitation.

'I think it's highly likely, yes.'

'And that he murdered your sister too?'

Kate nodded again. 'He must have thought she was me,' she said. 'Which means he'll be back once he finds out his mistake.'

Pauline glanced around her nervously. 'Then maybe we should get you home,' she said. 'You can't be too careful. I'll call you a taxi.'

Kate shook her head. 'Thanks, but I'll get Hayden to do the honours, if you don't mind. He's sort of watching over me and I don't want to hurt his feelings.'

*Don't want her to know that I'm likely to be staying at his pad either.*

Pauline patted her arm and smiled. 'Understand perfectly.' She stood up. 'And I must be getting back too. Ring me when you want to call round, won't you?'

Kate nodded, squeezing her hand in response. 'You can count on it,' she said with a smile, more relieved than she cared to admit that Pauline had made the effort to clear the air between them and that they were finally friends again in spite of all that had happened.

But her smile quickly evaporated as she returned Pauline's departing wave through the window. A dark blue Honda Civic car was parked on the opposite side of the road, a heavy-set man dressed in a grey anorak and pork pie hat sitting in the driving seat smoking a cigarette. Almost at the same moment he glanced towards the cafe, perhaps conscious of her stare, only to look away as a sort of reflex action when their gazes met. Guilt. Then, apparently unnerved, he tossed his cigarette out of the window, bent forward to start the engine and drove away, taking care not to look in her direction again.

Detective Inspector Roscoe should have been supervising the murder scene at Jury's Yard or her flat, but it seemed someone had decided that watching her was a greater priority. No prizes for guessing who that someone was and Kate wondered what Detective Superintendent Davey would say if he knew his DCI was waging a private vendetta against one of her own officers — but there again, perhaps he knew that already.

It had turned even colder by the time Kate left the café and she stood for a few moments on the pavement, watching the traffic trundling past and wrestling with more personal worries that crowded her mind. She should not have agreed to meet Hayden back at the nick, but made some excuse about having other things to do. She was afraid that she was getting too close to him — after all, they had been just colleagues before all this business and now she had slept in his house, used his shower, eaten his breakfast and had even been offered the loan of his second car. What did that make her? So they had not slept together yet, but the way things were going, it would not be long before that actually happened as well.

She realized she was wrong to have wound him up by stripping off in front of him at the hospital. It had been an act of stubborn defiance — a perverse desire to get under his skin and shock his pompous old-fashioned principles — but he may have seen it as a come on, which was the last thing she wanted. OK, so she *did* like him, liked him a lot, but for weeks she had been repeatedly telling herself that she was not looking for any new relationships — not since finding her long-term ex in bed with a couple of call-girls — and here she was sliding right into one. She needed time to get over that last betrayal and even more time to get over the nightmare of the past few days.

The decent thing to do, of course, was to telephone Hayden and cancel their arrangement, but she knew that that would lead to questions, protests, maybe even an argument, and she just couldn't face all the hassle in her present state of mind. So, feeling a heel, but desperate to find some space for herself, she called a taxi and fifteen minutes later paid him off about fifty yards from her flat.

The police were still there. She recognized Callow's Audi car straightaway, parked behind a marked SOCO van, and the uniformed officer on the main door of the building was obviously vetting all comings and goings. She ought to have known the place would still be a crime scene; it was only on TV that the police finished a forensic examination in a couple of hours. As the tenant, she had a right of entry, of course — to collect clothing or any personal belongings she needed — but that would mean seeking the authority of Callow first and she was in no mood for another sparring session with Hayden's Wicked Witch of the North. Not only that, but there was also quite a crowd of reporters and camera crews milling about in front of the building and they were the last people she wanted to tangle with.

Turning away from the scene, she headed across the street towards the town centre. She had no idea what she was going to do when she got there — Bridgwater wasn't exactly the most inspiring of places — but she had to waste some time before returning to her flat; probably after it was dark when most of her colleagues were safely tucked up in a bar somewhere. But if she thought she could simply slip away unnoticed, she was sadly mistaken.

'Kate Hamblin?' the unfamiliar voice greeted. 'Can I have a word?'

He was young, with the build of a whippet, and he materialized at her elbow as if from nowhere, a broad grin on his baby-face. She muttered an expletive and quickened her step.

'Local radio,' he explained, practically thrusting his mic into her face as he paced her effortlessly. 'You *are* Kate Hamblin, aren't you? Detective Constable Kate Hamblin?'

'No comment,' she snapped, pushing him aside as he tried to get in front of her to block her path.

'So who's the dead woman in your flat then?' he persisted. 'I hear it could be your sister.'

'Sod off,' she grated.

'Any connection between her murder and the killing of those two coppers?'

Kate tried to ignore him, but a quick glance across the road told her that he was about to become the least of her worries. His antics had caught the attention of his colleagues gathered outside the block of flats and their heads had gone up like a pack of African wild dogs suddenly scenting prey.

'Just leave me alone, will you?' she snarled, lashing out at him with such force that he lost his balance and ended up sprawled on his back in front of her. Seeing the look of shock on his face as he hit the pavement gave her a real sense of satisfaction, but it didn't last long. Out of the corner of her eye she saw that some of the other reporters had now broken away from the group and were heading across the road towards her at a trot.

*Bugger it. Now I'm really in shtook!*

Her instinct was to run — to head for the nearest side-street or alleyway and find somewhere to hide — but even as the thought flashed through her mind she knew it was out of the question. In her present physical state a brisk walk would have been painful enough without trying to do the minute mile. But just as the pack closed in for the kill, help came from a totally unexpected quarter.

She hadn't heard the vehicle approach, but the next instant the big Land Rover Defender had mounted the kerb beside her, its horn blasting and the door swinging open to slam into the reporter as he struggled up on to his knees, knocking him flat.

For a second she just stood there, staring into the vehicle, her mouth hanging open in astonishment. 'Get in,' Terry Duval shouted from the driving seat, a small black pistol in one hand levelled at her head. 'Like *now.*'

Duval only missed the rest of the pack by a matter of inches as the vehicle roared away with a squeal of tyres — fish-tailing for the first hundred yards before he decided to dump his pistol into his lap and regain full control. Then they had swung sharp left into a narrow side-street and were heading for the relative safety of the main road, leaving the press clamouring in frustration amid the choking black clouds of diesel smoke that trailed in the Land Rover's wake.

They had made it — got clean away before the vultures had realized what was happening — and in any other circumstance Kate would have felt an immense sense of relief, and not a little triumph, over such an audacious rescue. But strapped into the 'suicide seat' of an old, probably unroadworthy Land Rover driven at breakneck speed through busy streets by a desperate armed criminal gave her little cause for relief or triumph.

And now that the media threat to her was gone, another doom-laden thought occurred to her. She had been seen by half the country's press climbing into the vehicle of a wanted murderer. Whether or not the reporters had managed to clock who was behind the wheel, they had nevertheless all seen the Land Rover — some may have actually captured its number on camera — and it wouldn't take them long to find out who it was registered to. She doubted that any of them — including the dazed youngster they had bowled over — had seen the gun in Duval's hand, so it would have looked as though she had climbed aboard the Land Rover of her own free will in a bid to escape awkward questions.

Thinking of Callow and the suspicions her behaviour had already aroused among her colleagues, it dawned on her with a sickening jolt that even if she did manage to get out of this mess alive, the hole she had been digging for herself ever since the nightmare business had started was likely to become the grave of her career.

And as if to reinforce the point, seconds after reaching the main road and turning towards Bristol, the scream of sirens suddenly erupted from behind. Peering into the nearside mirror, she saw the glitter of blue flashing lights approaching from behind and closing fast.

# CHAPTER 18

The little thatched cottage looked deserted. Twister sat in the old green van he used for the conveyance of cadavers to the morgue or his funeral parlour and watched the place from the opposite side of the road. Even he had had to accept that the Land Rover was too conspicuous for what he had in mind this time. He just hoped the young girl who manned the telephones in his office during the day didn't receive any calls for his services while he was away. Albert Price, his deputy, who effectively managed the operation of the business for him, had taken the afternoon off to visit a sick aunt in Yeovil, so there was no one else in the office to handle any new bookings. He had already been tied up for several hours dealing with the last minute arrangements for the funeral of Mary May, which was due to take place the following day, and he couldn't afford any more distractions from the far more important task of recovering his electronic tracker.

He frowned thoughtfully as he studied each of the cottage's windows in turn. Like most old properties, it looked a bit gloomy inside, but no lights showed and there was no sign of movement. He could see the Mini parked on the gravel drive at the side, but Hayden Lewis's distinctive Jaguar was conspicuous by its absence. The bastard was probably at the nick.

So where was little Miss Katie? According to his information, she was still unofficially suspended — garden leave as they apparently called it — so, as he'd already surmised, she certainly wouldn't be at work. And after discovering the body of her sister in her flat, she would hardly feel like returning to the very place where it had happened — even if her colleagues were of a mind to allow her access to the crime scene, which he doubted. Not that she would be able to get away from the flak wherever she went. AM Radio had been full of it: the body of a woman found in the flat of local detective, Kate Hamblin, and believed to be that of her twin sister; the police refusing to officially confirm or deny whether it was linked to the murder of their two officers and the killing of the proprietor of a local vehicle recovery garage; and the claim 'from an inside source' that the latest two victims had both been found with their necks broken. It was the sort of story that was going to run and run, and he wasn't surprised when his mobile activated and he saw the number registered in the display.

He'd wondered how long it would take the organ grinder to ring him when news of the killings got out, but he wasn't in the mood for the inevitable slanging match and ignored the call. Instead, he pulled on a pair of gloves and climbed out of the vehicle, looking quickly left and right as he crossed the road. It was time to take a closer look at the 'chocolate box'.

As he'd already guessed, no one was at home and repeated knocking produced only the indignant screeching of a seagull, which had been perched on the thatched roof above the porch and immediately lifted off in a panic. He ducked through an arch of honeysuckle on the opposite side of the cottage to the driveway and followed a path to the back garden. He made a calculated judgment on there being no security system installed and forced one of the antiquated French doors. He waited tensely for a few moments and was rewarded by continuing silence. Good, no audible alarm. A quick glance round the small living room inside provided the final confirmation. No infra-red sensors either, so it was unlikely that there was any kind of security system covering the place.

Reassured, he went through the cottage with great care, methodically searching each room in turn and leaving not a single cupboard or drawer unchecked. But he drew a complete blank; there was no trace of his tracking device.

He scowled. It was vital that he recovered the thing. When he'd originally fitted the tracker, he hadn't anticipated that it might be discovered before he'd had the opportunity of retrieving it, so while he was reasonably sure he had not left any prints or DNA traces on the tiny box or the batteries that were inside, he couldn't be absolutely certain. With his form, even the slightest risk of a match being made by some switched-on forensic expert was one risk too many and even if he had nothing to worry about in that respect, were the tracker to be passed to the police inquiry team, at the very least this would raise some awkward questions, which could jeopardize everything.

The problem was what to do next. He had no idea if and when Kate Hamblin or Hayden Lewis would return to the cottage. Yet the only way he would be able to find out what had happened to his tracking device was by interrogating them in his usual persuasive manner. It seemed therefore that he had little option but to sit it out until someone put in an appearance. That, of course, could involve a very long wait, but then he had done it all before and this time he was determined there would be no mistakes.


Kate's gaze was fixed on the Land Rover's nearside mirror as if mesmerized.

'You've got a tail,' she blurted, her voice breaking up as she thought of the pistol still in his lap and the likely consequences of a confrontation with an unarmed traffic officer.

Duval's eyes flicked to his interior mirror. 'Don't worry,' he retorted, 'I'll soon lose him.'

She tore her gaze away from the mirror, biting her lip. 'What, in this thing? You've got to be joking. That's a high-performance traffic car.'

'No joke,' he threw back and without warning wrenched the steering wheel to the right, cutting across the road in front of an articulated lorry laden with cars.

Kate was presented with the nightmare vision of a towering mass of steel and glass bearing down on them. Then, a split second later, the cab of the lorry slewed round under the force of sudden violent braking and its own trailer swung out as if trying to overtake it in a deadly jack-knife that threw it across both carriageways like the annihilating arm of a demolition crane.

The screech of tortured metal and the crunch of impacting vehicles followed them into the side-street Duval had selected and he managed a fierce grin as he slammed the accelerator to the floor. 'That should hold 'em up for a bit,' he said. 'Bloody road'll be blocked.'

Kate felt sick. 'How could you do that?' she choked. 'All those innocent people.'

Duval snorted. 'Why should I care?' he snarled. 'No one gives a toss about me.'

'They will now,' she retorted. 'Every copper in the force will be looking for you now you've snatched me.'

'What choice did I have?' he retorted and, taking his eyes off the road longer than he should have done, allowed the Land Rover to clip a chunk out of the verge before he yanked it back on to the tarmac. 'Last night changed everythin'.'

'Last night? What do you mean?'

He scowled. 'Hadn't heard from you, had I? So I went to your flat to see if you was in. Found the door open an'—'

Kate took a deep breath. 'You found Linda?' she said, her voice cracking open like a nut.

He nodded. 'If that were her name,' he replied. 'Dead as mutton. Neck broke.'

Her expression hardened. 'You expect me to believe you just *found* her?'

He threw her another glance. 'Believe what you like, but I didn't stiff her, if that's what you're gettin' at — why would I? Thought she were you till I saw you just now in the street.'

She still looked far from convinced. 'And you didn't see anyone else at the scene, I suppose?'

He grunted. 'Oh, I saw someone all right. Come out the flat just before I quit the cupboard where I was hidin'.'

'And what did he look like?'

'Couldn't say. Didn't see his face. Just a big geezer in a hooded coat.'

'Convenient.'

'Yeah, well, what did you expect — his inside leg measurement?'

'So what were you doing back there just now — especially in the very motor the police are looking for?'

He turned off the road they were following into an even narrower lane, studying his interior mirror intently as he did so. 'Left me prints all over the flat, didn't I?' he replied. 'Went back to see if I could clean up before the stiff were found by someone, but I was too bloody late. Old Bill was there already.'

She released her breath in a deep trembling sigh, sensing in her water that he was telling the truth despite the glibness of his story. 'That makes things a lot more awkward.'

'Don't you think I can see that?' He glanced at her again, but tried to keep a weather eye on the road as well this time. 'So did you get the note?'

She made a tight face. 'Fat lot of good that will do you now,' she said. 'When SOCO lift your prints and match them to your criminal record, you'll be more oven-ready than a Christmas turkey.'

He scowled again. 'That's why I need the bloody thing; it's all I've got.'

She nodded slowly. 'We had a deal: you get the note and I get to take you in.'

He shook his head. 'Situation's changed. I'm splittin' altogether. But I have to have the note just in case things go pear-shaped.'

They could hardly get more pear-shaped than they are already, she mused, but decided not to labour that particular point. Instead she said, 'Then you'd better pull over so I can give you the note and you can let me out.'

He shook his head grimly. 'No way. I can't risk you callin' up your mates afterwards. Anyway, I might need you later as insurance.'

Before she could argue the point, her mobile suddenly shrilled.

'Leave it,' he rapped as her hand darted towards her pocket.

She hesitated. 'Let me at least look to see who it is.'

'I said leave it — better still, throw it out the window.'

'What?'

'Do it — *now*.'

Her gaze darted to the gun still visible in his lap and she moistened dry lips, deciding that a refusal was inadvisable under the circumstances.

They were following a long straight stretch of road, bordered on both sides by the familiar reed-fringed rhynes and, opening her window, she reluctantly tossed the mobile out and saw it bounce once on the road before springing off into some long grass. Now she really was in the cart, with no prospect of calling for assistance even if the opportunity did arise.

Closing the window again, she gripped her hands tightly together in a gesture of frustration at the hopelessness of her situation. She did her best to try and keep calm, but she couldn't help dwelling on the thought that was uppermost in her mind: what would happen to her when she finally handed the note over to Duval and she was no longer of any use to him? Would it be a bullet in the back of the head, or would she feel his calloused hands round her throat, crushing the life out of her before her weighted body was dumped in a rhyne or allowed to sink into the slime of a convenient peat bog?

And that critical moment was brought a lot closer when the Land Rover suddenly slowed and turned on to a track, bordered by yet another rhyne and bearing a dilapidated wooden sign, 'Danger. Keep Out'. Almost immediately they entered a stunted copse and a few yards further on the track emerged on to a broken concrete hard-standing scattered with rusted machinery and piles of rubble. Kate glimpsed half-buried narrow-gauge railway lines curling away between derelict sheds and beyond, a massive red brick building dwarfed by an even bigger pencil-like chimney.

'What is this place?' she queried nervously, as they pulled up between two of the sheds and he switched off.

'Old pumpin' station,' he replied. 'Abandoned twenty years ago.' He pointed the pistol at her again and nodded impatiently at the passenger door. 'Out — and no *Action Woman* stuff neither.'

She unclipped her seatbelt and slid from her seat on to the broken concrete, considering taking to her heels while he was still climbing out of his seat, then dismissing the idea as a complete non-starter.

He came round to her side of the vehicle and waved the pistol towards the big brick building with the chimney. 'Over there.'

She felt the barrel of the pistol pushing her forward as she picked her way among the debris in the direction he indicated, stopping in front of a pair of green doors. Ahead of her, beyond the rhyne, she saw a river curling away across country from behind the building. She had no real idea where she was, but assumed the river was likely to be the Parrett, though she couldn't be sure.

Duval reached past her to unlock the padlock securing the doors and gripped her arm tightly to pull her back a short distance before opening one of them wide.

'Inside,' he ordered.

The strong smell of damp and decay issued from the gloom. He produced a torch and directed it ahead of her. She glimpsed several rows of pipes and what looked like a rusted boiler with its hatch door wide open and hanging off. She also glimpsed a pile of blankets in one corner and a dozen or so opened tins and plastic food wrappers scattered around them — all the detritus of someone sleeping rough.

'Just like home,' he sneered, and reached above her head.

She heard the rasp of a match and a butane lamp sprang into life on a chain suspended from a low steel girder. Shadows crowded in on her and she shivered. She saw that they were standing on the lower section of a split-level floor, with a heavy machine of some sort — no doubt the pumping engine — occupying the upper level. Even though she knew nothing about pumping engines, she could see that this one was not connected to anything and appeared to be little more than a skeleton, with much of its parts missing.

Duval prodded her forward to the foot of a row of steps accessing the upper level and lit another lamp dangling from its chain. Now Kate could see that the floor beyond the engine plunged into a deep shaft and she shivered again.

'That's where they pumped the water up from the rhyne before dumpin' it in the river,' Duval said at her elbow and, no doubt sensing her fear, added meaningly, 'Good place to dump anythin' you want to get rid of . . .'

She turned to face him, her heels against the lower step. She could smell his rancid breath and flinched. 'So this is where you've been hiding all this time then?' she blurted, anxious to change the subject, but suffering a sudden spasm of reflux, which reduced her voice to an asthmatic wheeze.

He towered over her, the gun in his hand inches from her stomach. 'Just give me the note,' he rapped, ignoring her question and holding out his other hand.

She clenched her fists tightly by her sides. 'We had a deal.'

He took a deep rasping breath. 'Look, lady, I'm not going to play games with you. Give me the note or I'll just rip all your clothes off until I find it — your choice.'

She glared at him, her sense of betrayal overriding her fear. 'I tried to help you because I thought you were innocent,' she said bitterly. 'I don't know why I bothered.'

He emitted a sneering laugh. 'Help *me*?' he echoed. 'You didn't do it for me, love, so don't kid yourself. You did it to earn yourself some mega Brownie points for bringin' me in — nothin' more. Now, *the note.*'

She thought about knocking his arm sideways and running, but knew that that sort of thing only happened in films. He would just put a bullet in her back, search her clothing for the note, as he'd threatened to do, then dump her body down the shaft. All nice and tidy.

Feeling totally helpless, she fumbled in her pocket and produced the crumpled piece of paper. He snatched it from her before she could even straighten it out and moving away a few feet to subject it to a brief scrutiny under the butane lamp, he grunted his satisfaction. 'You done well, girl.'

Then, slipping the note into his coat pocket with his other hand, he studied her fixedly for a moment. 'Only problem is,' he said, 'what do I do with you now?'

But Kate made no reply, for, as she stared with a kind of morbid fascination at the little black pistol in his hand, she already knew what the answer to that question was going to be and it numbed every fibre of her being.

# CHAPTER 19

Crime reporter, Peter Devlin, was definitely not feeling his best. The door of Duval's Land Rover had missed his head by a fraction, but it had nevertheless bowled him over and he had struck his head on the pavement with some force. He now sported a nasty gash on his temple and a two-inch circle of rapidly worsening discolouration round the wound that resembled the skin of a bruised pear.

By rights he should have gone to hospital, but he had refused the offer from the young policewoman who had raced across the road from her station outside Kate Hamblin's flat to help him. Now, sat on the low wall of an adjacent garden, he held a handkerchief to his head, scowling as he passed the information about the incident to his editor on his mobile phone, while his colleagues, standing around in a bristling group with notebooks or microphones in their hands, listened attentively to what he had to say.

The hatchet-faced woman in the suit pushed her way through the crowd as he returned the mobile to his pocket, and stood over him, studying him with the intensity of a vulture waiting for a potential meal to keel over.

'DCI Callow,' she introduced herself. 'What was all that about?'

Devlin returned her stare. 'Bloody maniac in the Land Rover drove straight at me,' he retorted. 'Snatched your DC Hamblin and drove off.'

Callow's eyes narrowed. '*Kate* Hamblin?'

Devlin nodded. 'Guy pointed a gun at her and told her to get in.'

'A gun? What sort of a gun?'

Devlin shrugged. 'Pistol of some sort, I think. Glimpsed the thing as I was trying to get up again.'

'What did the man look like?'

'Dunno, only noticed the gun.'

Callow was unable to conceal her disappointment. 'You sure it *was* a firearm and she didn't just get in of her own accord?'

There was contempt written into Devlin's expression now, as he dabbed the gash in his forehead again. 'It was either a gun or the guy had one hell of an erection,' he retorted with heavy sarcasm. 'And before you ask, I didn't get the Land Rover's number.'

Callow nodded and treated him to a grim smile. She didn't need it. Having seen the Land Rover mount the pavement, then roar away from her vantage point in Kate Hamblin's flat, she already knew the number and who the driver was, but she had no intention of sharing that information with Devlin.

'Thank you for your assistance anyway,' she said and, moving away out of earshot of the reporters, she called up Detective Superintendent Davey on his mobile. 'Where are you, guv?' she queried.

There was a weary sigh. 'Well, I *was* heading home for a bite to eat,' Davey replied. 'What's up now? I only left you ten minutes ago.'

Callow smirked her malicious satisfaction. 'Sorry, guv,' she said without meaning it, 'but we have a bit of a problem.'

And that really was an understatement.

Hayden Lewis was worried, confused and — yes — angry. Where the hell had Kate got to? He had left her at the café over an hour ago and had been fully expecting her to call in at the police station for her lift when she'd finished her chat with Pauline, but she just hadn't materialized. Without a car though, where could she have gone? It would hardly be on a shopping trip, for Highbridge was pretty much the pits in that respect.

The sour-faced waitress wasn't much help either. 'Just upped and went,' she said.

'How long ago?'

'Dunno. Wasn't watchin'.'

'Well, did she leave with anyone?'

'Ain't got the faintest.'

Lewis muttered an oath and stomped from the café, slamming the door behind him. Once outside, he paused a moment to study the street in both directions, but there was still no sign of her.

Fumbling in his pocket, he tore his mobile free of the lining and tried to dial her mobile number, but rang off again as the answer voice started telling him to leave a message.

*Damn it! Now what?*

For a few minutes he hung around outside the café, walking up and down in a state of visible agitation. Then abruptly, as another thought occurred to him, he swung on his heel and headed towards the Bridgwater Road.

Pauline Cross answered the door to him almost immediately and she looked surprised when he asked if Kate was with her.

'She's not here,' she told him, shaking her head. 'I left her at the café. I did offer to call her a taxi, but she said she'd get you to run her home.'

'Never turned up at the nick,' he replied.

Pauline frowned. 'Why don't you ring her mobile?'

'Tried that,' he snapped irritably. 'Not answering.'

Now Pauline looked worried. 'I hope she's all right,' she said.

'So do I,' he agreed, then added as much to reassure himself as anything else, 'Maybe we've crossed paths and she's back at the nick now.'

But she wasn't and Dick Stacey, the office manager, broke the news to him as he pushed through into the CID office.

'Balloon's gone up,' he said. 'Duval has Kate and he's armed. Force chopper spotted them at an old pumping station near the Parrett and an ARV[3] is *en route*.'

Lewis felt something crawl down his spine. Kate in the middle of a stand-off between Duval and an armed police team? The thought horrified him. 'What pumping station?' he demanded hoarsely.

'Best you don't get involved,' Stacey advised. 'Guv'nor won't like it.'

'*What* pumping station?' Lewis almost shouted. 'Come on, man, tell me.'

Stacey made a face and crossed to a map of the Levels on the wall. 'There,' he said, pointing a nicotine-stained finger. 'That's if you want your head blown off.'

But Lewis didn't hear him. He was already crashing back through the door — for the second time since the investigation had begun bursting out of the office like a madman.

'Bloody women,' Stacey muttered.

Kate Hamblin heard the thud of rotor blades moments before Duval and she instinctively glanced upwards, even though she knew she couldn't see anything from inside the building. She felt her heart start to race, sure in her own mind that it had to be the police chopper, and desperately hoping that if it was, the crew would spot Duval's Land Rover parked in the open.

Duval's face had once more developed a heavy scowl and there was a strange glint in his eyes that Kate read as a mixture of anger and panic as he also threw a swift glance towards the roof. 'Get over here,' he snarled, the pistol in his hand lunging towards her like a striking snake.

Faced with no other option, she did as she was told.

[3] ARV — Armed Response Vehicle

'Turn around,' he snapped and, when she did so, closing her eyes tightly for a second when the barrel of the gun pressed into her neck, he leaned close to her ear. 'One silly move,' he warned, 'an' I'll blow your soddin' head off. Got it?'

She nodded weakly and he pushed her forward. 'To the door and let's take a look,' he said.

Keeping her in the shadow of the doorway, he peered over her shoulder to where he had left his Land Rover. The chopper was hovering directly over the vehicle, the big 'Police' sign clearly visible on the machine and a crew member leaning out through the open cockpit door to study the vehicle.

'Should have put the bloody thing in the shed like I usually do,' Duval breathed, then dug the pistol into her neck again. 'Who would be in that thing then?'

Kate swallowed. 'Pilot and observer,' she said.

'Would they be tooled up?'

'I don't know. Could be a couple of armed officers in the back.' He thought about that for a second. 'Then we wait to see,' he said, 'an' if there are, you get it first.'

As he spoke, the helicopter suddenly lifted and began to circle the site, skimming the ruined buildings, then dropping between them like a giant flying bug searching for prey. Duval pulled Kate back as the machine turned its attention to the pump house, peering in through the door just above the ground and shaking the building to its foundations. Behind her, she felt Duval tense expectantly. But then the chopper had lifted again and was racing away across the fields before banking sharply and hovering at a distance above the road into the site. At the same moment she heard the sirens and, as Duval pressed her forward to the door again, glimpsed the flashing strobes through gaps in the buildings, apparently stationary at the entrance to the site.

'What they doin'?' Duval demanded. 'Why don't they jus' drive in?'

Kate knew the answer to that, but decided it best not to enlighten him. The firearms team from the armed response

165

vehicle would be making their way across the site, step by step, searching each building in turn, their Heckler & Koch sub-machineguns sweeping across doorways and windows as they advanced. The team would need to establish where their target was holed up before they could do anything. Then there would be the usual warnings and the instruction for Duval to come out with his hands raised. That was when she would be most at risk, for she knew deep down that her captor would not surrender now, even if the police decided to put up a hostage negotiator to try and secure her release before resorting to the final option. The police firearms officers would be highly trained professionals, of course, but things could still go wrong and if they did, whether the bullet came from Duval's pistol or one of the H & Ks, it would make very little difference to her — she would still be dead and that was a sobering thought.

Duval was getting more and more twitchy as he peered through the doorway and that worried her too. She was well aware of the fact that just a few pounds' pressure on the trigger of a pistol was all that was required to discharge the weapon and a nervous finger could easily do that by accident. So she forced herself to relax, praying that Duval would hold it together long enough for her rescue to be effected. But her captor had no intention of allowing her colleagues to call the shots and he suddenly dug her hard in the neck with the pistol. 'OK, move.' he rapped. 'We're going for it.'

But he had left it too late. As Kate stumbled out into the gathering dusk, two figures in military style blue uniforms appeared round the corner of one of the derelict buildings and immediately froze into a combat stance, their weapons trained on them. 'Armed police,' one shouted unnecessarily as the other moved carefully to one side in a backup position. 'Stand still.'

Kate cried out as Duval grabbed her hair and pulled her head down on to her shoulder, the pistol pressed against her temple. 'Do anythin' an' I'll blow her head off,' he snarled. 'Now get out of the way.'

The first officer glanced quickly at his companion and motioned him back as he retreated a few paces. 'Don't be a fool, Duval,' he said, his tone hard and uncompromising. 'Put down the gun.'

Duval released an unnatural snigger. 'You throw yours down first,' he retorted and pushed Kate forward in the direction of his Land Rover, which was just visible between two of the derelict buildings to their right.

The helicopter now thudded in towards them, adopting a holding position fifty feet above their heads. Duval threw an angry glance up at the machine. 'Tell that thing to piss off,' he yelled at the policemen.

The lead officer spoke quickly into his personal radio and seconds later the chopper veered away across the fields to hover over a distant clump of trees.

They were now within a few feet of the Land Rover and out of the corner of her eye Kate saw that the second of the two police officers had disappeared, while his colleague had turned slightly and was following their progress along the barrel of his H & K.

Kate knew that once she got into the Land Rover with Duval she was finished. He would have no need of her half a mile down the road and would simply toss her out of the vehicle with a neat little bullet hole in her head. She had to act fast — and she did that just as Duval, backing towards the vehicle and using her as a shield, released his grip on her hair to open the driver's door.

How he had expected to be able to climb up and pull her in after him was difficult to fathom, but he never got the chance. Suddenly lurching backwards to knock him off balance, she threw herself sideways, hitting the ground with agonizing force as her already badly bruised ribs screamed their outrage in a silent mind-numbing white-out.

The shout of 'Drop your weapon' seemed faint and unreal as she fought against the waves of intense pain and nausea that tore through her like high voltage electrical discharges, but the double crash of the firearm was real enough.

So was the figure, just feet away from her, slamming back into the Land Rover under the impact of the shells and slowly slithering down the side of the vehicle like a broken ragdoll. Duval ended up in a sitting position against the front wheel, head turned in her direction, eyes wide open and fixed on her in the shocked realization of death.

For several minutes she was unable to tear her gaze away from him or the two bloodied holes in his chest from which dark rivulets streamed like oil from a leaking barrel; staring at it with the same kind of morbid fascination that draws rubber-neckers to grisly accident scenes. Not for the first time since this horrific business had begun, she felt strangely detached from the reality of what was going on around her; lost in a macabre unreasoning world of her own in which the white bloodless faces of Andy Seldon, Alf Cross, her poor sister, Linda, and the hapless Ray Jury all jostled for a place. Now there was Terry Duval too — not much of a human being, but still another life brought to a violent end. So much tragedy, so many lives extinguished and each one linked directly to her. Irrational though it was, she couldn't help feeling an almost overwhelming sense of guilt, a grow-ing conviction that she was jinxed and the unwitting catalyst in it all. And as she stared at Duval, she imagined that his lips curled into a momentary sneer of satisfaction.

Then the horrific illusion was gone and one of the police-men was bending over her, gently but firmly helping her to her feet. 'You OK, love?' he queried, peering into her face.

For a few seconds she just stared at him, as if unable to comprehend what he was saying. 'You shot him?' she even-tually managed to choke through the vomit welling up in her throat. 'You killed him — just like that?'

'Had to,' he replied and he stiffened defensively before resorting to the standard response he would have to use later during the inevitable IPCC[4] inquiry. 'He was armed and pre-sented an imminent threat.'

[4] IPCC — Independent Police Complaints Commission

His colleague straightened up from the corpse, Duval's pistol in his hand and his face grim. 'Not that much of a threat as it turns out, mate,' he breathed. 'The bloody fool's pistol was made of plastic.'

The red Mk II Jaguar didn't like the narrow lane. Its low-slung body had been designed for smooth even road surfaces along which it could snarl at maximum revs, not the undulating ribbons of broken tarmac that looped their way across the Somerset Levels, and at over fifty miles an hour, it was a miracle that the Jag stayed on the road at all.

But Hayden Lewis didn't care. Kate was far more important to him than even his beloved classic car and the news flash he had just picked up on his car radio about a reported shooting on the pumping station site had scared the hell out of him.

A police road block had been hastily set up a couple of hundred yards from the site entrance and he only just managed to pull up in time, the Jaguar lurching to a stop inches from the marked police traffic car parked broadside across the lane.

The uniformed sergeant wore an angry scowl as he marched up to the car. 'Bit of a hurry, were you, sir?' he rapped, then stiffened when Lewis thrust his police warrant card under his nose. 'And *you* should certainly know better anyway,' he added, his face darkening even more.

Lewis almost knocked him over as he flung his door wide. 'What's happened?' he exclaimed, making to push past him.

The sergeant threw an arm out to bar his progress, his eyes glinting. 'It's an armed incident,' he snapped. 'No one's allowed through — not even you.' He nodded towards the mouth of an intersection to his right. 'You can rejoin this lane further along if you turn right at the top.'

Lewis made no move. 'Is Kate OK?' he said, a stubborn set to his jaw.

The sergeant took a deep breath. 'Look, I don't know any "Kate",' he retorted. 'I was pulled off the motorway to set up this bloody roadblock and that's all. Now, I suggest you Foxtrot Oscar, OK?'

'Sounds like good advice to me,' another voice joined in and Lewis turned sharply to meet the cold stare of DCI Callow who had suddenly materialized at his elbow.

'Ma'am,' he acknowledged without enthusiasm.

Callow treated him to a frosty smile. 'So why are you still here, DC Lewis?' she queried.

Lewis stood his ground. 'I want to know if Kate's all right,' he persisted.

Callow raised an eyebrow. 'Do you now?' she replied. 'How very touching. Well, for your information, she is absolutely fine, which is more than can be said of Terry Duval. He got a fatal dose of lead poisoning, courtesy of the ARV team.'

Lewis felt her eyes boring into him and sensed she was looking for a reaction from him in relation to Duval's death. But he made sure he disappointed her. 'I want to see her,' he said instead.

Callow frowned. 'Correct me if I'm wrong, DC Lewis, but weren't you assigned by DI Roscoe to incident-room coverage?'

'Yes, ma'am, but—'

'Then what are you doing swanning around the countryside?'

The traffic sergeant sensed the escalating antagonism between the two and discreetly edged out of the way.

'I wasn't swanning around — with respect,' Lewis contradicted. 'I heard Kate was in trouble and came straight out here.'

'So chivalry is not dead then?' Callow sneered. 'Well, let me set your mind at rest. DC Hamblin is currently *en route* to Highbridge for a debriefing with Detective Superintendent Davey.' Her chagrin at not being part of the debrief was clearly evident in the spiteful expression on her face. 'But that has nothing to do with you, so I suggest you return to your assigned duties immediately before I lose what little patience I have left.'

Lewis glimpsed movement across the adjacent field and saw a big 4 x 4 he recognized as one of the force's ARVs emerge from among a collection of buildings on the pumping station site and turn towards the entrance gate.

He tensed and Callow stepped smartly in front of him. 'One more step,' she warned, 'and you'll be off CID and back to wearing a funny hat.'

Lewis hesitated, watching the ARV bump its way along the track at a crawl. He knew that the threat of being returned to uniform patrol duties was not an idle one and he checked himself in time. He would be no good to Kate off the department and if she was to be debriefed at the station, then there was every chance he would be able to see her there anyway.

Unfortunately, however, Callow was ahead of him and, as he climbed back into his car, she leaned on the sill of the open window, her frosty smile back with a vengeance. 'In fact, DC Lewis,' she said, 'with Duval now sadly demised, I expect the incident room to be run down very soon, which means we don't really need you there anymore. So take the rest of your shift off — you must have quite a few hours' overtime left on your card.'

Lewis shook his head as he started the engine. 'I'd rather work on, if you don't mind,' he replied.

She leaned right into the car. 'Read my lips, Lewis,' she rasped. 'You are off duty as of now. Go anywhere near the nick and I'll have your balls. *Capiche*?'

Lewis glared at her. 'I don't think you can force me to take time off,' he said.

Another humourless smile. 'I can do anything I like,' she said. 'And you'd better believe it.'

# CHAPTER 20

Twister was feeling restless and frustrated. It would soon be dark, but there was still no sign of Hayden Lewis or Kate Hamblin. Where had the bloody love-birds got to? He suddenly felt very uneasy, a little voice in his head telling him he should give up on the whole thing. But quitting went against the grain. One of them at least *had* to put in an appearance sooner or later; he would just have to be patient. As he settled back into his chair, however, after first removing the bulbs of the chandelier, he broke a golden rule and lit a cigarette. The smell would be a dead give-away if someone opened the front door, he knew that, but he needed a drag like nothing else and anyway, by the time they sussed they had company, it would be too late. He just had to remember to take the cigarette butt with him afterwards. Didn't want to risk that being picked up by some eagle-eyed plod and sent for DNA analysis.

He had finished his cigarette and pocketed the butt when his mobile telephone rang. He checked the number on the display and frowned. It was the organ grinder again and he decided it would be better to answer this time.

'Twister,' he announced with a weary resignation.

'What the hell's going on?' a familiar voice snarled.

'Meaning?' he replied, his tone dull and indifferent.

'*Meaning* the two new murders I've just heard about — the breakdown man and Hamblin's sister. Press are saying that, behind the scenes, they are being linked to the same killer.'

'So?'

'Were they your handiwork?'

"Fraid so.'

'Are you crazy?'

'Maybe, but it's nothing to worry about — I'll be better soon.'

'This isn't funny, Twister.'

'Who's laughing?' He hesitated. 'Look, the girl was a mistake, OK? How was I to know she was Hamblin's twin?'

'And this Ray Jury character — was he one of the family too?'

'Hardly. Just a bit of collateral damage, that's all.'

'Collateral damage? What's got into you? You were only supposed to knock out a bloody surveillance team — not half of Somerset.'

He yawned. 'Yeah, well, it'll all be over soon anyway.'

There was anxiety in the caller's tone now. 'Why do you say that? Where are you?'

He smirked to himself. 'Nice little thatched cottage in Burtle actually.'

'Burtle? What the hell are you doing there?'

'Waiting for a certain police lady and her boyfriend.'

There was a sharp intake of breath. 'You prick! You'll blow everything.'

'Thought you wanted Miss Fancy Knickers out of the way?'

'That was before you went on this last killing spree. We can't afford more corpses with their necks broken. Snapping necks is hardly Duval's MO anyway. He's a bloody arsonist, not some kind of martial arts hitman.'

'Fine, so I'll arrange a nice fire this time. Could be fun and it will put Duval back in the frame.'

'Just drop the idea, will you? I'm not convinced Hamblin is the threat we thought she was and, despite your best efforts to cock everything up, there's still a realistic chance that this whole business will turn out just as we'd planned. So no more killings, OK?'

Twister didn't answer and the caller added, 'Are you listening to me? I said it's over. Finished. Have you got that?'

He took a deep breath, reluctantly deciding to come clean. 'It can't be.'

'What are you saying?'

'Hamblin and her boyfriend have something of mine and I need it back.'

A heavy pause. 'Something of yours? Like what, for instance?'

'Like the electronic tracker I put under her car. She and this guy, Hayden Lewis, found it after the crash.'

A despairing groan. 'I can't believe I'm hearing this. You seem to be making a profession out of incompetence. If your fingerprints or DNA are on that thing—'

'I'm pretty sure there won't be *anything* on it, but I can't afford to take the risk. I have to find out where the tracker is and get it back.'

'Well, it's pretty obvious where it is, isn't it? Police forensics will have it.'

'I doubt it. Hamblin is *persona non grata* with the firm and seems to be playing her own little game. I don't reckon she'll trust official channels, so the thing is likely to be still in her possession.'

'In which case, it's best left there — especially if getting it back means knocking her and her boyfriend off afterwards.'

'It's all right for you,' he retorted. 'There's nothing to connect you to any of this and in your position, no one would suspect you anyway, but I'm wide open if that tracker happens to lead Old Bill to me.'

'But as you've just said, that's pretty unlikely, isn't it? And anyway, you should have thought about that before sticking the thing on her car in the first place.'

'Easy for you to say that, sitting there on your fat arse while I do all the dirty work.'

'That's what I hired you for, isn't it? Not that I'd have bothered if I'd known what an amateur you are.'

Twister's face darkened. He was growing tired of the constant insults. 'So what do you suggest?' he said coldly. 'There's a lot of money riding on this job.'

'I'm not in the game of suggesting anything — I'm *telling* you, forget the girl and the tracker and get out of that place before it's too late.'

But he was no longer listening and abruptly snapped the flap of his mobile shut, cutting off the call, as headlights grazed the front window of the living room and car tyres crunched in the gravel alongside the cottage.

'Seems like it's already too late,' he murmured to himself and, switching his mobile off altogether, he left his seat to position himself behind the front door, which opened directly on to the living room, flexing his powerful hands as he waited for the key to turn in the lock.

Detective Superintendent Steve Davey was on a high. That much was obvious when he showed Kate into DCI Callow's office. Davey's eyes were bright with almost evangelical zeal and he wore his characteristic boyish smile like a badge of commendation.

Plainly, Duval's shooting had not fazed him in the least. In fact, he seemed positively delighted with the result and actually hummed to himself as he poured them both a cup of tea from the pot he had had sent up from the shift kitchen.

What followed was nothing like the interrogations Kate had been subjected to throughout the inquiry and it was certainly nothing like any debriefing she had experienced in her career before. There was no aggressive questioning, no in-depth probing and certainly none of the interview trickery she had learned to expect. In fact, the whole thing was conducted in the sort of relaxed informal style employed by psychiatrists with their clients and, as the debriefing progressed, it dawned on her that it was actually more to do with shoring up any possible weaknesses in the inquiry team's pre-judged conclusions about the case than anything else.

Davey wanted — no, his career reputation *needed* — a speedy detection and he was desperate to ensure that nothing prevented that from happening. Duval's death meant no long-winded interviews, no questions asked about some of the anomalies that had arisen during the investigation, and no protracted court proceedings. Naturally, there would be an inquest, plus the standard IPCC investigation into the actual shooting of Duval, but that was it. All nice and tidy. A result to be proud of — provided Kate Hamblin didn't rock the boat, of course.

No wonder Callow had been excluded from the debriefing. The last thing Davey wanted was for any loose ends to be opened up by the vicious incisive questioning of someone who had a personal axe to grind and, as for Kate herself, she was in a real cleft stick. Allowing Davey to bury the truth and the real killer to go free went against everything she believed in, but for the present she had no choice. To make a stand meant revealing her involvement with Duval, resulting in the destruction not only of her own career, but that of the faithful Hayden as well. So she had no choice but to bite her tongue and go along with the charade, nodding sagely in all the right places and trying to control her trembling fingers as she finished her cup of tea.

'So, Kate,' Davey summarized, standing up to indicate the debriefing was now over, 'I think we can safely say we have achieved a very successful result in this inquiry.' He smiled with the sincerity of a crocodile. 'And much of it is down to you.' He patted her on the arm, adding the lie: 'I'll make sure you get a mention in dispatches, of course.'

'Thank you, sir,' she responded and left the room quickly before she was sick.

The thin bearded SOCO man was waiting for her on the stairs and he thrust a large padded envelope into her hands as if he were relinquishing hold of a bomb. 'You're mates with Hayden Lewis, aren't you?' he queried.

She hesitated, wondering if this was some sort of trick. 'He asked me to do a rush job for him on the quiet like,' he explained, turning back down the stairs. 'Give that to him, will you? I can't raise him.'

'What on earth is it?' she called after him, weighing the envelope in one hand.

He half-turned. 'You'd better ask him,' he retorted. 'I just want shot of the bloody thing.'

Then he was gone, clattering down the stairs as if pursued by the hounds of hell. Frowning, Kate stared after him, then abruptly shrugged. She'd had enough excitement for one day and all she wanted to do now was sleep. Hayden's damned envelope could wait.

Ducking into the empty CID office, she picked up the telephone and dialled his home number. The telephone rang and rang, but all she got was the BT answer phone service.

Two of her plainclothes colleagues, one her own DS, wandered into the office, threw her hostile glances and left again after checking their in-trays. 'So much for camaraderie,' she muttered to herself and dialled Hayden's mobile. Once again, a metallic voice responded, telling her to leave a message. She glanced at her watch and headed for the stairs.

Her DI, Ted Roscoe, was in the incident room and he looked up from a text-crowded computer screen. 'And what are you doing in here?' he demanded. 'You're supposed to be on leave.'

'Debrief with the guv'nor, sir,' she replied, taken aback by the hostility in his tone. 'Just going home — no chance of a lift, I suppose?'

Roscoe's heavy face creased into an even deeper scowl. 'Too busy,' he retorted. 'Plenty of cabs about anyway.'

One of the officers manning the bank of VDU consoles threw her a sympathetic glance as Roscoe stalked from the room. 'They'll all come around in time, Kate,' she said. 'Look, I'm about finished here. I'll give you a lift, if you like.'

Kate smiled her thanks and waited while she signed off. 'No idea where DC Lewis has got to, I suppose?' she asked.

The other shook her head. 'He was in here this afternoon, but I don't know where he went afterwards.'

Grabbing her civilian anorak, she led the way downstairs to her ancient Peugeot 205 in the police station yard, moving a pile of shopping from the front passenger seat so Kate could sit down. 'You and Hayden an item?' she grinned as she pulled out of the yard.

'An item?' Kate echoed, then chuckled in spite of herself. 'Now that is a terrifying thought.'

And she frowned as they headed out of Highbridge in the direction of home, another thought troubling her. So, where are you, Hayden, she mused? And why the hell aren't you answering your phone?

But she would have been a lot less preoccupied with Lewis had she been aware of the fact that a car, which had exited the police station yard just seconds after their departure, was now tailing them at a discreet distance along the Bridgwater Road.

Roz Callow had returned to the station in a foul mood, determined to have it out with Davey as to why she had been excluded from the debriefing, but her mood had lifted dramatically when, using her security card to enter the building by a side door, she had glimpsed the SOCO man handing Kate the padded envelope. Now hunched over the wheel of her Audi like some hungry praying mantis, she smiled grimly as she recalled the conversation she had overheard. 'So why would you want shot of that envelope, my friend,' she murmured to herself, 'and what sort of a rush job were you doing for Mr Hayden Lewis anyway?' Could it be something to do with whatever it was the 'love birds' had found under Hamblin's car perhaps? A certain something that needed to be checked out forensically? It would be easy enough to find out, of course, by leaning on the SOCO man, but that would have to come later. Right now she was much more interested in what Detective Constable Hamblin did with her padded envelope and where the envelope went, DCI Callow was determined to go too.

Hayden Lewis at first thought there had been a power cut when he opened his front door and found the lights were dead. But then he detected the smoke from Twister's cigarette still hanging in the air and noticed the half-open French doors standing out clearly in the blaze of moonlight.

'Gordon Bennett, I've been done,' he breathed and strode across to the doors to take a closer look.

He hadn't expected that the intruder would still be on the premises lurking in the gloom behind him, but a faint sound alerted him as he bent down to examine the lock on the doors and he pivoted round just in time. The powerful hand chopped the air instead of his neck as the policeman dived to one side, out of harm's way, throwing the assassin off-balance. But Twister had been trained to recover quickly and he was on to his target even as Lewis scrambled to his feet, both hands locking on to his throat in a deadly grip, searching for the vital pressure points.

But Lewis was no push-over. As he slammed back against the sideboard, he managed to snatch a wine glass from the tray he had left on top. Smashing it against the wall, he slashed his assailant across the wrist with the broken stem before the other realized what was happening, forcing him to release his grip and stagger backwards with a sharp cry of pain. The wound was bleeding badly. Twister could feel the blood pouring down his wrist into his glove and almost certainly soaking into the carpet (so much for leaving a clean crime scene), but the injury only served to heighten his focus and, kicking the coffee table Lewis had overturned in front of him out of the way, he slammed into the policeman with annihilating force.

Lewis hit the floor hard and was only briefly aware of Twister's knee in his back and the blood dripping on to his neck in a steady stream before powerful fingers found the pressure points they had been seeking and he passed out completely.

# CHAPTER 21

Kate was startled to find a uniformed police officer standing outside the door of her flat when she got home, and she was only vaguely aware of the double blast of her new-found friend's horn as the young policewoman drove away again.

The policeman checked her warrant card carefully and nodded. 'SOCO haven't quite finished their examination of the crime scene,' he said. 'Guv'nor wants it kept intact for the time being.'

'And which guv'nor would that be?'

'DCI Callow, miss,' he replied.

She gave an understanding smile. 'And what am I supposed to do in the meantime?' she queried. 'Sleep in a cardboard box in the street?'

The constable looked uncomfortable. 'You can collect any personal items you need,' he said, 'as long as I accompany you.'

'Well, thank you,' she said with heavy sarcasm. 'You can have the thrill of watching me go through my knicker drawer.'

She could have argued the point, but it wasn't worth the hassle. Instead, she quickly changed her clothes in the bathroom, putting on a pair of warm woollen trousers and a sweater before stuffing some underwear, tops and toiletries into a holdall, while her colleague waited discreetly outside.

'All done?' the policeman asked, staring at her bulging holdall with raised eyebrows.

'Not quite,' she replied, pulling on her woollen coat. 'Presumably I can't use my telephone and as I seem to have lost my mobile, you can call me a taxi, OK?'

'So you've got somewhere to go then?' he said, reaching for his mobile.

'Oh yes,' she replied, frowning again as she wondered why Hayden hadn't answered her calls. 'I just hope someone is home.'

Twister was exhausted and his cut wrist, now covered by some lint and a wide bandage he had found in a kitchen drawer, hurt like hell, even though the touch of first-aid he had recalled from his army days seemed to have reduced the bleeding substantially. A slightly deeper incision, he thought, and Lewis might have ruptured an artery, which wouldn't have been at all funny. The injury had made it difficult for him to replace the light bulbs in the chandelier, but he had finally managed it, taking care to wipe them afterwards with a damp cloth to remove any minute bloodstains he might have missed. He had also cleared up the broken wine glass, burying the fragments under a bush in the garden before carefully wiping up the blood he had dripped on to the kitchen floor and work surface. There was not much he could do about the living room carpet, however, apart from covering the bloodstain with a mat from the bedroom. With a bit of luck, no one would suspect that the mat was hiding something, but he was not that confident.

Now sitting with the curtains pulled and the lights lit in the armchair opposite the detective, after trussing him up with sticky tape and securing him to a straight-backed chair he had brought through from the dining room, he watched him through half-closed eyelids. Give the copper his due, he had put up a pretty good fight and the ex-SAS man admired him for that. But Twister had admired plenty of his targets in the past too and that hadn't stopped him killing them — as he knew he would be killing Lewis once he had got hold of the information he needed. So he waited patiently for him to come round, irritated by the delay, but accepting there was nothing he could do about it. And even as he shook a cigarette out of the packet, he was rewarded by a loud snort as the detective opened his eyes and stared at him blankly for a moment.

Twister lit his cigarette and smirked. 'Nice to see you back at last,' he said.

Lewis spat something out of his mouth with a muttered: 'Who the hell are you?'

'The electronic tracker,' Twister responded, without answering his question. 'Where is it?'

'Tracker?' Lewis feigned bewilderment. 'Don't know what you're talking about.'

His captor hissed his disapproval. 'I have searched this entire cottage very thoroughly,' he breathed, 'and there is no sign of my property. But I know you and your girlfriend found it, so what have you done with it?'

Lewis grinned, delighted to see the heavy bandage round the other's wrist and to know that he had managed to inflict some damage on him at any rate. 'Worry you does it, this missing tracker?' he mocked. 'Afraid it might be the loose end that nails you in the end?'

Twister rose to his feet and leaned over his prisoner. 'Play games with me and you will be sorry,' he warned. 'Now, I'll ask you again, what have you done with the tracker?'

Lewis shrugged. 'Damned if I know, old sport. What does it look like?'

Twister nodded slowly. 'Decided to play hardball, have you, my friend?' he said. 'Well, we shall see what your girl-friend has to say about that.'

Lewis's bravado evaporated. 'You leave her out of this,' he grated, struggling against the tape which bound him to the dining room chair.

Twister laughed. 'Leave her out of it?' he echoed. 'But she is so very much a part of it, DC Lewis — a key player one might say.' He held up a mobile phone in the light of the lamp. 'Interesting contact list you have on your mobile and I must admit that so far I have had a lot more success interrogating that than I have you. So shall we give little Miss Katie a call — let her know we've had this little chat?'

He dialled slowly, then waited, the speaker activated and his gaze fixed intently on Lewis's sweating face with grim satisfaction. 'In fact, I think it would be nice if we asked her to join us, don't you?' he mocked. 'A sort of reunion party.'

The mangy looking fox had had a bad night. The twin barrels of a twelve-bore had sent him packing from a nearby farmyard and the rustlings in the marshy undergrowth had produced nothing so far save a couple of agile mice. The night was still young, but Reynard needed to fill his belly and the signs were not good.

Padding along the frozen tarmac, following the line of the rhyne, he heard the strange sound issuing from a clump of long tangled grass on the verge and stopped dead, his nose questing the cold night air and his ears pricked up suspiciously. The loud shrilling sound was nothing like he had heard before, but the possibility of a meal drove him forward to investigate further.

At first he saw nothing but the stiff points of tufted grass, tinged with bluish fire in the splashes of moonlight, but then something else attracted his attention — something that glittered unnaturally like a live thing. He approached it cautiously on his belly, nose now parting the grass in front of him as he went, then tensed over the thing, ready to snatch it in his jaws if it tried to flee.

But the silver-coloured box remained motionless, its little illuminated window staring back at him with a robot-like coldness. The fox sniffed it once, but concluding that it was not worth eating, abruptly lost interest. And as he padded away, disappointed, the police issue mobile Kate had thrown out the window of Duval's Land Rover suddenly stopped ringing and the display shut down.

Hayden Lewis was feeling violently ill in the back of the undertaker's van. Gagged and still tightly bound with tape, he had been zipped up inside what seemed to be a none too clean body bag, with just the upper part of his face uncovered and a familiar nauseating smell wafting off the plastic. Twister had left him for just a few minutes to collect his battered vehicle and park it down the side of the cottage in front of the Jaguar — presumably so he could check the Jag for his tracker before loading his prisoner in the back of the van under cover of darkness — and though the detective had struggled furiously with the tape while he was gone, he had found it impossible to release so much as an ankle.

Lewis was actually more than a little surprised that he was still breathing. He had convinced himself he was about to die from the moment Kate failed to answer her mobile telephone. The killer had been left with no reason to keep him alive once it became clear that his prisoner could no longer be used to put pressure on Kate and as the policeman was also able to identify him, imminent elimination had seemed inevitable. Yet for some reason he was still in the land of the living and he clung to the old adage that while there was life there was hope — even though he knew full well that his reprieve was almost certain to be only temporary and that he was likely to be wearing the evil-smelling body bag for good very soon.

For Twister's part, he was in something of a dilemma. The policeman was certainly a liability and snapping his neck there and then would obviously have been the safest bet, but that would not have helped him recover the tracker. As long as Lewis was alive he felt he had a hold on Kate Hamblin. With him dead, attractive though that proposition might be, he would lose the only bargaining counter he had.

Staying on at the cottage in the hope that Kate would eventually turn up there was not an option, however. In the first place, it was possible that, contrary to his earlier assumptions, she had actually gone home to her flat in Bridgwater with no intention of popping over to Burtle, and secondly,

Lewis's tiny pad might be convenient at present, but it could prove to be a liability if some of the detective's colleagues were to turn up, wondering where he was, or a friendly neighbour decided to call by to borrow some milk.

There was a sharp reminder of the risks he was running as he drove away from the cottage too. A police patrol car appeared suddenly a couple of hundred yards down the road, travelling towards Glastonbury, and it slowed noticeably as it passed his van, the driver's white face caught briefly in his headlights, apparently turned in his direction to study him before accelerating away. He breathed a sigh of relief. He realized only too well that an old closed van like the one he was driving was bound to attract the interest of the police and a random stop-check was the last thing he needed — especially if that stop-check resulted in a police officer taking a look in the back.

He was on edge for the rest of the journey and he couldn't have been more relieved when he finally pulled into his yard in Highbridge and jumped out to close the gates behind him. Safe at last — but then his mobile rang and it wasn't good news as far as he was concerned.

'You cut me off,' his co-conspirator accused. 'Been trying to get you ever since. Where are you?'

'Just pulled in at home,' he replied, returning to the van and pausing with one hand on the handle of the rear doors.

There was a heavy sigh of relief. 'So you did as I said? Thank heavens for that anyway. Have you heard the news?'

'Hardly.'

'Duval's dead.'

'What?' He stiffened and snatched his hand from the door as if the handle was hot. 'How did that happen?'

'Seems he snatched Kate Hamblin from the street. Police ARV cornered him in some disused pumping station on the Levels and put a couple of bullets in him.'

'Bloody hell.'

A chuckle this time. 'Don't sound so shocked. It couldn't be better news for us. We should now be in the clear. Duval was the murder team's number one suspect and with him dead and nothing else to go on, they're bound to lay all your hits at his door. I've a feeling it's going to be case closed very soon.'

He felt sick. 'I doubt it.'

A tense silence, then slowly, harshly, 'Why, what the hell have you done now?'

'What I said I had to do. I've got Hamblin's boyfriend wrapped up in the back of my van. Just going to dump him indoors.'

The voice erupted from the mobile with an explosive hiss. 'You stupid bastard. I told you to leave it.'

His eyes were cold and hard. 'And I told you I do things *my* way.'

'I'm coming over.'

'Best not to.'

'I said I'm coming over — don't do *anything*.'

Twister didn't answer, but abruptly ended the call. Then, opening the back doors of his van, he directed a small torch on to Lewis's sweating face. 'I thought we'd have a proper little talk now,' he said. 'And I *know* you'll give me some answers this time.'

CHAPTER 22

Kate paid off the taxi directly outside Lewis's cottage, relieved to see that his Jaguar was parked in the sideway, which suggested he was at home. She was surprised that the cottage was in darkness, though. If Hayden was the person she imagined, he should have been slumped in an armchair after finishing his tour of duty, a large glass of brandy in one hand and the stereo on, playing something from Wagner. That would at least have explained why he hadn't heard her ring him from Highbridge police station. But there was no sound of music as she approached the front door and after repeated knocking produced no result, her misgivings mounted. If his car was there, where the hell was Hayden? It wasn't that he could just stroll round to the supermarket if he had run out of milk or bread. Burtle was way out in the sticks and, as far as she knew, the village pub was about all it had. No, something was wrong — she could feel it in her water — and she made her way down the sideway towards the back of the house with more than a little trepidation.

She found the half-open French doors immediately and stopped dead. Rustlings in the undergrowth at the end of the small garden drew her attention for a second, but she relaxed when a large bird erupted from a bush and flapped away across the moor with an unnerving cackle of alarm.

Pulling the right-hand door fully open, she stepped cautiously into the blacked-out living room, feeling for the main light switch which she knew was on the wall beside her somewhere. Seconds later she found it and the chandelier flickered into life. She stood for a moment, studying the room with narrowed suspicious eyes. Nothing. No body, bloodstained walls or a man in long coat and baseball cap; just an empty room with a softly ticking grandfather clock and a long expired open fire. She laughed at herself for even thinking such things.

She went to the bottom of the stairs and peered up into the gloom. 'Hayden?' she called. 'You there?'

More rustlings — this time, she fancied, in the thatched roof — but no answering shout. Frowning, she turned back into the room, dumping the padded envelope she had brought with her on to the coffee table.

Perhaps Hayden had simply gone down the pub for a drink or popped to see a friend in the village? Well, surely he had taken his mobile with him wherever he had gone? He was on call, for heaven's sake, and he would never have been irresponsible enough to leave his phone behind. Yes, but he had been stupid enough to leave his French doors open, hadn't he? She gave a rueful smile. Maybe he had lived in Burtle too long and the relaxed country ways were getting to him.

Crossing the room to the pseudo Victorian telephone (typical Hayden) on its half-moon table beside the front door, she dialled his mobile number again. But, although the phone rang and rang, there was no response until the answer service kicked in and she was advised to leave a message — just like before. This time she did.

'Where the devil are you?' she shouted into the phone. 'It's Kate and I'm at your place. Call me back.'

Tiny feet pattered across the floor upstairs and she jumped, staring at the black maw of the staircase and half-expecting something to scamper out into the light. It didn't.

'Damn it, Hayden,' she said, slamming the telephone down on its cradle, 'where the hell *are* you?'

She sighed heavily. Well, wherever he was, there was nothing she could do until he chose to ring her or put in an appearance, so she had no option but to wait for him to make the move. Slumping into a corner of the settee, she leaned her head against the high cushioned back and closed her eyes for a moment. She hadn't intended going to sleep, just to rest her sore eyes, but she would certainly have drifted off anyway had the sudden sharp crack of a timber a few minutes later not made her jump. She shot up in her seat and listened intently. Another crack. She relaxed. *Just the house settling, you silly girl.* She smiled ruefully. Maybe it was, but she couldn't afford to nod off completely, could she?

Shaking her head quickly to disperse the inner cobwebs, she wandered into the kitchen, snapping on the strip-light and pouring herself glass of water. It was as she was returning to the living room, sipping from the glass at the same time, that her gaze fell on the padded envelope and she remembered the SOCO's words: *'You're mates with Hayden Lewis, aren't you? Asked me to do a rush job for him on the quiet like . . . Just want shot of the bloody thing . . .'*

She weighed the envelope in her hand and felt something bulky slide from top to bottom inside. The thing was clearly addressed to Hayden and had nothing to do with her, but her curiosity was aroused and, making a snap decision, she carried it out to the kitchen and slit open the flap with a carving knife from one of the drawers.

Feeling guilty, but convincing herself that she was fully justified after Hayden had kept her waiting for so long, she emptied the contents out on to the kitchen work surface — then simply stared at the bundle of papers and the familiar electronic tracker with a sense of shock. Hayden had promised to try and get the device checked out and it seemed he had done just that. 'You little star,' she breathed, as she flicked through the fingerprint forms, photographs of the tracking device and its batteries taken from different angles

189

and, most important of all, the attached report and comput-
erized copy of a criminal record file.

The words in the report jumped out at her: *No finger-
prints found on external body of tracker or inside device . . . Part print
discovered on one of batteries . . . Not conclusive result, but search
suggests probable match with attached . . .*

As she turned to the criminal record file, she froze.
The photograph was of a bearded man in his late thirties,
wearing a dark jacket and white open-necked shirt, who had
apparently been convicted of fraud some years before. He
didn't look like a murderer, but she would have recognized
that bearded face anywhere; it was indelibly imprinted on her
memory from the night he had run her off the road.

'Larry Wadman,' she breathed, leafing through the papers
and speed-reading, as she had done for Terry Duval not long
before: *Thirty-seven years old . . . Nickname Twister . . . Ex SAS
. . . Dishonourably discharged . . . One time gangland enforcer and night
club bouncer . . . Targeted unsuccessfully by Regional Crime Squad . . .
Convicted of benefit fraud and tax evasion while working as night club
bouncer . . . Eighteen months imprisonment . . .*

Scouring the file, she found a number of different addresses for him — in Manchester, Liverpool and
Birmingham — but, like the file itself, all were several years
old. Frowning, she leaned back against a tall cupboard. So
now what? She had her 'face', but no idea where he lived. It
was torture.

She returned to the file and laboriously went through
it again. At first still nothing and then, as an afterthought,
she turned back to the envelope. There was a note from the
SOCO inside that she had missed: *Thought you might like to
know, your man currently living in Highbridge. Has an undertaker's
business, Wadman & Son. I know because he buried my father two
months ago.*

Wadman's Undertakers? She had passed that place often
enough in the course of her duties, though she had never
actually been inside. She stared at the note again in disbelief.
A killer who was the local undertaker? Why on earth would

an undertaker want to murder a police surveillance team? He was supposed to deal with people *after* they were dead, not actually initiate the process — unless, of course, he was a bit short on clients and needed to create a few more. But then why go to the trouble of killing police officers? It just didn't compute. After all, there had to be enough sick old people around to fit the bill.

She shook her head quickly to expunge the thought, ashamed of herself for allowing her mind to come up with something like that. It was gross. But then she saw something else that was even more gross — spots of what looked like dried blood down the door of one of the cupboards and, lying in the corner, a tiny piece of red-soaked tissue. Fears crowded her mind. Maybe Hayden had cut himself badly on something and had been rushed to hospital? And here she was wasting time reading a damned crime file.

She rang Taunton Hospital first and, drawing a blank, tried Weston-Super-Mare. No trace of any person being admitted by the name of Hayden Lewis. Bristol's BRI was the only other likely casualty unit worth trying, but again, she met a brick wall.

So where had the blood come from? There were no signs of a struggle in the living room, suggesting Hayden had disturbed an intruder, and, as his car was still here, she was at a loss to know where he could have gone.

It was then that she noticed the rug Twister had laid over the stain and bent down to look at it. That certainly hadn't been in the living room when she had last been to the cottage and it didn't go with the carpet either. Curious without really knowing why — perhaps female intuition — she lifted a corner and pulled it back. The blood had soaked right through the pile, but the ragged brown mark was still visible. She gave a sharp intake of breath and froze for a second, her gaze fastening on the French doors — the fact that they had been left half-open now assuming a new significance.

Straightening up, she walked slowly towards them, knowing deep down what she would find, but hoping she would be proved wrong because of what that would mean. The doors were old and the frames of both in poor condition. Nevertheless, when she bent down to examine the lock, she could see at a glance that it had been forced, slivers of rotten wood lying on the carpet in the gap. Her stomach churned. The killer had been here, maybe hiding in a corner waiting for Hayden to come home. He must have overpowered the detective and taken him away with him; it was the only plausible explanation. But for Kate, the principal worry was where the blood had come from — whether it was Hayden's or the killer's — and she knew there was only one place she could find that out. Grabbing a set of car keys with a Jaguar fob from a hook beside the stairs, she headed for the front door.

The cellar was as dank as the Levels. A single light bulb hung from the ceiling, flickering spasmodically as it stirred in a draught, reminding Lewis of a scene from an old spy thriller he had once seen. The place was full of rubbish. Bicycle frames, tea chests, broken chairs — even a couple of lidless coffins leaning grotesquely against one wall. Hitchcock's *Psycho* could have been here or Michael Myers from Michael Carpenter's *Hallowe'en*, and he shivered involuntarily, once more straining futilely against the tapes which still held him fast.

Before leaving the cottage, Twister had cut Lewis free of the dining room chair, so that he could get him into the body bag and out to the van, but if the detective had expected that this would present him with an opportunity to overpower his captor or make good his escape, he was sadly disappointed, for the rest of his sticky bonds had been left intact. And now in the cellar, he had been strapped to yet another chair — one that was nowhere near as comfortable as his own either. But at least it meant he was free of the body bag — for the time being anyway.

'Comfy then?'

Lewis hadn't heard Twister come down the wooden stairs behind him in his thick-soled suede shoes and he started at the sound of his voice. 'Better than the lounge at the Ritz,' he replied over his shoulder, recovering quickly.

The killer came round the chair and stood over him, flexing the fingers of his right hand with his left. 'So what have you got to tell me, Detective Constable Lewis? A lot, I hope.'

Lewis shrugged. 'Where would you like me to start, old sport?' he retorted drily. 'My police career, my early childhood, or perhaps even my time at public school?'

The blow was sudden and very hard. Lewis suspected that his nose was broken — fractured at the very least. Twister drew up another chair with the back towards him and sat down. There was no animation in his expression; no anger, no glee — not even the semblance of any human emotion — just the cold dead eyes studying the detective with the analytical interest of a biologist about to dissect a frog.

'Let's start again, shall we?' the ex-SAS man said softly. 'I know you and your girlfriend took the tracking device and I want it back. All I need to know is where I can find it.'

Lewis's eyes flicked to the large muscular hands now resting on the chair-back as Twister waited for a response. The policeman's nose spurted blood and there was a terrible pain in his eyes from the blow. He recognized his captor for what he was and he felt a frozen hand clutching at his insides. He wasn't a coward, but he realized that he wouldn't be able to defy this excuse for a human being for long; pain is an excellent persuader and he knew without being told that the cold-eyed monster sitting in front of him would have a lot more of it in his armoury.

'Can I have a tissue?' he said through gritted teeth.

One was produced as if by sleight of hand and Twister almost tenderly wiped his nose. 'Well?' he asked, returning his hands to the back of the chair. 'Are you ready to stop playing games?'

Lewis nodded, knowing he had to come up with something convincing, but realizing only too well that to reveal that the tracker was with scenes of crime would mean a permanent place in the body bag. Twister had to believe that the device was still in play for him or he would cut his losses and disappear; it was in the nature of the beast.

'It's locked in my drawer at the nick,' he said.

One of the hands started to twitch, but remained on the back of the chair.

'And why would you put it in there?'

'To hide it.'

Twister raised an eyebrow. 'Hide it?' he echoed, inviting an explanation. 'In a police station?'

Lewis swallowed some blood and Twister gently wiped his mouth. 'Kate and I are in the mire with our colleagues,' he began, then, encouraged by an understanding nod from his captor, continued more confidently, 'so we couldn't hand the thing to SOCO to check for prints because it would have raised too many questions as to why it was put on Kate's car in the first place and it might also have looked like we murdered Ray Jury to get it back.'

'Go on.'

Lewis's mind was racing. 'We intended getting it checked out ourselves on the quiet through a SOCO contact I know who owes me a favour.'

'And did you?'

Lewis shook his head, trying to meet the other's hard gaze. 'He wasn't on duty. I was going to see him tomorrow.'

'So the device is still in your drawer?'

'Yes.'

Twister considered his story carefully and treated him to a watery smile. Lewis was acutely conscious of the muscular hands flexing on the back of the chair and tensed, ready for the next blow, but it never came. Instead, a mobile telephone suddenly 'beep-beeped' an alert from one of Twister's pockets, indicating he had a message.

With a muttered exclamation, he checked first one pocket and then the other until he found it. Lewis's eyes widened, recognizing that the telephone was his own and guessing who the call would be from. Twister studied the display, then flicked a button and frowned. 'You had the damned thing on divert,' he hissed, and held the phone to his ear, listening to the message.

Lewis could hear Kate's angry voice even from where he was sitting and smiled faintly in spite of himself.

'Seems your girlfriend rang you half an hour ago,' Twister went on, snapping the lid of the phone shut. 'From the phone at your cottage too. Wanted to know where you were.' He studied Lewis again through half-closed eyelids. 'Shall we ring her back and tell her, *old sport?*'

Lewis watched him while he dialled. *'Don't answer, Kate,'* he willed silently and he clenched his teeth so tightly that it sent spear-points of pain up his injured nose into his eyes. But his fears proved groundless, for a few seconds later Twister returned the mobile to his pocket.

'No reply,' he breathed, his voice flat and unemotional. 'Just an answer message. She must have already left. So, Mr Detective, what do you suggest we do now, eh?'

But Lewis just stared into those cold reptilian eyes and felt his stomach muscles tighten in another spasm.

# CHAPTER 23

DCI Callow could feel her patience evaporating, along with her resistance to the cold. She had parked her car three to four doors down from Lewis's cottage after seeing Kate's taxi drive off and she had been standing in the gateway of the house next door — concealed behind a large oak tree — for the best part of forty minutes. Yet in all that time there had not been a movement or a sound from inside the little thatched cottage.

Lewis's distinctive Jaguar had been parked in the drive alongside the house on her arrival, so she had naturally assumed he was at home and, as she hadn't seen Kate actually knock on the front door and then head round the back afterwards, since she had still been parking her car at the time, there was no way of her knowing that Kate was alone inside.

Nevertheless, her febrile imagination did its best to unsettle her. So, the stupid cow had run home to her boyfriend, had she? Even now the pair were probably sharing a nice bottle of wine while they studied what was in the padded envelope. Maybe there was even a bit of shagging going on too, eh? Yeah, right — and she smirked through her near frozen facial muscles. She couldn't see Miss Tin Knickers doing anything as common as shagging. Sex was strictly for the lower orders. She glowered in the darkness, feeding off her own sour mood.

OK, so she shouldn't have made a play for the silly bitch when she'd joined the team; ought to have known she was straight. But to actually be given the cold shoulder by a snotty little tart like that really got to her. What made Miss Kate Hamblin think she was so special? Her numbers weren't even dry yet. And if Roz Callow had anything to do with it, they never would be — she would be out on her delicate little ear. All that was needed was enough dirt to throw at her and though she had got away with the little game she was playing so far, maybe, just maybe her luck was about to run out.

Callow was so preoccupied with her hate agenda that she failed to hear the front door of the cottage open and close, and it wasn't until the footsteps crunched into the gravel within spitting distance of her that she realized her target was on the move. The engine of the Jaguar started immediately and the DCI only just managed to shrink back into the gateway before the powerful car emerged with blazing headlamps and a grinding of gears, turning in the direction of the village of Mark.

Hell's bells, she couldn't lose her now; that would be too much. Unused to running, Callow was panting heavily when she climbed back behind the wheel of her Audi.

The Jag's tail lights had already faded by the time she pulled away, but if there was one thing this DCI could do well, it was drive and she demonstrated that now, catching up with Kate just as the Jag swung off the Burtle road to head towards Highbridge.

Callow frowned. Where the hell are you going now, she mused? Surely not back to the nick? That would be a real bummer after she herself had endured forty-minutes' purgatory standing in the cold under a bloody tree. For a while it certainly looked that way though. After entering The Causeway, a mile and a half from Mark village, Kate continued left at speed through Watchfield and eventually on into Highbridge itself. Now she slowed, but passed the police station without the slightest flick of her brake lights and shortly afterwards swung right again into a side road.

Knowing the road went nowhere, Callow pulled into the kerb just before the junction and parked outside the darkened premises of Wadman & Son Funeral Directors. Then, switching off her police radio, she followed the wall of the building round the corner on foot. Within a few yards she spotted the Jaguar's exhaust smoke issuing from the mouth of a cul-de-sac running parallel to the main road behind the building. She crept closer and, slipping into the shadows in front of two large wheelie bins, peered round the corner. The car was parked opposite the rear gates of the funeral directors, its engine ticking over with a low growl and Kate sitting motionless in the driving seat. What on earth was she up to at this time of night, Callow mused — especially here? And why was Hayden Lewis not with her? After all, it was his car she was driving. She compressed her lips into a thin, hard line. Somehow she knew that finding out would be well worth the wait and, flicking up the collar of her coat against the cold, she leaned against the wall, determined to do just that.

Kate had no idea she was being tailed, not because Callow was such an expert at mobile surveillance, but because her mind was sick with worry over Hayden. The realization that his cottage had been broken into and her discovery of the bloodstains had really shaken her and she had spent a further ten minutes checking out the garden in the light of one of Lewis's torches to satisfy herself that he wasn't lying somewhere seriously hurt.

She should have called out her police colleagues, of course — in the same way as she should have alerted them to what was going on from the very start of the murder inquiry. After all, that is what she would have expected of anyone else in the same circumstances. But she had been through all this mind-searching before and it was far too late to do the official thing now. What had she got to tell them now anyway?

That Hayden was AWOL, his French doors had been forced and there were traces of what looked like blood in the living room and kitchen? And what if she was wrong and it wasn't blood, but a spillage of red wine, or Hayden had cut himself on a glass, then gone to a friend in the village for a plaster? Maybe there hadn't even been a break-in — Hayden had forced the French doors himself because he had forgotten his front-door key? There could be a perfectly reasonable explanation for everything and perhaps she was simply being neurotic. Somehow she didn't think so, however, and anyway, she now had a face and an address for her suspected killer and that had to be followed up as a priority — regardless of what had happened to Lewis.

She sniffed nervously as she stared at the solid wooden gates. A dilapidated sign fixed to the adjoining wall which bordered the road to the end of the cul-de-sac read: 'Wadman & Son, Funeral Directors. Do not obstruct.' She snorted. Obstruct? If it had been left to her, she wouldn't be within ten miles of the bloody awful place.

Easing the car forward, she took it to the end of the cul-de-sac, squeezing between a fish and chip van left half on and half off the verge and a Ford tipper lorry parked close to Wadman's wall. Then, mounting the verge behind the lorry, she reversed into the end space of a three-car-parking bay, concealed by the projecting bulk of a smart looking caravanette.

Switching off, she continued to sit there for a few minutes, trying to pluck up the necessary courage to force herself from the warm security of the vehicle to carry out a quick reconnoitre. Then, finally making up her mind, she pocketed a small torch she had found in the glove compartment and opened the door. It was a bitterly cold night and the road surface already sparkled with frost. But the sky was clear, with myriads of stars, and the veined face of the moon blazed with an intensity that blinded her for a moment. Not exactly the ideal night for a burglary, she mused, staring at the heavens from under one upraised arm and futilely hoping to see a few clouds moving in on that near featureless white face. The brilliance of the moonlight soon turned out to be the least of her problems, however. Checking the gates of the undertaker's, she discovered that they were bolted on the inside and a small pedestrian door in the right-hand gate also proved to be securely locked.

Drawing her coat more tightly about her, she stood for a few moments in their shadow, considering her options — not that she was exactly flush with those.

Going round the front and knocking the proprietor up was obviously not a good idea and trying to force an entry through the small pedestrian door with whatever implement she could find in the Jaguar's boot was likely to cause so much noise that it would wake up half the neighbourhood. That left her with just one alternative — scaling the wall — which, in her present poor physical condition, was certainly not something to be attempted lightly. But at least one helpful lorry driver had provided her with a leg-up, lessening the amount of pain the climb was bound to involve, and further-more, as the tipper was half-filled with rubble, it would put her even closer to the top of the wall.

Getting up on to the back of the lorry, however, proved to be more difficult than she had anticipated. For a start, the tipper was a lot higher off the ground than she had imagined and the wheels and sides were also covered in a slippery icy crust. She was forced to make several attempts before she was able to secure a foothold on top of one of the rear wheels and hoist herself up. But it was well worth the effort, as the summit of the rubble proved to be an ideal vantage point.

She found herself staring into a rubbish-strewn yard with a gloomy looking two-storey building at the far end, apparently fronting the main road, and a big garage with busi-ness-like steel doors extending back from it in her direction. The place was very still, one light showing in a downstairs window. She shivered and very nearly jumped down from the crates to drive off into the night. Then she thought of all those who had died — Andy Seldon, Alf Cross, Linda and the poor breakdown man, Ray Jury. Most of all she thought of Hayden who, as far as she was aware, was still alive, and she knew she had to stick with her plan despite the obvious risks.

Gritting her teeth against the searing erosion of her ribcage that now seemed to be underway again, she gripped the top of the wall with both hands and hauled herself up, digging the toes of her boots into the rough stone. Then she was straddling it, one leg each side as she looked down into the yard, wondering if she should simply jump off despite her injured ribs and hope to land safely, but distrusting the dense shadows below where the moonlight failed to reach. In the end, left with no alternative, she pivoted round to face the road and again gripping the top of the wall with both hands, swung her right leg over to join the left before lowering herself down the inside as far as she could and letting go.

She landed clumsily, jarring her ribs again, but managed to stay on her feet and avoid doing herself any serious damage by bending her legs on impact. Then, straightening up with one hand clutching her chest as the other dug into her pocket for her painkillers, she leaned back against the wall, trying to manufacture enough saliva to swallow her tablets. Anxiously studying the back of the funeral parlour at the same time, she listened for the slightest sound, fearing that there might be a dog on the loose. But nothing moved, apart from a noisy motor cycle on the main road, and she breathed a tremulous sigh of relief. So far so good — the first phase of her illegal trespass completed and she had got in without detection.

But she was wrong about that and on the corner of the cul-de-sac, DCI Callow's malicious smile said it all. 'Gotcha,' she murmured as she reached for her police radio.

Twister had spent the best part of half an hour pacing the small cellar, smoking one cigarette after another in a mood of increasing agitation. It was plain that he was in a dilemma and it didn't take the wisdom of Sherlock Holmes for Lewis to deduce that he was the cause.

In the end the psychopath seemed to come to a decision and he bent over his captive, staring fixedly into his eyes. 'Does anyone else have the key to your desk?' he said.

*Thank God. He had bought the bogus story.*

Lewis shook his head. 'Wouldn't be much sense in putting the tracker in there if someone else had access,' he replied.

Twister acknowledged the point with a brief nod and straightened up. 'Where is your key?' he said. 'Do you have it on you?'

The detective thought quickly. If he said 'yes', he could be inviting trouble as there was no way his captor could just pop into the police station to retrieve his property and anyway, Lewis wasn't sure he had a key on the ring in his pocket that looked like a drawer key. On the other hand, if he said 'no, it's at home', the killer might decide to drive back there to collect it himself and, as far as Lewis knew, the only keys he possessed, apart from those on the ring in his pocket, were his spare car ignition keys hanging on a hook in his cottage.

'How are you going to get into the nick to unlock the drawer anyway?' he prevaricated, conscious of the beads of sweat breaking out on his forehead. 'There is a security door and you would be challenged if someone saw you.'

Twister treated him to a mirthless smile and suddenly Lewis realized he had been outwitted. 'There is no locked drawer, is there?' he said softly. 'You were just playing for time.' His smile faded and the empty expression was back in his eyes. 'Well, Mr Detective,' he went on, 'your time is up.'

Lewis caught the glint of steel and stared in horror at the cutthroat razor in the other's hand. 'First, I shall cut off your left ear,' Twister said, 'then your right. And if that doesn't work, I shall turn to even more sensitive areas.' His face was now inches from the policeman's. 'So, tell me, where is my tracker?'

CHAPTER 24

The big steel doors of the garage were securely locked. Kate made a face in the moon-dappled shadows as she carefully tested them. No way in there then, she mused, and peered round the corner pillar to study the rear of the main building from which the garage projected some thirty feet. As she had noticed before, a light burned in one of the downstairs windows, but otherwise the place was in darkness — apparently as dead as the people in its fridges.

She shivered again, then crept slowly along the garage wall towards the light, pausing every few seconds to scrutinize the building and listen for any sounds of movement. Once her foot struck what looked like a discarded beer or cider can, lying with the multitude of other rubbish that was scattered over the concrete hard-standing, and it shot away from her with a loud clatter, freezing her into immobility. But the noise seemed to have gone unnoticed, for no additional lights came on and no one came out to investigate. Essentially that was a relief, but it also occurred to her that maybe no one had materialized because there was no one in the building to start with. After all, why *would* anyone be in a funeral parlour this late in the evening except through shortage of breath? Perhaps she had got it all wrong and Larry

Wadman had taken Hayden somewhere else entirely. It could be that she was wasting her time here, but there again, what other options were open to her?

Watching where she put her feet this time, she moved off again and kept going until she reached a wide paved area close to the back door of the building.

The light burning in the window turned out to be a flickering ceiling globe illuminating a small shadowy room with a crucifix glinting on a pedestal at the far end. The floor was fully carpeted and there was a narrow window (internal, it had to be) above the crucifix that seemed to be composed of coloured glass. This had to be the so-called chapel of rest — and it was just her luck that someone happened to be resting there at the moment. A long table covered by a cloth occupied the centre of the room and an open coffin stood on top of it, wreaths leaning against the sides and the end nearest to her — the unfortunate incumbent obviously having been prepared for viewing before their final journey.

She didn't fancy climbing into a room with a corpse and tried the handle of the back door first, but, as she had expected, it was locked. The top panel of the door was glass and she pressed her nose against it to try to see what was on the other side, but it was pointless; the glass had a heavily frosted pattern and whatever lay beyond was in darkness anyway. Smashing the glass as a means of entry was out of the question, so reluctantly she turned her attention to the window, gently tugging on both corners of the frame. It creaked, but remained steadfast, even though she could see that the stay at the bottom was already sheared. *Damn it!* Patting her pockets, she felt for anything she could use as a lever. Usually she carried a mini make-up case in her coat pocket to cater for emergency repair work, but the very time she needed the little leather case, she had come without it. Then she remembered the wallet in her back pocket and tugged it free. Her credit card was just about the right thickness, but was it strong enough? All depended on the window catch.

She was actually in the process of inserting the card into the narrow gap between the window and the outer frame, when the light blazed through the half-panelled glass door. *Hell's bells!* Someone was coming.

Unbeknown to Kate, the sound of the tin can clattering across the yard, while unnerving for her, had bought a temporary reprieve for Hayden Lewis. Although the cellar lacked fanlights of any sort, there were two vents located high on the wall close to the ceiling and the noise, though muffled, had been loud enough to penetrate the room — and, more importantly, to distract Twister.

'Seems we have a visitor,' he murmured, closing the razor with a snap and returning it to his pocket. 'And a none-too-quiet one at that.'

He studied his captive thoughtfully. 'I don't want to gag you,' he said. 'You might choke with your nose the way it is and we don't want you dying on us just yet, do we?' He thrust his face close to him. 'But make one sound,' he added, 'and I'll come back and cut your tongue out. Just remember that.'

Then he was moving swiftly across the cellar to the stairs, his soft-soled shoes making hardly any sound. The stairs creaked once and then Lewis heard the door at the top close with a sharp 'ping'. He was alone and unashamedly shaking in his shoes.

Saved by the bell — or in this case, what sounded like a tin can. But for how long, that was the point? Lewis thought about ignoring the killer's warning and shouting to attract the intruder's attention, but straightaway decided against it. First, it was unlikely that they would hear him and, secondly, even if they did, how would they know where he was? There was also the question of why they were on the property at all. It was unlikely to be for a legitimate purpose and if they were up to no good, they would hardly be keen on coming to his rescue, would they? Furthermore, he had no doubt that the killer would make good his threat to cut out his tongue and even though he knew he was likely to end up with his throat cut eventually anyway, he had no desire to hasten that moment.

No, his only chance lay in freeing himself and for the next few minutes, he strained against the tapes that held him with all his strength. But it was hopeless — they loosened hardly at all — and in the end he gave up trying. If this had been a movie, he mused, he would have been able to pitch the chair over on to its side and cut the tapes on a conveniently placed knife or saw-blade, but this wasn't a movie and he knew that if he did pitch over, he was more likely to crack his skull open on the concrete floor than anything else.

So what *did* he do apart from just sit there in the dank gloom of the cellar and wait for the killer to return to finish him off? Well, there was one other option open to him and though with his inbuilt scepticism it had to be a long-shot, he came to the conclusion that anything was worth a try. Closing his eyes and drawing on as much of his schoolboy memory as he could summon, he began, slowly, and at first hesitantly to mumble an incoherent Lord's Prayer.

Kate's heart was hammering against her ribcage like an out-of-control tumble-drier as she quickly slid her credit card upwards until the antiquated window catch prevented it going any further. Then, wiggling it under the catch and twisting it slightly to one side, she tried to prise the tiny brass lever upwards. Instead, she felt a corner of the card snap off. Sucking in a mouthful of oxygen, she tried again. Keys now jangled on the other side of the door and she heard a curse as someone dropped them on the floor. *Come on, Kate, get the bloody window open!*

Perspiration stood out on her forehead despite the coldness of the night air and she was conscious that her hand was shaking. Then, as a key slammed into the door lock, she felt rather than heard a 'click' and the window catch flicked open. Success, but only just. Willing the window not to stick, she gripped the edge of the frame again and pulled.

To her relief, it swung back easily with just a faint scraping sound and at the same moment the door opened, sending a shaft of yellow light out to join the moonlight. Kate only just managed to scramble up on to the sill, using a projecting water pipe as a step, before a heavy shadow was thrown across the paving just feet away.

But then she was through the window and crouching on her knees among the folds of a heavy curtain, one hand reaching up to gently pull the window to behind her and wincing at the waves of pain surfing through her ribcage.

Gritty footsteps on the paving directly outside now. She closed her eyes tightly, her heart making peculiar squishing noises like a misfiring water pump, as she prayed that the insecure window would escape detection. Silence for what seemed an age and then, with the pressure building up inside her making her want to scream, the footsteps moved away across the yard, gradually fading.

For a few moments she remained where she was, almost too frightened to move, but, then forcing herself to straighten up, she peered round the curtain into the moonlight. She saw the heavy-set figure at once. He had his back to her and seemed to be checking the gates at the far end of the yard. Time to move before he came back.

The heady perfume from the wreaths enveloped her as she advanced further into the room and she wrinkled her nose in disgust. Ordinarily she loved flowers, but somehow the smell of them in this place was overpowering, their rich cloying scent nauseatingly intoxicating. Yet even as her senses swam and her stomach heaved, she was drawn by a kind of morbid curiosity towards the coffin and the next instant found herself standing directly under the flickering ceiling light, staring down at the corpse.

The old woman was dressed in a plain white robe with her arms dutifully folded across her shrunken breasts and her sparse grey hair combed out over the tiny pillow-like strands of steel wool. The ends of the thin bony fingers and the lips and marbled face had a bluish tinge, indicating that deterioration had already set in. Kate shuddered, drawing back quickly, as if she half-expected the eyes of the corpse to open and the mouth to twist into an obscene rictus grin. Being a police officer, she had seen death many times — had attended any number of grisly crime scenes and post-mortems — yet had always managed to remain professionally detached from it all. But now, in her present heightened state of anxiety and with the emotional baggage she was already carrying, the suffocating atmosphere of this heavily perfumed room really got to her, almost inducing a sense of panic.

Spotting a pair of white doors, framed by swags and tails, on the far side of the room, she headed straight for them, but her haste was ill-advised. Decorative brass vases containing artificial white lilies stood on pedestals on each side of the doors and the one to her right was almost buried in shadow. As a result, she walked straight into it, bowling the pedestal over and sending the vase crashing into the wall with a reverberating clang. Cursing her stupidity, she quickly righted the pedestal and replaced the vase on top of it, but she felt sure someone must have heard the noise and she strained her ears for the sound of approaching footsteps, ready to scramble back through the window should she hear anything. But there was nothing and, taking a deep breath, she reached for the brass knob of one of the doors — only to freeze in the act of pulling it open. The knob itself was already turning in her hand. Someone was holding it on the other side.

Twister had heard the loud crash as he'd headed back across the yard. So his visitor was in the chapel of rest, was he — how appropriate — and he flexed his fingers in anticipation.

Turning the hall light off to avoid being silhouetted in the chapel doorway, he approached the double doors cautiously and reached for the handle. He immediately felt resistance on the other side. Well, well, well, he mused, great minds think alike, it seems. He withdrew his hand and, stepping back a couple of paces, waited for the intruder to emerge into the hallway, but nothing happened and, gripping the handle again, he found it turned easily.

The room beyond was empty, that much seemed apparent, and he scowled, crossing swiftly to the window. He could see that it was at least a quarter open even before he got to it. Pushing it wide, he stared at the paving below the sill before scanning the yard again. Someone was playing silly buggers with him and he didn't find it at all funny. There had been two attempted break-ins on his property over the past few weeks, one involving the use of an acetylene torch on his garage doors. What they had been after was a mystery, unless there was a market in stolen hearses or body parts, but he would have loved to have got hold of the culprit or culprits red-handed. A little recreational violence, he'd always felt, was good for the soul.

He saw the broken stems of his plastic lilies when he returned to the door and swung round again to study the chapel, not entirely convinced that his intruder would have had time to flee via the insecure window. But there was nowhere for anyone to hide — except maybe under the table bearing the coffin. Turning up the dimmer switch controlling the lights, he dropped on to his hands and knees to pull the cloth aside and check under the table. Crouched on the floor just inches away from him under the cloth, Kate held her breath and waited for the inevitable.

# CHAPTER 25

The thunderous knocking was so sudden that it made Twister jump and he cracked his head on the upper frame of the table as he scrambled to his feet. A pulsing blue light radiated off the walls and ceiling of the chapel like the intense eerie glow from a flying saucer in a science fiction film. Striding across the room, he stared through the window and saw that the top of the wall at the far end of the yard was bathed in blue light. The next instant the heads and shoulders of a couple of uniformed figures appeared in view, apparently having climbed the wall from the other side. Powerful flashlights raked the yard before the figures disappeared again.

More heavy pounding. He swore savagely. The bastard police seemed to be at the front door of his place as well as the back. He felt his stomach muscles tighten. What the hell did they want? Surely they couldn't be on to him? He had been so careful not to leave any incriminating traces behind. Yeah, but what about the tracker? Maybe they'd had it all along and their forensics had picked up a print? Well, if that was what had brought them to his door, there was no escape anyway; they were all round the place. All he could do was try and bluff his way out.

Throwing the chapel door wide, he walked into more pulsing blue light. It poured into the hallway through the wide-open door of the reception office. He shielded his eyes as he strode into the river of blue. A police car was parked directly in front one of the big windows that faced the main road and he glimpsed a white face pressed against the glass for a moment before it disappeared again and the pounding resumed.

He turned the key in the door and opened up. A hatchet-faced woman stood on the pavement, flanked by a uniformed police sergeant and a constable. She made to push past him, but he threw a muscular arm out in front of her. 'And where do you think you're going?' he snapped.

She flashed a wallet in front of him. 'DCI Callow,' she said. 'I've just seen someone climb over your back wall.'

He raised an eyebrow. 'So?'

She pushed against his arm without success. 'Well, we have to check it out. You've obviously got an intruder.'

He emitted a humourless laugh. 'As long as no one is trying to *leave*,' he said. 'I'd be a bit worried if one of my clients tried to do that.'

But she didn't appreciate the joke. 'Let me past,' she rapped, bristling with aggressive authority. 'Don't you understand — someone is in the process of breaking into your property?'

Twister smiled. Now he knew he was not the reason for the visit, his confidence had returned in abundance. 'He won't find much in here,' he retorted, 'unless he's into necrophilia.'

'We still need to give your place the once over.'

'And you have a warrant, I suppose?'

She stared at him in astonishment. 'A warrant? Why would I need one of those? We're here for your benefit and we're already wasting time.'

He nodded. 'Well, I don't need your help, thank you, and I certainly don't want your lot stamping all over my clean carpets. I've got a funeral tomorrow.'

The DCI was so taken aback that for a moment she seemed lost for words.

The sergeant sensed the tension building and coughed discreetly, his own uneasiness palpable. 'If the gentleman doesn't need us, ma'am, perhaps we should — er — go.'

'Go?' Callow almost spat the word. 'We'll do nothing of the sort. There's a bloody crime in progress.'

Twister shrugged. 'Well, you're not coming in anyway,' he said firmly and started to close the door.

Immediately Callow's foot shot out and jammed itself in the gap. Twister's smile vanished. 'If I were you,' he said softly, 'I'd remove that foot. Unless you'd like to discuss your illegal entry with my solicitor.'

'Ma'am,' the sergeant put in hastily, touching her arm. 'We'd best be on our way.'

For a moment it seemed that Callow would ignore her colleague and force the issue. But then abruptly warning bells jangled in her brain, bringing her sharply to her senses. She was well out of order here and she knew it. Reluctantly she stepped back from the doorway.

'Thank you, Chief Inspector,' Twister said, as he closed the door. 'Now you have a good night, won't you?'

The sergeant was already turning towards his patrol car, speaking quickly into his personal radio. Callow heard the words 'All units resume patrol', as if it were part of some impossible dream. This couldn't be happening to her. She'd had Hamblin totally banged to rights and now at the crucial moment had had the rug pulled out from under her, leaving her powerless to do anything. What the hell was the funeral director's problem? Most people would have been only too pleased for the police to check their property out in such a situation. But he had seemed so rabidly anti. She just couldn't understand it.

She watched the sergeant open the door of the patrol car and in her frustration nearly called out to him to tell him the full story — that the intruder was not just some random burglar, but one of their own. But she stopped herself in time. That wouldn't change anything — they would still be unable to gain entry — and unless she managed to catch Hamblin red-handed, she would have no case at all anyway. Blurting out what she had seen without a prisoner at the end of it would only make her look stupid and raise uncomfortable questions as to what she had been doing following Hamblin in the first place.

She acknowledged the sergeant's wave with a curt nod and watched the patrol car head off towards Bridgwater, shortly followed by the big police van that had been sent to the back of the premises. She was alone, spitting feathers, but determined to nail Kate Hamblin, whatever the cost. OK, so she couldn't catch her actually on the premises, but little Miss Perfect would have to come back out to the car eventually — maybe with a bagful of nicked gear too — and that would be just as good a collar. Returning to her original spot in front of the wheelie bins, she leaned against the corner of the wall with her gaze fixed on the back gates and slipped two extra strong mints between her bared teeth as she waited.

Kate scrambled out from under the table even as Twister left the chapel, but she hesitated in the even stronger pulsing blue light which now poured down the hallway beyond the chapel's open door. What on earth were her colleagues doing here? They couldn't possibly know about Wadman — or could they? Maybe the SOCO who had handed her the envelope had had second thoughts and reported his discovery elsewhere. But even if he had, how could the inquiry team have connected Wadman with the murder investigation?

Seeing her colleagues actually on the spot, she was tempted to rush to the front door to enlist their help, but then she heard DCI Callow's voice shouting about an intruder and her spirits sank. *Hell's bells!* The evil bitch must have followed her to Wadman's place and seen her climb over the wall. Well, she could expect no help from this particular DCI, that was a fact. All Callow was likely to do was arrest her for burglary and, whether the charge held up or not later on, by then Wadman would have had time to finish poor Hayden off, if he was still alive in the first place, and dump his body somewhere far away. No, she had started this thing on her own and, whether she liked it or not, she would have to finish it the same way.

Taking a calculated risk — hoping that Wadman and her colleagues would be too engrossed in their stand-off to spot her among the rippling blue flashes produced by the police car's powerful strobe — she edged out of the doorway, then suddenly cut across the hallway to another small door opposite, brushing against a wheeled stretcher left against the wall. No one shouted after her and the door opened easily, the darkness inside exhaling an unpleasant rancid smell reminiscent of rotten meat mixed with the sharp bite of antiseptic, that seemed to envelope her like a poisonous miasma as she closed the door again behind her.

The thin beam of her torch touched on the white tiled walls and floor of a small oblong room, with a stainless steel table in the centre straddling a gully that cut into the floor for half the room's length, and ended in a sunken drain. A pair of glass-fronted cabinets fitted with shelves holding numerous bottles, a selection of books and what looked like surgical instruments, occupied one wall and a nest of stainless steel taps hovered over a peculiarly shaped sink in the far corner.

The place had a distinct hospital feel to it and when she moved closer to the cabinets, the titles of the books seemed to leap out at her: *Human Anatomy, Embalming For Morticians, Chemical Preservatives*. She shuddered. She had been in enough mortuaries in her career to know that she stood in just such a place now — one that almost certainly doubled as an embalming room — and, swinging her torch towards the opposite wall, her suspicions were confirmed when the beam bounced off a row of three steel refrigerator doors.

For a moment she kept the beam trained on the doors, unable to take her eyes off them and thinking of Hayden. Surely not? He couldn't be . . . ?

Driven by a kind of morbid compulsion, she crossed the room and grasped the handle of the first door, her stomach churning as she pulled it open. She was met by a blast of cold rancid air, but the three steel trays provided for the cadavers inside proved to be empty. It was the same story with the next refrigerator, but when she checked the last one, she got a shock she certainly hadn't expected. The trays inside had all been removed (she could see them leaning against the side of the refrigerator) and in their place someone had actually stacked three cardboard boxes, labelled Chardonnay.

She shuddered again. A cadaver fridge used as a cold store for wine? How gross was that? But at least Hayden's corpse was not inside, which was the main thing, and she muttered a brief prayer of thanks to whoever happened to be listening in such an awful place.

Her gratitude turned out to be premature, however. Even before she could turn round, she heard the crack of a floorboard in the hallway outside and a second later the squeak of the door handle. She had company!

With no time to look for somewhere to hide, she did the only thing she could think of under the circumstances. Crouching right down, she clambered backwards into the icy maw of the fridge, pulling the door to behind her and holding on to the inside catch to prevent it swinging open again — this time praying that whoever was entering the room would not notice that the fridge door was ajar and decide to push it shut completely. Then, propping herself on top of the boxes of Chardonnay, she sat shuddering in the icy darkness, listening to the scrape of shoes on the tiled floor and the sound of heavy breathing as the fridge's forty degree breath seeped into her bones and the rancid smell of death enveloped her in its sweet nauseating embrace.

DCI Callow felt even colder than she had during her vigil outside the cottage in Burtle. The frosted lids of the wheelie-bins had now developed a hard crust that felt like a burn when she touched them and she was convinced her legs and feet were going the same way. But she was determined to continue her vigil, even though there had been no sound or sign of movement since her colleagues had left fifteen minutes ago. After all, the prize was well worth it, wasn't it? Kate Hamblin on a plate facing a charge of burglary. It was an ideal outcome. Disgrace and obscurity for the meddlesome cow who had had the impudence to interfere in matters that were no concern of hers and a nice tidy detection and 'case closed' for the detective super and his top-notch DCI.

Despite the cold, she was smiling as she reached into her pocket for another extra-strong mint, but her smile froze like the muscles in her legs, first because she discovered that she had run out of mints and second because she had detected the approach of a slow-running engine.

Ordinarily, she would have taken little notice of the vehicle, merely shrunk back into the shadows beside the wheelie-bins until it had passed, but when she glanced over her shoulder, she saw that it was actually creeping along the road towards her without any lights. Her curiosity now well aroused, she watched from a crouched position as the car pulled up on the opposite side of the road just a few yards beyond the entrance to the cul-de-sac.

Seconds later the driver, dressed in an anorak and woolly hat, climbed out into the night air and, shutting the door carefully behind them, pointed what was obviously an infra-red central door-locking device at the vehicle. Then, as the car's indicators flashed twice, the dark figure turned and walked briskly across the road towards the mouth of the cul-de-sac, pausing briefly a few feet from where Callow crouched to glance quickly in both directions. For one agonizing second Callow feared she had been spotted and her hand closed on the warrant card in her pocket in readiness for the anticipated challenge. That challenge never came, but for an instant the face of the new arrival was clearly visible in the moonlight and the DCI's jaw practically hit the pavement when she saw who it was. Before she could say or do anything, however, the other had moved off again, turning into the cul-de-sac and stopping before the undertaker's gates. There was a clinking sound as a set of keys was apparently produced and then the figure was gone, ducking through the small pedestrian door in the right-hand gate and closing it to behind them.

Callow was in shock. She could hardly believe what she had just seen — and, more importantly, *who*. She could not have imagined anyone less likely to be slipping into the back of a local undertaker's at this time of the night than the individual in question, yet that is exactly what they had just done — *and* used a key to gain entry too, which suggested that they had to be on pretty good speaking terms with the undertaker himself. First Hamblin scaling the wall and now this. What on earth was going on? Suddenly what had started out as a simple tailing job had turned into something a lot more complicated and Callow's curiosity, stimulated by years of detective work, was at fever-pitch. She had to satisfy the twitch in her nose and get to the bottom of it all, whether that was against the rules or not.

Quitting her hiding-place, she followed the wall closely all the way round to the double gates, wondering grimly what one of the local residents might think of her antics if they happened to be looking out of the front window of one of the terraced houses opposite. To her surprise, the pedestrian door was ajar — the nocturnal visitor had apparently not shut it properly afterwards — and she hesitated. If she went any further and was discovered, she would be seen as a criminal trespasser and tarred with the same brush as Kate Hamblin. Yet standing out there in the cold, she was no good to anyone; she might as well be at home in bed.

She pushed the door open and ducked through into the yard beyond.

After the police had left, Twister's first move was to recheck the chapel of rest. He didn't expect to find anyone there and he wasn't disappointed. The space under the table was empty. If someone had been hiding there, they were long gone, which was hardly surprising under the circumstances.

His main concern was *where* they had gone. It was unlikely that they had fled altogether as the police would have spotted anyone trying to exit via the yard wall. That meant they still had to be on the premises — no doubt having slipped past him into one of the other rooms while he had been preoccupied with Old Bill at the front door. Excellent! A nice little game of cat-and-mouse, with the prize of a kill at the end of it. What could be better? Once more flexing his powerful hands, he smiled to himself as he crossed the room to close the window. Hayden Lewis could wait; this issue was much more pressing and he was conscious of the fact that he hadn't felt so alive for years.

Returning to the hallway, he stood for a moment listening to the loud ticking of the ancient grandfather clock in its alcove at the foot of the stairs as it thudded on relentlessly through the night like the timer on an explosive charge. There wasn't another sound.

He checked the cellar next, smiling again when he saw the look of dread in Hayden Lewis's eyes the moment he appeared. 'Patience, Mr Detective,' he murmured close to his ear. 'I'll get back to you again shortly, I promise.'

At the top of the stairs he gently pushed the cellar door to behind him rather than closing it completely, conscious of the sound the door would make when the catch was engaged, then quickly crossed the hallway to the old embalming room and mortuary.

Flashing the torch round inside, he saw at once that the room was empty, the broad beam reflecting back at him from the stainless steel table and fridges and glittering on the bottles and surgical instruments in the glass-fronted cabinets.

Returning to the hallway, he pushed through the door into the workshop, satisfied himself that it was also empty and flicked on the lights in the big garage. The two Daimlers stood out black, shiny and sinister under the strip-lights, contrasting with the battered green van and his mud-plastered Land Rover. He walked round each vehicle in turn, even looking under them, but there was no sign of anyone.

Frowning, he switched off the lights and made his way back to the hallway and it was just as he was closing the workshop door that he heard the distinctive crack of rafters and a couple of soft footfalls above his head. His smile returned and, moving with almost cat-like grace, he headed for the staircase leading to his flat.

# CHAPTER 26

Twister paused for a moment on the landing before pushing the door of his flat open. The noises he had heard had not been repeated, but instinct told him that he had not imagined them — someone was definitely inside — and the confirmation came when he snapped on the light of his living room and saw the figure in the dark overcoat standing at the single window, looking down into the street.

Even before the figure swung round to face him, he knew who it was and he scowled as he relaxed his tensed muscles. 'How the hell did *you* get in?' he demanded.

His visitor shrugged. 'You gave me a set of keys, remember?'

'Yeah, but I told you not to come here tonight.'

'Good job I did — what were the boys in blue doing outside as I arrived? I had to park my bloody car further down the road until they'd left.'

Twister lit a cigarette. 'They said they'd spotted an intruder climbing over the yard wall.'

A disparaging snort. 'Why would anyone want to screw an undertaker's?'

'How should I know? Anyway, the only person I've been able to find in here so far is you.'

The other's mouth tightened. 'Probably because there wasn't any intruder in the first place.'

'How's that?'

'Use what little brains you've got, Twister. It was a ruse, can't you see that? An attempt to get into the house. They're on to you.'

'Impossible.'

'So how come they just happened to be on the spot to see this so-called intruder?'

'No idea. The bitch detective told me she had clocked the guy personally.'

'What detective?'

'Some inspector — Cannow or Carlow, I think her name was.'

A sharp intake of breath. 'Detective Chief Inspector Rozalind Callow? She's the last thing you need — where's Lewis?'

'In the cellar.'

'You dick-head, you should have got rid of him by now. Callow will be back, you can bet on it — maybe with a search warrant next time — and a dead copper on the premises would be a bit difficult to explain away.'

'He's not dead yet. He's' — and he grinned — 'helping me with my inquiries.'

His visitor failed to see the joke. 'The way you're going, you'll be helping the police with theirs pretty soon too and I can't let that happen.'

Twister raised an eyebrow. 'Meaning what exactly?'

'*Meaning*, I'm terminating your contract. Cutting you loose. You've become too much of a bloody liability.'

Twister couldn't help sniggering as he towered over his visitor. 'And how do you propose doing that?' he sneered.

'Easy,' came the confident reply and he felt a tongue of fire rip through him as a long-bladed knife was driven hard into his abdomen.

Roz Callow was nervous — very nervous. She had followed her quarry right inside the house via a convenient back door, which had been carelessly left ajar like the pedestrian door in the gate. The place was in total darkness. Even the probing fingers of moonlight had suddenly been withdrawn as the moon itself was swallowed up by the beast of the night, but a ghostly glow emanated from a doorway at the top of a wide staircase and she glimpsed the smudge of a figure on the landing, though she couldn't identify it before it was absorbed by the light.

It was obvious that the nocturnal visitor knew exactly where they were going, indicating a familiarity with the place that, to the DCI's mind, was more than a little unsettling and she hesitated before the 'Private' sign and loop of chain that blocked her way. As she had already recognized, she was well out of order entering the property in the first place, but to compound that felony by penetrating further could prove to be a serious error of judgement. In her present obsessive mood, however, reason held little sway and what had started out as a vengeful opportunity had now become much too personal to abort.

The stairs drew her on, but as she climbed, she couldn't help thinking with a shiver of Hitchcock's cult-horror masterpiece, *Psycho*, and the scene where the private detective was attacked on the landing of a very similar staircase by a nightmare figure with a knife.

As it transpired, there was no knife-wielding madman waiting for her in the upper gloom of this landing, but when she stepped cautiously through the open doorway of the flat above, she walked into a nightmare that was even worse.

Kate felt a tremendous sense of relief when she heard the door of the embalming room open then close again with a dull clunk, indicating that her mystery visitor had left. Even then, however, despite the intense cold that was rapidly solidifying the blood in her veins and seemed to have already slowed her heartbeat almost to a stop, it was several minutes before she managed to pluck up the courage to push the door open.

The room was deserted, although the lights had been left on, suggesting that someone would be back before long. She needed to get out of the room as quickly as possible, but that was easier said than done. Easing herself from the refrigerator with great difficulty, she found that her legs were incapable of supporting her and, slumping to the floor, she was forced to remain there for several minutes while she waited for the feeling to return to her frozen muscles and sinews. From somewhere above her head she heard heavy footsteps and waited for the embalming-room door to be thrown open again with the yell that meant discovery, but it never happened and as the building settled into a strange heavy stillness, she at last began to feel the uncomfortable burning sensation in her legs and feet as the circulation was slowly restored.

Using the edge of the mortuary table for support and wincing at the sudden painful surge of hot blood through her veins, she finally managed to stand up and after a few more minutes make her way slowly to the door. She opened it very carefully. Silence. The hallway beyond was now pitch black. A warning voice in her brain told her to get out of the place as quickly as possible, but she ignored it. Lewis had to be somewhere in the building and she was determined to find him. The problem was where to look next.

A grandfather clock ticked loudly in an alcove at the foot of the stairs — a quick flick of her torch beam revealing its pale sombre face before passing on to fasten on another door on the other side of the alcove. She was actually turning towards the door when she spotted the light. It was just a tiny gold thread reaching out across the floor, but in the darkness it was plain enough and, moving closer, she saw that it continued as a vertical line up the wall beneath the staircase. She ran her fingers down the wall, found a small knob and gently pulled.

The small door was only ajar and it opened easily. Beyond, she glimpsed steps leading down to some sort of dimly lit cellar. She hesitated, recognizing the folly of going any further. Anyone could be down there and she could find herself trapped with no possible way out. But what if that was where Hayden was being held? She couldn't leave the place before she had satisfied herself one way or the other.

She ducked her head and began the descent, conscious of the slight movement of the wooden treads beneath her feet, as if the stairs were not as secure as they could have been.

She saw the seated figure even before she had reached the bottom, bound with so much tape that he resembled a partially unwrapped Egyptian mummy. She didn't need to see his face to know it was Lewis — his mop of unruly blond hair was a dead give-away — and when she went round to the front of his chair, the look of relief on his battered bloodied face was immediate. 'Hi, old girl,' he said in a weak slurred voice. 'What kept you?'

Callow stopped short just inside the small living room, her eyes widening when she saw the man she had only been speaking to a short time before lying on his side in front of the settee, a pool of blood forming under him and one hand gripping the handle of the knife that protruded from his belly. The figure standing over him cast her a sidelong glance and, bending down, roughly yanked the knife from his body, allowing his hand to drop back to the floor with a thud, before straightening up again.

'Hello, Roz,' Pauline Cross said quietly, stepping over her victim to within a couple of feet of her. 'Sorry you had to see this.'

Callow gaped at her in horror. 'Pauline?' she gasped. 'What have you *done*?'

The other shrugged. 'Terminated his contract, that's all,' she said, glancing back at Twister with contempt. 'He was becoming a bit too much of a liability.'

Callow seemed to have difficulty comprehending what she was saying. 'His contract?' she echoed in a strangled voice. 'What the hell are you talking about?'

Pauline smiled indulgently. 'Said he was ex-SAS, you know,' she went on, 'not just a simple undertaker, but a trained killer no less. He did my brother's funeral, you see — that's when we first met — and we had a bit of a fling afterwards.'

'A fling?'

Pauline threw another contemptuous glance at Twister's inert body. 'If you can call it that,' she said. 'Turned out he was no better between the sheets than he was doing what I'd hired him for—'

'You — you *hired* him?'

Pauline made a rueful grimace. ''Fraid so,' she said, ignoring the point of the question, 'and, to be fair, he did show a bit of promise at the start. It was his idea to frame Terry Duval for the Transit job. Seems he'd nearly walked in on the little pervert torching a farm near Glastonbury, and he thought that, with his history, Duval would be the perfect suspect — especially as he was already under police surveillance.' She sighed. 'He was right about that too. Trouble was, poor old Twister just couldn't help cocking things up and in the end I decided I couldn't risk him leading your mates to me.'

Callow felt her legs start to shake and she gripped the arm of the settee to steady herself. 'You murdered Alf?' she gasped. 'You killed *your own husband?*'

Pauline sighed. 'Not personally, but I suppose it amounts to the same thing.' She sniggered, a chilling unbalanced sound. 'Funny really, but poor old Alf's a lot more use to me dead than when he was alive — at least he *will* be when the insurance company pays up. Pity Andy had to fry with him, but then a bit of collateral damage can't be helped sometimes, can it?'

Callow stared at the bloodstained knife, as if mesmerized by it, then began to back slowly towards the door, shaking her head in disbelief and choking back the bile rising in her throat. 'All those times we were together you were actually planning his murder?' she whispered, then retched.

'On — on that last night, while we were having sex in Alf's bed, you knew he was about to be blown to pieces?'

Pauline snorted. 'Don't moralize with me, girl,' she retorted. 'You wanted him out the way as much as I did. What was it you said — if only he wasn't around, we could be together for good?'

Callow shook her head several times, a look of horror in her eyes. 'Good God, I didn't mean it *that* way.'

Pauline shrugged again. 'What does it matter what you meant or how he was got rid of? Means justifies the end and all that.'

'But — but you used me.'

Pauline sighed. 'Had to, Roz. Needed someone like you on the inside to let me know what was going on, didn't I? How else would I have found out all the detail about good old Operation Firetrap and been able to keep ahead of the inquiry team afterwards, eh?'

Callow was just a couple of feet from the open doorway now, gripped by a terror she had never known before and trying to put her revulsion to one side as she realized the deadly peril she was in. 'But you said you loved me,' she blurted, desperate to keep Pauline distracted while she felt behind her for the door handle.

'And I do, Roz,' Pauline soothed, moving with her, 'and I do. Trouble is, I love money even more, you see' — her face hardened — 'and I just can't risk you turning me in.'

Callow managed to side-step the first vicious thrust of the knife, but the second ripped right through her coat and she felt a searing pain as the blade cut into her side. Then her fist smashed into Pauline's face, sending her staggering backwards. Before the crazed woman could recover, she had hauled the door shut between them and literally thrown herself at the staircase.

Such was her panic, that she was halfway down before Pauline erupted on to the landing and she would have got away completely had she not suddenly lost her footing. Uttering a wild scream as her leg twisted under her with a loud snapping sound, she tumbled headlong down the remaining stairs and slammed into the base of the grandfather clock in its alcove at the bottom where she lay still.

Pauline took her time descending the staircase, but there was a triumphant gleam in her eyes as she bent over the DCI's prostrate form and lifted her head by the hair. She could feel a faint pulse in her neck and for some reason this excited her. Her mouth was dry as she placed the edge of the blade across the milk-white throat. 'Sorry, Roz,' she murmured and tightened her grip on the knife, savouring the moment. In fact, she was so absorbed in what she was about to do that she failed to hear the rustling sound behind her and the knife slipped from her nerveless fingers as the muscular arm encircled her own neck.

A blast of bad breath enveloped her as Twister rasped in her ear, 'Key rule of assassination, sweetheart,' he said. 'Always make sure your victim is actually dead.'

And with a sudden twist of his powerful hands he snapped her spine.

Twister was in trouble; he knew that only too well. The knife had plunged deep into his abdomen and some of the internal tissue had forced itself out through the wound when it had been withdrawn. But, going by the colour of the blood seeping from the hole in his gut, which he had plugged with his handkerchief and some of the tape he had used on Hayden Lewis after snapping Pauline Cross's neck, he was reasonably sure that his liver had escaped damage. Had it been otherwise, the blood would have been streaked with black and that would have amounted to a death sentence. Though reassured by his brief examination, however, he knew he still needed urgent medical treatment. It wasn't the first nasty wound he had ever received, of course. His time in the SAS had seen to that and his body was already badly scarred from encounters with knives, bayonets, machetes and on one occasion even some razor wire. But he was not as fit as he had been then and he knew it was touch and go as to whether the physical  toughness and resilience to severe pain, which had ensured his survival in the old days, would be enough to see him through the vengeful task he was desperate to complete before he handed himself over to the backstreet doctor who had tended him — and many other fugitives like him — in the past.

He'd really thought he had killed that double-crossing bitch, but somehow he hadn't done as good a job as usual. Returning to check her seemingly lifeless body — crumpled over the corpse of the lady copper — he'd been astonished to detect the faint tickle of a pulse in her neck. For a moment that had thrown him — but only for a moment. Catching sight of one of his wheeled stretchers in the beam of the torch as he clambered over the two bodies into the hallway, he had been furnished with his most sadistic idea yet. Finishing madam off with another quick twist of the neck would have been the obvious thing to do under the circumstances — send her off to her Maker before blood loss, organ failure or septicaemia sent him there himself — but that would have been much too easy and now that Fate had presented him with a further opportunity to punish her, he was determined to make the most of it.

'Well, sweetheart,' he rasped, coughing up some blood from a torn lip as he crouched down beside her and stared into the immobile wide-open eyes with the aid of his torch, 'so you're still alive, are you? Paralysed, but still with us. Now, there's a thing.'

Just to make sure, he also checked her wrist, detecting the same feeble flicker. Striking a match, he cruelly held the flame against her cheek, until a sickly scorching smell became apparent, and he was pleased to see that she didn't stir a muscle.

'Can't move, can you?' he gloated. 'Can't shout, cry — not even blink. But,' and he pressed his face closer to hers, 'I bet you can still *feel*, and that's good, because I've got a real treat in store for you.'

And he planted a sneering bloody kiss on her forehead.

## CHAPTER 27

Kate stood stock still. The blood-curdling scream from somewhere above her head had been followed by a heavy thudding sound, then a crash and a discordant jangling. It suggested that something — or *someone* — had fallen down the main staircase and collided with the clock she had noticed in the hallway earlier. But if it was a *someone*, who could have taken the tumble, she wondered? Larry Wadman perhaps? The scream had sounded as if it had been made by a woman, but, muffled by the solid wooden ceiling of the cellar, it was impossible to be certain.

Her heart was pounding again as she strained her ears for any further noises, but there were no more and she released her breath in an explosive gasp. Her professional training dictated that she should investigate the disturbance, but she had no intention of doing any such thing. She had enough on her hands already in this creepy house of horror without poking her nose into something else.

Lewis was sagging in his bonds, head bent forward on his chest. His face was a bloodied mess and his nose, which looked as if it had been broken, was badly swollen and still dribbling blood. He was obviously in great pain and the resilience that had helped him to keep going up until now seemed to have deserted him, resulting in a gradual loss of consciousness.

Getting him up the steps and out of the cellar, she knew, was going to be a real problem, but before that she had a more pressing challenge to overcome. Whatever the sticky tape was that the killer had used on him, it could not be unravelled in the normal way and she had wasted precious time trying unsuccessfully to prise it apart. What she needed was something sharp enough to cut through it, but she had absolutely nothing on her that would serve the purpose.

Suspecting that she was fast running out of time and expecting the cellar door to be thrown open any moment as the killer returned to finish the job he had started, she made a frantic search of the cellar itself, but failed to turn up any kind of discarded blade among the rubbish that littered the floor.

It dawned on her then that if she had nothing to hand with which to cut Lewis's bonds, then she would have to get a blade from somewhere else and the only place she could be certain of finding one in a hurry was the embalming room upstairs. The very thought of venturing back in there filled her with dread, but she knew she had no other realistic alternative and, throwing another anxious glance at Lewis's sagging body, she turned for the stairs.

She found the hallway still cloaked in a heavy darkness, but it was far from empty. The squeak of dry wheel bearings was accompanied by the sound of dragging footsteps. Through a crack in the half-closed cellar door she glimpsed a solid black mass — a powerfully built man — hunched over what appeared to be the same sort of wheeled stretcher she had spotted earlier as he pushed it slowly along the hallway towards the rear of the building. As the figure passed by, she picked up the sound of laboured breathing, punctuated by sharp grunts, suggesting that the man was in pain or the exertion was proving too much for him. She watched as he was absorbed by the gloom, then saw him reappear briefly a moment later in a sudden wash of insipid light — the chapel of rest? A door slammed and the light was snuffed out. She was alone again, but for how long?

Crossing the hallway with the speed of a frightened hare crossing a main road, she found the door of the embalming room and slipped inside. The surgical instruments glinted at her through the glass of the twin cabinets; cold, sinister and infinitely gruesome. She found a key in the lock of the first cabinet and gently tugged it open. The wicked looking scalpel attracted her attention immediately and she lifted it carefully off the shelf, grimacing as she thought of what it must have been used for maybe not that long ago.

She closed the cabinet and was on the point of returning to the hallway when she heard the familiar squeak of wheels. She switched off her torch and once more stood motionless in the darkness, waiting for the stretcher to pass by. Instead, it stopped and she heard something slam into the door. Bloody hell, caught with her knickers down again — and in the same sodding place.

There was no time to hide — not even in the fridge — and all she could do was to slip behind the door before it flew open, the handle jabbing into her stomach, and crushing her against the wall. She gritted her teeth from the impact, holding back the cry that rose to her lips as the blow reawakened the pain in her bruised ribs. Then the light snapped on and, peering round the edge of the door, she watched the stretcher lurch past her, wheels now squealing on the tiled floor. Wadman — she recognized him from his CRO file immediately — seemed to have difficulty walking and he leaned heavily on the stretcher for support, bent over on one side as he forced it across the room towards the refrigerators.

The stretcher was not empty either and she stared with unutterable revulsion at the thing in the long white robe that was being transported — just its blue-tinged bare feet visible to her as Wadman opened the door of the first refrigerator and adjusted the height of the trolley so that he could slide the corpse on to the metal tray inside.

Tearing her gaze away from the gruesome operation, she noticed something else — Wadman was bleeding badly. His light coloured shirt seemed to be saturated on one side, and he had left a trail of dark spots behind him on the tiled floor. She couldn't imagine how he had come by his injuries — maybe it had something to do with the disturbance she had heard — but that was the least of her concerns. On the plus side, it meant he was partially incapacitated, which gave her something of an edge, but she had no illusions as to how dangerous he still was. An extremely powerful man, she would stand no chance at all in a physical confrontation with him. Her only hope was that his injury had slowed him up enough for her to keep clear of those deadly hands.

It was at that moment, while he had his back towards her, that she decided to make her move. Gently pushing the door away from her and holding her breath in case the hinges creaked, she crept from behind it. The door made no sound, but to her alarm her knee cracked as she crossed the tiled floor. She froze and glanced quickly towards Wadman. But he still had his back towards her and, fully occupied manoeuvring the corpse into the fridge, seemed unaware of her presence. Risking all, she quickly tiptoed out of the room and into the comforting darkness of the hallway.

There was no challenging shout or the sound of footsteps coming after her, but as she jerked the cellar door open and ducked through the opening, she heard a loud metallic crash from across the hall, which she assumed to be the fridge being slammed shut. Standing there for a moment with her back against the door and her eyes tightly closed, she forced herself to wait for the adrenalin rush to subside. And it was as she stood there that she heard the squeak of the stretcher's wheels once again, this time moving down the hall towards the front of the building.

What on earth was Wadman up to? Obviously badly injured, bleeding and hardly able to stand upright, why on earth was he trundling a stretcher about in the darkness instead of seeking medical help for his injury? His behaviour didn't make sense — unless, she mused with a shudder, he was stocking up his freezers with more victims of his murderous proclivities. Whatever the truth was, one thing was very clear to her: somehow she had to get Lewis out of the place before that stretcher returned and stopped outside the cellar door.

Roz Callow was in considerable pain. She knew she had broken her leg and suspected she had also suffered other injuries as a result of her fall. Her left arm was trapped under her body and there was a creeping numbness at the base of her skull which was threatening to plunge her into a smoky oblivion. She had to resist it, to stay conscious until she could summon assistance, yet she was terrified to move or make a sound in case she attracted the attention of Pauline's killer. He was out there somewhere in the darkness, she knew that only too well. He had already taken Pauline's body — picked her up and loaded her on to some sort of wheeled stretcher before carting her away — and it was almost certain he would be back. On the face of it, playing dead seemed the safest bet, but what if he decided to check her out when he returned to make sure she was legit — just like Pauline? That really would mean curtains.

Forcing her right hand under her body, she felt for the police radio trapped beneath her in her coat pocket. If she could just get hold of it in time . . . A door slammed at the far end of the hall as her fingers touched the top of the metal casing — or was it the bottom? *God help her!* The bloody thing was up the wrong way. She forced her hand deeper into her pocket, but even as she managed to tear the radio free and fumble with the control buttons, she heard the unmistakable squeak of the stretcher's wheels. Wadman was coming for her.

Kate's hands were trembling as she sliced through the sticky tape binding Hayden Lewis, her eyes constantly darting apprehensively towards the stairs and the cellar door. Lewis was still only partially conscious, but he managed a crooked grin as she cut the tape away. 'Mind my important bits, Kate, won't you?' he said before drifting off again.

Having heard the stretcher squeaking back along the hallway just minutes before, Kate tried hard to hold down the panic welling up inside her. She was only a quarter done, but the last thing she needed was to make a mistake with the scalpel and sever an artery — not that Lewis looked as though he had much blood left in him to start with.

As the tape fell away from him, however, she couldn't help agonizing once again over the next phase of her crazy rescue plan — single-handedly getting a near unconscious colleague up the steep rickety stairs, through the back door and across the yard to the street under the very nose of a psychopathic killer. In her heart of hearts she knew she was on to a loser, but she had to at least try. If only she'd managed to keep hold of her mobile telephone, she could have short-circuited this whole thing and called up the cavalry, but Terry Duval had put paid to that when he'd ordered her to dump the phone out of the window of his Land Rover. As for Lewis, she'd already learned from him that his mobile was in Wadman's hands, so that was that; she could expect no help from anyone.

She cut the last of the tape away from Lewis's legs and shook him — at first gently and then a lot harder. 'Wake up, man,' she said hoarsely. 'We've got to get you out of here.'

Lewis opened his eyes and gave another weak smile. 'Just when I was beginning to enjoy myself,' he murmured before his head dipped again.

Kate swore and once more shook him awake, pulling him forward in the seat by his shoulders. 'Stand up, you prat.' she hissed.

He lurched in his seat, as if making some sort of effort, then fell back again. 'Hayden.' she snarled close to his ear. 'Do I have to grab your balls to get you on your feet?'

That registered all right and he jerked upright on the chair with a short laugh. 'You really know how to please a chap, don't you?' he said and, reaching for her shoulder with one hand, he pressed down on the edge of the chair with the other to hoist himself up. Kate realized that it wasn't just the injury to his nose and the blood loss that was a problem. Trussed up for so long, his legs had been weakened through lack of circulation and it would take a while before he was able to rely on them with any degree of confidence.

Twice he tried to stand up and twice fell back on to the chair again before finally managing it. Even then, he still had to lean on Kate as he stood there swaying unsteadily. After the chest injuries she herself had suffered, his weight proved to be a major problem and she had to grit her teeth tightly to prevent herself crying out as she led him slowly towards the stairs. He made it without falling over and relieved some of the pressure on her shoulder when he transferred his grip to the banister rail, but he still needed support climbing the stairs and he nearly overbalanced several times before they reached the top.

So far so good, she mused, breathing heavily from her exertions, but there was an even more difficult job to come. Leaving him propped against the wall, she opened the cellar door very slightly and peered through the crack. Silence, but she was not reassured and peered intently into the blacked out hallway for several seconds before she was satisfied. 'Come on,' she whispered and, pulling the door right back, held out her arm for him to lean on as she guided him through the opening, the scalpel held out in front of her in her other hand.

*Squeak, squeak, squeak.* The familiar sound raised the hairs at the back of her neck. She froze, darting quick frightened glances into the gloom on both sides. The heavy darkness totally concealed whatever was lurking there. She heard a grim laugh and suddenly realized that the pair of them were clearly illuminated by the light streaming out of the cellar doorway. She pulled Lewis to one side of the door, kicked it shut, then held him up against the wall to prevent him falling over again.

'Well, if it isn't little Miss Katie,' a harsh voice called out. 'Now, that is a nice surprise.'

She thought quickly, her skin wet and clammy. Wadman had the upper hand. He knew exactly where they were, whereas he himself could be hiding anywhere in the hallway. Maybe he was just feet away, creeping slowly towards them like a big black spider with poisonous dripping fangs. The analogy wasn't pleasant and she felt her skin crawl.

*Squeak, squeak, squeak.* She whirled round. The sound was coming from her left — from the direction of the front door. She shrank against the wall, edging along it in the opposite direction, pushing Lewis ahead of her.

'You can't get out of here, you know,' Wadman mocked, though she noticed that his breathing was ragged and his words ended in a bubbling sound, as if he were suffering from a bad attack of catarrh.

'Doors all locked, Kate,' he went on, 'and I have the keys.'

She thought about the window in the chapel of rest, but knew she would never be able to get Lewis through it in time. 'It's all over, you know that, don't you?' she blurted, playing for time and trying to pinpoint his position. 'Give it up.'

Another hard laugh. 'Funny, that's more or less what Pauline Cross said,' he replied. 'Before she stuck me, that is.'

In spite of her predicament, Kate stopped short and gaped into the blackness in disbelief.

'Pauline?' she choked incredulously. '*Pauline* stabbed you?'

A pained grunt. 'She did that all right. Bloody hurts too. Knocking off Alf was her idea, see. Nice insurance pay-out at the end of it. Only she got greedy.'

*Squeak, squeak, squeak.* Much closer now, but somehow Kate could not get her legs to work.

A cold hand had reached into her head to clasp her brain in a vice-like grip, rooting her to the spot. Pauline a murderess? Impossible. She'd doted on Alf. They'd been together for years. And yet . . . and yet . . . it all added up. The way she had recovered so quickly after Alf's death, then made a point of following Kate to the café to quiz her in such detail about the murder enquiry. Alf had not been the most discreet of people, so she would have known all about the operation and where the surveillance vehicle was to be parked. It would have been so easy for her to plan the whole thing.

She shuddered, the horrific implications of it all chasing round inside her head. 'I — I don't believe you,' she whispered into the darkness, trying to convince herself more than anything else.

'Then maybe you should ask your DCI,' he mocked. 'She's been having it off with the bitch for weeks. Maybe they planned it all together.'

Kate was immune to further shock. Her numbed senses lacked the capacity to absorb anymore, but even as the sharp crack of a floorboard jerked her back to reality, it was already too late.

The powerful smell that suddenly reached out of the darkness towards her was sweet and raw — the smell of death. Even as she instinctively threw herself sideways into Lewis, bowling him over and losing her grip on the scalpel, which slipped from her fingers, a solid towering mass slammed into the wall beside her with a reverberating crash, recovered and launched itself at her again.

This time there was no escape and she found herself pinned against the wall by the stretcher in an agonizing blast of pain. Then Wadman was on her, powerful hands closing round her face, foul breath enveloping her as his wet lips brushed against hers in a mocking caress.

She felt her head being twisted sideways, tried to resist, grasped his wrists with both hands, kicked out at his legs, but all to no avail and, as her face was forced against the cold wall, she prepared herself for the sudden violent wrench in the opposite direction that would snap her spine.

It never came. The sudden crash was a deafening combination of ripped metal and splintered wood. Immediately the grip on her face relaxed. Laser-like white beams cut through the flood of flashing blue light that once more stained the walls and ceiling and shouting voices accompanied the sound of heavy boots hammering into the hallway. The cavalry had arrived — and this time they had no intention of knocking!

Seconds later the hall lights blazed into life, searing her eyes. There were uniformed figures all around her. Gradually her eyes accustomed themselves to the glare and her gaze took in the demolished front door, the crumpled form of Hayden Lewis on the floor beside her and the pale face of Roz Callow staring blankly at the ceiling from the wheeled stretcher as it was gently pulled away from her by a scowling DI Roscoe.

It was a good few minutes before it fully dawned on her weary tortured brain that it was all over. Sanity had finally been re-established in her turbulent nightmare world and, miraculously, she had survived probably the closest call of any she had experienced in her short eventful police career. But her relief was soon tempered by another more sober realization — Larry Wadman was nowhere to be seen. In the pandemonium, he had seized his opportunity and escaped into the night.

# CHAPTER 28

Kate stared at Detective Inspector Roscoe in disbelief. 'Vanished?' she echoed, her voice shaking with emotion. 'He can't have just vanished.'

Roscoe made a face. 'Seems like he scarpered out the back door as we come in the front,' he growled. 'Bastard could be anywhere by now.'

'Not with his wound he won't be — what about the blood trail?'

Roscoe shrugged. 'Pitch black out there,' he said, 'and bloody moon's deserted us. Dog van's *en route*, but it's likely to be another half-hour before it arrives.'

He scowled, thrusting his head forward aggressively. 'What the hell happened here, Kate? We get a radio alert from Roz Callow and when we turn up, what do we find?' He tapped the fingers of one hand with the index finger of the other. 'A pool of blood in the flat upstairs, what looks like some sort of explosive and a load of detonators and timers in a bedroom cupboard, a flaming knife lying in the hallway — *plus* the DCI sparko on a stretcher and Hayden Lewis lying on the floor with a busted nose.' He took a deep breath. 'And you claim it's all down to some psycho undertaker now on his toes somewhere after being stabbed by Alf Cross's missus — *who*, incidentally, also seems to have gone AWOL.' He shook his head. 'Sounds like some soddin' off-the-wall TV who-dunnit to me.'

Kate shivered in the draught from the open front door. 'A who-dunnit that happens to be real,' she said, her tone pure ice. 'Maybe you should ask Pauline Cross for her take on it — *if* you can find her.'

Roscoe lit a cigarette and drew in the smoke so deeply that he ended up in a heavy coughing fit. 'Lads going round to her place as we speak,' he wheezed. 'Not that I expect them to find her at home if what you say is true.'

Kate watched as two ambulance men wheeled DCI Callow on a stretcher to the front door. 'You could always have a chat with Roz in the meantime,' she said drily. 'I'm sure she would be only too happy to "help you with your inquiries".'

He grunted, ignoring the sarcasm. 'Tried to,' he said, following her gaze, 'but she's away with the fairies right now. From what you've already told me, though, you can bet your life the guv'nor will be on her case the moment she gets back from cyber space — and I wouldn't want to be in her shoes then for anything.'

He studied her critically, pulling on his cigarette. 'You OK?' he observed. 'You look like a corpse.'

She gave him a thin humourless smile and thrust her hands into the pockets of her coat. 'Well, thanks,' she replied, 'I very nearly was.' Turning her back on him, she walked over to a wheelchair being pushed after the stretcher by an ambulance woman. Lewis looked up at her, his face an even worse mess now than it had been, with mauve patches under both eyes in addition to his bloodied nose. He forced a smile when she touched his hand. 'You should see the other chap,' he said, reading her thoughts. 'He's a right mess.'

She gave a short laugh. 'I'll come to the hospital just as soon as I've finished here,' she replied. 'Don't try chatting up any of those nurses while my back's turned, will you?'

He chuckled. 'Might be difficult fighting 'em off,' he replied and waved weakly as the ambulance woman wheeled him out through the front door, 'especially with my good looks.'

Then it was Roscoe at her elbow again. 'Guv'nor's on his way,' he said, nodding at the radio in his hand. 'He'll need to be fully briefed on this.'

She turned to study him sourly. 'You mean he finally wants to hear what I have to say?' she queried and, turning up the collar of her coat, she headed for the half-open back door. 'Well, he knows where to find me, doesn't he?'

Roscoe gaped, then abruptly recovered and went after her. 'You can't just *leave*,' he exclaimed, holding the door shut.

She wheeled to face him. 'And why not?' she retorted. 'After all, I'm officially on holiday, aren't I?'

Hauling the door open and pushing him aside in the process, she drew back her shoulders and marched briskly out into the yard. The rear gates were now wide open and a couple of uniforms gave her an appraising glance as she stepped past them into the lamp-lit street. She smiled grimly. Nothing changed, did it? Still less the one-track mind of the average male — copper or not. But she didn't care. She was still alive — alive and finally exonerated — which was all that mattered. It was time to look forward to a new beginning. OK, so Wadman was still at large, but, with his wound, he would probably turn up dead in a ditch in a couple of days. As for Pauline Cross and Roz Callow, they were matters for the inquiry team to sort out and were not her concern anymore. She smiled, feeling good about things for the first time since the murder inquiry had begun. It was all over at last, justice had been served in respect of Andy Seldon and Alf Cross and she was free to think about herself for a change. Maybe she and Hayden *would* get together after all and, with her career back on track for the first time in days, her future was starting to look promising again.

The Jaguar's sleek body gleamed with frost and she had to exert some pressure on the driver's door before it swung open with a loud 'crack'. She didn't notice the dark smears on the windscreen or the small card trapped under the right-hand wiper blade until she had slipped behind the wheel. Then, frowning, she climbed back out again and pulled the card free.

At first she thought someone had left her a snotty note because she had parked the Jag in their space, but when she studied the card in the light of her torch, she felt a cold clammy hand descend on her shoulder.

The front of the card was just like any other printed business card, but there the similarity ended, for it was neatly inscribed with the name and address of 'Wadman & Son, Funeral Directors' and, turning it over, she saw that there was a handwritten message scrawled on the back. 'Sorry I missed you, Kate,' it said. 'See you soon . . . Twister'.

# AFTER THE FACT

The funeral of Mary May was not very well attended. That could have been due to the fact that Bristol were playing at home, of course, with many would-be mourners choosing to go to the match instead, but it was more likely that few people had actually known the reclusive old woman in the first place and therefore her passing had attracted little notice, even in the village where she had lived for much of her life.

In any event, her send-off proved to be an unremarkable formality, fraught with problems and memorable only in the fact that it was the very last internment to be managed by the funeral directors, Wadman & Son. The funeral director himself had vanished, the hearse had developed a puncture and was late and it was pouring with a sleety rain, which hammered the windows of the little chapel and gushed from the overfilled gutters in milky torrents. Even the sandwiches supplied for the wake back at the village hall had been put out too early and were already curling at the edges as the hearse finally turned up at the crematorium.

'Funny business about Mr Wadman, isn't it?' one of the mourners commented to Albert Price as she arrived, shaking the rain over the polished wooden floor from her black umbrella, her sharp eyes alight with curiosity.

'Most peculiar,' he agreed, still suffering from shock and knowing very little about the circumstances, apart from the fact that the funeral parlour had for some reason become a crime scene and he had been lumbered with Mary May's funeral as a result of Larry Wadman's dramatic disappearance.

The only saving grace was that the coffin, which he had left open in the chapel of rest the day before just in case any relatives or friends wanted a last viewing, had been sealed with its long brass screws, presumably by Larry, ready to be loaded into the hearse. The police had therefore allowed the funeral to go ahead, as planned. But Price still could not get his head round what Larry had been doing in the funeral parlour so late in the evening, *or* why he had chosen to disappear. Mary May had already been properly prepared for her final journey, so there had been nothing for Larry to do, apart from polish his shoes for the big day. All very strange and what was so frustrating about it all was the refusal of the police to enlighten him or to allow any of the staff inside the funeral parlour, save the pall-bearers who had had to collect the coffin and load it into the hearse. And today would have to be the day when Mrs Price was due to clean the mortuary refrigerators, wouldn't it? Most inconvenient!

Inside the light oak coffin, with its polished veneer and smart imitation brass handles, Pauline Cross stared into impenetrable blackness — as she had done for the past twelve hours. Paralyzed from Twister's deadly attack, but still fully conscious, she had been aware of every movement as the coffin was placed in the back of the hearse by the pall-bearers, but totally helpless and unable to utter a sound or so much as lift a finger.

Even after a night of futile effort, she still desperately tried to will the motor cortex in her brain to awaken; to stimulate the nerve impulses that would force her frozen muscles and sinews to work; to enable her to hammer on the lid of the coffin with her fists and scream through her parched cracked lips 'I'm alive. I'm STILL ALIVE.' But her body remained inert, her vocal chords silent, her physical system in total suspension.

The service was short and simple, the eulogy a stammering self-conscious delivery by an estranged daughter who had not seen her mother for the past eight years after a monumental family row, but had now made the trip from deepest Wiltshire to pay her last respects — and, of course, to stake her claim to Mary's house and meagre savings.

In the tight claustrophobic confines of the long wooden box, which had been made to take a much slighter frame than her own, Pauline mentally prayed for deliverance as the funeral service commenced; to be forgiven her sins just like the Bible promised, granted that one last chance the scriptures were always crowing about. And, as she did so, she suddenly saw Alf's white face loom before her immobile gaze — none of the hate she would have expected in those brooding brown eyes, just pain and sorrow as he stared down at her with a tenderness she would never have thought he possessed. Andy Seldon joined him too, peering closely at her and shaking his blond hair in gentle reproof. She tried to shake her own head, tried to close her wide-open eyes to shut out her ghostly visitants, but her facial muscles remained taut and unresponsive and, as if sensing her torment, both faces then abruptly began to fade, becoming tiny specks of light in her sea of stygian blackness and she was alone again, wondering if her sanity had deserted her in the same way as the rest of her vital functions.

And it was at this point that the clergyman began speaking, his muffled voice on the crematorium microphone intoning the final words of committal; extolling the virtues of eternal life and the promise of redemption in the hereafter.

She felt the loud clonk as the coffin started to move on the catafalque, heard the piped music begin to play, which was abruptly cut off following the 'crack' of a steel door closing. Then, after a brief pause, the sudden roar of powerful burners and within her tortured brain a voice screamed and screamed.

## THE END

**Thank you for reading this book.**

If you enjoyed it please leave feedback on Amazon or Goodreads, and if there is anything we missed or you have a question about, then please get in touch. We appreciate you choosing our book.

Founded in 2014 in Shoreditch, London, we at Joffe Books pride ourselves on our history of innovative publishing. We were thrilled to be shortlisted for Independent Publisher of the Year at the British Book Awards.

www.joffebooks.com

We're very grateful to eagle-eyed readers who take the time to contact us. Please send any errors you find to corrections@joffebooks.com. We'll get them fixed ASAP.